"I'm going to take a soak in my tub. Care to join me?" he asked.

I blinked. It wasn't a tub, but a round, large sunken pool with tiles made of the same deep blues as the Aegean Sea and smack in the center of his room like some ancient Grecian spa. I'd literally dreamed about bathing with him in it a million times—our bodies wet and steaming as I rode his muscled frame and devoured his sensual lips with my mouth.

King lifted one dark, silky brow. "My, my, Miss Turner. You *do* have quite the dirty mind. I hope to sample the fruits of its labor before my time is up. Perhaps tonight?"

I shook my head, feeling ashamed. My imagination was out of control. "No."

"Such a shame, as I think we both might enjoy it." King shrugged and began walking toward the house, dissolving into thin air right before my eyes. "I hope you like the dress, Mia."

"I didn't agree to go with you."

"Do not be late," his disembodied voice called out. "It displeases me."

Pompous jerk. I hung my head and covered my face before blowing out a slow breath. I tried not to be excited about tonight, but I was. I tried not to hate myself for it, but I did.

What Are Reviewers Saying About King?

5 STARS. "King's is everything it promised to be and more. It's dark, mysterious and gritty with a touch of sensual and a dash of snarky humor..." - **tjlovestoread.wordpress.com**

5 STARS for King's. "I can honestly say I was so charmed by this book I didn't put it down once for 4.5 hours straight." - **smartmouthsmut.com**

KING'S. "I give this book 11 on a scale of one to 10. This book catches you right from the beginning and does not let go."- **bookwormsanonymousmyfavoritethings.blogspot.com**

5 STARS. "Just when I thought I had seen it all in King's, Pamfiloff ups the ante in King for a Day." - **bookchickwithkick.com**

5 STARS for KING FOR A DAY! "The writing was so suspenseful and well done that I couldn't put it down..." - **guiltypleasuresbookreviews.com**

"Heart-racing, mind-jumbling, infuriatingly-beautiful, steaming-hot and where-the-hell-is-the-next-one! That's exactly how *King's* made me feel and ultimately left me." - **thebookbell.wordpress.com**

"Ok so can I just say HOLYSH**BALLS BATMAN!!!!!!!!!! I did not even see this coming I really thought I might know who KING was but I was nowhere near close." - **bookwormsanonymousmyfavoritethings.blogspot.com**

ISBN-10:0990304841
ISBN-13:978-0-9903048-4-5

Cover Design: EarthlyCharms.com

Editing: Latoya Smith, Tessa Shapcott, and Pauline Nolet

Interior design: WriteIntoPrint.com

KING (of) ME

The King Trilogy
Book Three

Mimi Jean Pamfiloff

Mimi Boutique Imprint

DEDICATION

I'm going for cheesy and dedicating this book to two people I've never met: the women who inspired my love of wicked, sexy, tormented, bad boys. Anne Rice, thank you for getting me hooked on vampires at a very young age and for writing some of the best anti-heroes ever. Paranormal Romance would not be what it is today without you. Charlaine Harris, thank you for reintroducing me to Paranormal Romance twenty-five years later. Without you, I wouldn't have woken up and learned to love books again.

KING
(of)
ME

CHAPTER ONE

Sex with a ghost. Sex with a ghost. Am I really going to do this? I stared into my champagne glass, my hand trembling as I focused—tried to focus, anyway—on the delicate bubbles fizzing to the surface. It was all I could do to keep from getting up and running from the nearly empty restaurant or stealing yet another look at my date. His unsettling, raw masculinity nearly undid me every time, despite knowing that his exterior was a façade.

How did I get myself into this?

"Miss Turner," he said in that deep, dark, disapproving tone, "look at me."

I knew I had to face this situation head-on, so to speak. There would be no running away.

You can handle it. Hell, I'd endured a heck of a lot worse these past few months—physical threats, being kidnapped, watching my brother get murdered; however, my mental armor wore thin.

Doesn't matter. You're in the home stretch now.

I finally willed myself to gaze across the table at the imposing, exquisite, and dangerous man, his sleek muscular body draped in an expensive tux.

Stunning.

I listened to my heart beat exactly three times and then sucked in a shallow breath, willing my heart to continue pumping.

The way the candlelight danced over his finely sculpted cheekbones, chiseled jaw, and sensual lips mesmerized me. I couldn't help it. Then there were those dark lashes and his thick, wavy black hair that fell just behind his ears, and...Well, let's just say his appearance made it easy to forget who he was: an ancient, dead king cursed to roam the earth for eternity. His modern camouflage wasn't simply exquisite; it was flawless.

Sweat began to trickle down my spine beneath my little black dress, forcing me to shift in my seat. *Breathe, Mia. Breathe.*

"Stop the incessant fidgeting, Miss Turner, and tell me how you like the champagne." He stared unblinkingly at me with his icy gray eyes.

Trying to project an air of calmness, I casually brushed my crazy blonde waves from my face and picked up my menu, finding sanctuary from my thoughts on page two. "Um. The champagne is good. I like it."

Idiot. Even I, with my whiskey palate, knew this was a five-hundred-dollar bottle of fermented grape juice fit for the gods.

Or a king.

Able to hear my thoughts, he smirked, and two tiny but deep dimples puckered in his stubble-covered cheeks. "Do you know what you'd like to order?"

"Not really." I didn't normally eat this sort of stuff—quail egg sushi rolls with a ginger plum reduction, or wild sea bass with a lilac honey glaze. It sounded pretty good, but for one hundred dollars a plate, I didn't feel right rolling the dice on my menu selection.

You're going to have sex with King tonight, and you're worried about what to order?

"That is exactly right, Miss Turner." He pinned me with his cool eyes. "Ordering the wrong dish isn't the end of the world. Sex on the other hand..." He scratched his unshaven chin. "I expect my order to be perfect. Or there will be consequences." He flashed a wicked little grin.

Dammit.

"Stay out of my head," I said.

"Let us cut the crap, Miss Turner. I can hear you. I can either pretend not to, or we may both simply acknowledge that this is a fact. If I pretend, however, I will not be gaining any..." he reached for the words, "yards. Yes—yards with you."

"So we're playing football now?" I supposed the sports metaphor felt appropriate. He wanted to win and would mow down anyone who got in his way. Right now, he needed to win me. All of me. Why? I'd get to that in a moment.

"No. Our game is far more serious than that." He dipped his head a notch and gazed hungrily across the candlelit table, pushing my body temperature up ten more degrees despite my effort to ignore the hold he had over me.

"The game of life," I muttered under my breath.

"Greater than that."

What could be bigger than life? I wondered.

"The eternity of death," he replied to my thoughts with a curtness that needed no explanation. He was, after all, dead and had been for over three thousand years, searching for an escape from the cruel, horrifyingly painful curse cast upon him by his unfaithful wife, Hagne. Hagne had been a Seer of Light like myself with the ability to see people's energy. Sometimes I saw imprints left behind by objects, too. Obviously, I suspected Seers were capable of much, much more—case in point: Hagne's curse—but I'd never know. I was the last Seer. Which was why King had an interest in me far beyond anything casual. And if I were to be honest with myself, a part of me, the part that lived in the darkest recesses of my mind, wanted him back.

"Do you plan to answer me this evening, Miss Turner?" King asked.

I pushed my mind away from any thoughts of sex and tried to focus on the conversation. "H-h-honesty. What else? If you can't stop hearing my thoughts, there's no point in pretending."

He smiled in that sexy, sinful sort of way that could melt a woman's panties off her body—like it or not. Yeah, he was powerful.

"I meant, what dish will you be ordering? I already knew you would choose honesty. You're not one to advocate lying."

He was right about that. I couldn't tolerate dishonesty. Which was why I struggled with what was to come after dinner. Why did he insist on making sex part of our new "deal"?

King leaned in. "Mia, how many times must I explain this? The Artifact will allow me to bring back one life, just one. Do you want your brother returned to you or not?"

I looked toward the panoramic view of San Francisco, the lights of the Golden Gate Bridge off in the distance. "You know I do."

Long story short, Justin had been murdered. And while some might argue whether he'd deserved to die, at the end of the day, he was family. My family. And returning Justin to my parents was the only way to make my family whole again. But to bring him back, I needed to break King's curse. To break his curse, we had to get a hold of the Artifact—a rock that King's ex-wife had used to bind his curse. To break the bond between King and the Artifact, a Seer had to undo it.

That's where this all got weird. Utterly and truly weird. According to him, the bond could only be broken with love.

Yeah, pretty damned strange. Definitely complicated.

However, I'd spent a lot of time thinking this one over. If Hagne used hate to create his situation, then it only made sense that the opposite energy would undo it. Sort of like an antidote.

Now, how breaking King's curse would translate into a dead person—any dead person—returning to life? That was where things became even stranger. He claimed that once his curse was broken, the Artifact would allow one life to be brought back as a sort of "do over." King had obviously planned for his life to be the lucky one, but he'd made me an offer I couldn't refuse. In exchange for ending his torment, he would allow my brother to return in his place. This meant that King would cease to exist, but in the end, we'd all get something we wanted. The only trick now was getting a hold of the elusive Artifact. *And...*I sighed, *I have to find a way to open my heart to him in order to deliver "the antidote."*

Easier said than done.

"Not difficult at all," King said. "You must simply put your youthful, spirited mind to it."

I made a little huff. *I may only be twenty-six*—a baby in his eyes—*but I know hearts don't follow the mind; it's the other way around.*

He tisked in disagreement. "There, you see. A sign of your youthful naivety; your mind is far more powerful than you give it credit."

"My mind is busy trying to accept that either way I'm screwed."

"I should hope so, Miss Turner." He cocked one dark, silky brow. "After all, is that not why you are here with me tonight? For the screwing?"

I narrowed my eyes at him. *Funny.* "You know what I meant, King. You've backed me into a no-win situation."

"How so?"

He knew the answer. He was too smart not to. But he wanted to hear me say it. He liked watching me squirm.

"If I successfully find a way to..." I swallowed, "love you, then your curse will end and you'll..."

"Cease to exist?"

I nodded. *Yes, I'll get to enjoy the heartbreak of caring about someone and losing him.*

"Ah. But you will get your brother back in my place."

"Yes." *But if I don't break your curse, I lose Justin.* There was no right in this equation. There was no easy out or perfect ending. *A Greek tragedy in the making.*

"I cannot argue," he said casually, seemingly uninterested in my heart-wrenching dilemma. "It is quite the predicament."

I looked at him and forced myself not to react to his indifference or to his exquisite masculine shell that made my body want and need things it shouldn't.

"I have a question," I said. "Are you just using this as an excuse to sleep with me?"

"Perhaps." His voice dropped an octave. "But if you are to love me, then we must become acquainted. And I assure you, the gift of..." he paused, "fucking is one of my finer qualities. I fear, perhaps, my *only* fine quality. Why not begin with our best attributes forward?"

"Stop. We both know you're exaggerating," I argued. "And before you go there, I'm not talking about the sex." I was, however, talking about his "finer qualities." I'd learned that King was sporadically capable of incredible compassion. A leftover from his pre-curse days, I supposed. What I would've given to know that version of him—King with a heart. This King was ruled by his obsession with the Artifact. He'd lied, manipulated, and bullied me into doing things just to get closer to it, which is why the man couldn't be trusted when it came to that damned rock.

Yes, I planned to play this out very carefully.

"I am worse than you could ever imagine," he said. "You will see for yourself soon enough." He looked toward the doorway where the waiter stood at attention. It was eerie to see the five-star restaurant overlooking the city empty. Like we'd shown up too early. In reality, it was ten o'clock at night, and King had reserved the entire place just for us.

"Yes, sir. What may I bring you?" asked the waiter.

King handed him the menu. "I'll have the steak Diane. Rare. She'll have the same."

"Very good, sir." The man scurried away.

Steak? I was leaning toward a salad, something that won't make my stomach bulge out while we're—I swallowed—*having sex.*

King chuckled at my thoughts. "You're beautiful, Mia. And I am looking forward to showing you how much I mean that." He sipped his champagne. "By the way, the steak will help you keep up your strength. I am ravenous in the bedroom."

My spit stuck in my throat as I pictured the two of us, our naked bodies writhing together on the large bed of whatever luxury penthouse suite he'd procured for the night. King was beyond gorgeous. He was every woman's sexual fantasy—large, hard, and lean—but on the other side of the coin, sleeping with a ghost. *A dead man—*

"Enough." King slammed his fist on the table.

I jumped in my seat. "I can't help how I feel."

"You've touched me before. You've wrapped your hand around my cock. You didn't seem to notice any difference then, so stop behaving like—"

"Don't. Don't speak to me like I'm your dog, or your woman, or your wife, or your anything."

"Oh..." He chuckled. "But you will be."

"Excuse me?"

"My wife, that is."

I blinked. *Did I hear him correctly?*

"Yes. You did," he responded.

"I never agreed to that."

"You agreed to give me redemption and freedom from my hellish existence."

"Marriage is out of the question." And it had nothing to do with what I'd agreed to. In fact, I was seriously beginning to doubt his argument for having sex, too.

"You think you have a choice in the matter?"

"Yes." I always had a choice.

"Wrong. You will fuck me tonight. Then you will marry me, love me, and end my curse."

My jaw dropped. "You're seriously commanding me to do those things?"

"What the hell do you think?"

I think you're insane.

"I don't give a fucking hell what you think. You'll do as you are told, Miss Turner, because that was always our deal."

I was about to retort when a poignant question entered my head: Why all this fuss masked in a flurry of threats and bullying? Because shocking me was one of his classic moves. *The bastard is planning something.*

Tugging on his silver cufflink, King glared from across the table. "You dare question my integrity? We have a deal, and I never welsh."

"But we're not talking about just any deal, are we?" An uneasy something built inside my stomach. King was manipulating me like a rat in a maze. That was how he operated—always in control, even when he made you feel like you were driving. But you never were.

Okay. Perhaps I needed to retreat and rethink the terms of our arrangement. I agreed to end his curse, but the "how" was open for interpretation, especially given that I needed to feel some sort of affection for the man in order to do it.

I took a deep breath and willed myself not to be swayed by his raw, backbreaking sensuality. "King,

I'm sorry, but I'm not doing this tonight." I stood and placed my napkin on the table.

"Where the *fuck* do you think you're going?" he growled in a menacing tone that rattled my rib cage.

"I'm not falling for another of your mind games. If we're going to break your curse, it's going to be on my terms. Mine."

He slowly rose from the table, a predatory look in his silvery eyes. "I don't think so."

I shook my head at him. "You can't bully me into feeling something for you. If you want this to work, you're going to have to accept it."

I turned toward the door, feeling goddamned proud of myself. I'd stood up to the ancient, powerful king without becoming tongue-tied. I said exactly what I'd meant to say and—

I felt a pull on my arm, and my body flew through the air, landing with a crash onto the table. Our champagne glasses tumbled to the floor, as did the candle and silverware.

He pinned me by the neck, face down. "Who the fuck do you think you're talking to, Mia? Huh? A man who gives a shit what you think or want?"

I grunted in agony as he pushed my arm behind my back and ground my neck into the table. "Get off, King!"

"Sir?" the waiter asked, obviously wondering what the noise was all about.

"Leave!" King barked. "Or I will kill you."

"Help!" I screamed.

"Uhhh...Call if you need anything, sir." The waiter disappeared into the kitchen.

Sonofabitch wasn't even going to lift a finger for
me?

"Don't go! Help," I screamed again.

"I'll help you, you fucking bitch." King pressed
my neck harder into the table with one hand and
began shoving my dress up with the other.

I felt the hem pass my hips, exposing my black
lace thong. I'd put it on tonight, anticipating I'd
have the nerve to follow through.

"Don't, King."

"Shut the fuck up. I should have done this the
night we met." He shoved down my panties, and I
couldn't believe he was doing this. The evil fucking
bastard would never find salvation from his curse,
but perhaps he'd never wanted it. A man who truly
wanted love would never do this. Never.

"Don't, King. Or I swear, I'll—"

"What? Curse me again, you bitch? You cannot
hurt me now because *you* are nothing," he roared.

I flung myself up from the bed, covered in sweat,
panting and crying. *Oh my God. Oh my God.* I
clutched the pink pajama fabric covering my chest,
my head swiveling from side to side. I wasn't in any
restaurant, nor was I being violated—thank God. I
was lying on a bed in King's palatial estate in Crete.

"Nice dream, Miss Turner."

I yelped.

In the corner, King comfortably sat in a leather
armchair. He wore faded jeans and a white linen
shirt partially unbuttoned and exposing the tan
chiseled planes of his pectorals. A wicked smile
occupied his full lips.

I felt my face turn rage-red. "You…you…"

"Don't blame me." He held up his palms as if surrendering. "That was all your twisted little brain. I merely observed." He leaned back, smothering a smile. "However, I must admit, you have a dirty, dirty mind."

If I could kill him with my bare eyes, I would. *God, I hate you.*

He laughed, his chest and shoulders shaking as his head tilted toward the sky, before he returned his unapologetic gaze to my furious eyes. "Then we have our work cut out for us, don't we, Miss Turner?" He stood and strolled casually toward the door of the master suite and then stopped right before twisting the handle. "I'll see you downstairs to discuss the real terms of our new deal. And so we are clear," he narrowed those stunning, pale gray eyes, "sex, even your scandalous version—as tempting as it may be—won't be part of it. I know how disappointing that must be, but I'm sure you'll get over it." He flashed a wicked, cocky grin and left.

I growled out a breath toward the closed door. *Sonofabitch.* As if *not* sleeping with him was some great loss. And how the hell could I help what I dreamed? Clearly my brain was letting off steam, my dream a metaphor for how I felt ruinously cornered by the situation.

I sighed, knowing that feeling sorry for myself wasn't going to solve a thing.

Just stay focused, Mia. Keep your eyes on the prize. Getting my brother back was all that mattered, and my new ruthless outlook on life—compliments of living in King's world for a few months—would help me do that.

Don't forget who you're dealing with: the goddamned devil. A devil who knew how to push every single one of my buttons, and had.

But you're not that same girl anymore.

No. I wasn't.

And this time, I was playing for my own prize.

CHAPTER TWO

I showered quickly and threw on a pair of jeans and a plain tee. The weather outside was tepid with a slight mugginess to it (I supposed typical for late fall in Crete), but with my curly blonde hair in desperate need of a trim, I was in permanent anti-frizz ponytail mode. At least I'd been getting a little sleep, despite the nightmares, and my blue eyes were finally rid of their bloodshot edges.

I headed downstairs from King's extravagant open-aired suite, thinking how much I'd miss the place once this was all over. I had to hand it to him: King had excellent taste—balcony overlooking the turquoise and sapphire-blue ocean, steaming sunken pool in the center of the room, murals of Greek goddesses, and neoclassic pillars. The entire estate was "Grecian spa meets the Four Seasons," complete with private beach, tennis court, helicopter pad, twenty-foot-high fountains, and lush fruit trees. A palace fit for a modern-day king from old money—very, very old money—who didn't think twice about spending it.

Still, I wondered why King had built the place. Stefanos Spiros, the head of the Spiros family who'd been King's loyal servants for generations, once hinted the house had been built for me. I didn't believe that. I mean, I'd only met King a few months prior, and this home had been built a few years ago.

Regardless, goose bumps broke out over my skin every time I thought about that conversation. Stefanos had called me King's "queen." So archaic. The real rub, however, was that from the first moment I'd met King, he claimed me as his personal property. Even went as far as placing his stamp—a "K" tattoo—on my left wrist. Later, I'd learned he could control and track me with it, which seriously pissed me off. I wasn't his. I never would be. And a tattoo wouldn't change that.

Neither will a house, I thought, *because I'm not for sale.*

I entered the large open living room with white modern furniture and panoramic windows overlooking the ocean. King stood with his broad back to me, staring out across the waves, a glass of champagne in one hand and unlit cigar in the other. "You are correct in your assumption, Miss Turner."

"Can we go back to 'Mia'? I think we're a little past the formal stage at this point."

He nodded, but did not turn to face me. "As you wish."

"Which assumption?" I asked.

"It is true; I had everything constructed in anticipation of your arrival, hoping you might want to call it home."

I sat on the white couch and folded my hands neatly in my lap, mulling that over. There was no use in pretending his statement didn't affect me, because King could hear my thoughts. There were no secrets. In fact, because he'd crawled around inside my head and body on several occasions, he knew more about me than I did.

"So how did you know I was coming?" I asked.

He stood perfectly still and spoke quietly, as if reliving the memories in his head. "I felt you growing closer with each day, just as I felt the Artifact's presence."

I quickly shut down any thoughts or emotions blooming inside my chest that might urge me to believe I meant something to him. I didn't. To him, I was a means to an end and nothing more.

"All right," I said. "So I'm here now, in the home you built for me—"

"For us," he corrected and turned to face me. I wished he hadn't, because I found it extremely difficult to stay focused when he looked at me. Fact was, the man did things to me—to my body. Even now, completely in control of my emotions, I felt the sensual heat pooling between my legs and deep inside, like some messed up Pavlovian response. Only, my brain and heart were not on board.

Idiot body.

But that was the conundrum about King I couldn't figure out. It wasn't like I ran around swooning for hot men, completely discounting their flaws. In fact, I'd always gone for the nice guys whom some might overlook because they weren't considered handsome by traditional standards. I always, *always* felt attraction for the insides first.

With King, however, something pulled me in. It was a feeling that radiated from some unknown place, drawing me closer while my rational mind kicked and screamed, telling me to stay away. After I learned about his curse, I began to believe that the conflicting emotions might make sense. He was once a man, a good man, and that part of him was still in there somewhere. Anyway, I wanted to believe that the physical attraction I felt was for the man—the real man—he once was. Of course, I'd never know. That person was gone or, at least, changed forever by this curse.

"I'm sorry you had the home built for 'us,'" I said. "Because there is no 'us.' There's just me and you, and one of us will soon be over." I know that pointing out his life would soon end sounded cruel, but King was made from the very fabric of cruel. He understood it and thrived on it.

"Yes." He grinned. "You are correct, and I look forward to the day my existence will end and you will have back your beloved brother. In the meantime, there is much to be done."

This was what I really wanted to hear: what he expected from me in this new deal of ours. As in my dream, to end his curse we needed the Artifact, and then I had to provide "the antidote" by finding something inside him to love. Not a simple thing. Thankfully, there were many kinds of love.

"You may assume," King said, replying to my thoughts, "that the breed of affection required to break my curse is not the sort one might feel for a puppy."

I laughed. "Well, thank goodness for that. Because puppies are irresistible." He frowned and was about to speak, but I held out my hand. "Just a joke. I get it. Problem is, I can't force myself to fall in love. So what I really need to know is your plan. What is it you need me to do?"

He nodded solemnly. "There is no plan."

Right. King always had a plan.

"Not this time, Mia. I have no scheme, no magic, no devices to force this on you."

"Seriously? You've got nothing?"

He shrugged.

"You're counting on me to just...swoon and fall in love with you?"

He nodded.

"Then we're screwed." Because without the aid of some of King's otherworldly gifts, I wasn't going to be falling for him.

He lifted one brow. "You really know how to hurt a man."

"I'm sorry, but it's the truth."

"We could have sex and go from there."

My jaw dropped. "But you said—"

"That was a joke, Mia."

"Oh."

He scratched his chin. "What I propose is something far simpler."

It was my turn to raise a brow.

"I will take you away, just you and I alone for the next six days. You may ask me anything you like, we can spend time together without interruptions, and you will get to know the real me."

My body broke out in a cold sweat. "You mean…a vacation?" Was he mad?

"Think of it as an extended date."

My breasts and core began to heat, fluttering and pulsing from just thinking about being alone with him. I could only imagine the overwhelming urges I'd have to resist if I actually went away with him. It was not a good idea. He had too much control over my body.

I shook my head no. "We should stay here and just…" I didn't know what we'd do. "You've seriously got nothing? No love potions or anything?"

He shook his head no and crossed his arms. "The love must be genuine, or it will not work."

"I'm not going away with you. I don't trust you." I didn't trust myself, either.

"You will have to try," he said starkly.

"Trust takes time."

"There is no 'time.' We have one week."

Oh no. This didn't sound good. "Whyyy?"

King looked away, grinding his jaw. I thought how strange it was that a ghost would do that. Then again, everything King did felt real and just as alive as any man. "I have made a deal with the 10 Club."

What the hell? "You made a deal with those soulless assholes?"

"Yes. Did I not just say that?"

"What deal, King?" I spat.

"I agreed to surrender my possessions."

I sprang from my seat, ready to throttle the man. "I'm one of your possessions! Why would you do that?"

For the record, I didn't agree I belonged to him, but what I thought didn't matter. According to the 10 Club, a depraved, elite social network of sorts for billionaires who used each other to acquire things that couldn't be purchased through any normal means—power, sex slaves, and other strange objects—I *was* his property.

"I anticipated you might react that way, Miss Turner, but let me explain: your disturbing dream was not so inaccurate."

Mia. It's Mia. Why is that so hard for you?

He ignored my thought and continued, "I do plan to marry you. This week, in fact. I'd hoped you'd warm to the idea after a few days alone with me."

I had to ask, "Why?"

"I wish to legally transfer my possessions to you while I still live. The 10 Club will get nothing when I sign everything over, because I will own nothing."

The 10 Club already had rules about ownership after one's departure from this world. Basically, the significant other got everything. What he had done, however, was barter his possessions in exchange for something he wanted now. Of course, he intended to use a loophole to avoid giving them anything. That was sneaky. Why wasn't I surprised?

"Why not transfer everything to my name without getting married?" I asked.

He looked at me as if I were daft.

"What?" I asked. It was a legitimate question.

"Miss Turner, I may be a ghost, but I assure you, my billions in assets are not."

"Meaning?"

"Even if I'll no longer be here to enjoy it, I am not about to give away half my wealth to taxes. Transfer of assets between spouses circumvents this issue."

Taxes. I thought that over for a moment. I supposed it made sense, but something still didn't feel right.

"What about me?" I asked. "You'll still 'own' me when you sign over your big-nothing to the Club. Doesn't that defeat the purpose?"

"I plan to remove my claim on you. You will become my wife instead—no longer my property, but my partner."

It was quite the grand gesture, but he had to be working another angle.

"I am not," he said, "working another angle. My wish is to see you safe and well looked after once I am gone. Marriage is merely the vehicle to accomplish this."

I narrowed my eyes. "Married. You're serious."

"Of course."

"And you think that once the 10 Club finds out what you've done, they won't come and take what they want anyway, including my life?" These bastards did what they wanted, when they wanted, except when dealing with each other, in which case they still did what they wanted, but were simply a bit more careful. Anarchists in suits. With yachts and Mercedes. And planes. Maybe a few small countries, too.

"I will ensure there are other measures in place to stop them," he said calmly.

None of this made sense, which meant the man was definitely up to something. If I had any chance of making my way through this, I had to lay out my cards and get him to agree to things that were valuable to *me*. "No deal."

King looked amused and crossed his thick arms over his partially exposed chest, a chest I was trying my damnedest not to look at. "What is it that you want?" he asked.

The old Mia, the one who hadn't watched a twisted, sick criminal named Vaughn gut her brother like a fish, would have danced around the answer. She might have even asked nicely. But the new Mia, who'd had her life turned into a never-ending stream of chaotic crap, knew she had to watch out for herself. *And I don't care what anyone thinks anymore. That's for sure.*

"I want them destroyed," I said. "I want the 10 Club dismantled."

"You do still care. Proof being your request."

"Stay out of my head." I shot him an angry look. "I'm not here to engage in a mental exploration of my feelings. I'm here to lay out the terms of our deal." I held up a finger. "That was number one. There's more."

"While I am intrigued by the rationale behind your requests, what you ask is impossible."

"Impossible is dead people walking around for thousands of years and driving cars. Impossible is bringing someone's deceased brother back to life with a rock."

His eyes glowed with a subtle humor. No, I didn't care why.

"Those are improbable," he said smugly, "not impossible."

"So is ending the 10 Club," I argued.

"Point taken; however, what you ask means having to kill them all. That would take years. We don't have years; we have seven days."

Yeah, thanks to you.

I thought about the situation for a moment. "Okay. Then kill their leaders, starting with Vaughn." They'd be crippled without any formal organization. The members paid an enormous sum of money into a pool each year to buy their unfettered freedom, making them above the law of any government. Without someone at the helm, someone powerful and ruthless they all feared, the club would fall apart under the weight of their own selfish, evil, cutthroat agendas.

"An excellent point, Mia. By the way, you never inquired as to why I made the deal to surrender my belongings in seven days."

"Why? Wait, don't tell me. It has something to do with the Artifact."

"Very good," he said a little too haughtily. "In fact, it has everything to do with it."

"So you have it?" I gasped as I spoke.

"Indeed, I do."

"Ohmygod." Why wasn't he dancing a jig? This man had been hunting the Artifact for, well, I didn't know how long, but I guessed it was thousands of years.

"However," he added, "that was not the only reason I made the deal."

I stared in anticipation. This news was already big. Huge, in fact. We had the goddamned Artifact! All I needed now was…well, to trust the guy and find some way to love him.

That's what all this vacation and marriage crap is really all about. Now that he had the rock, he'd planned to woo me because he needed me to develop some sort of romantic feelings for him. *Always one step ahead.*

King's handsome face sparked with an arrogant grin, indicating I was right. "I also bartered for my wedding present to you." He dipped his neatly groomed, full head of black hair, gesturing toward the kitchen. "Right this way."

My mind twirled in ecstatic circles as I followed King down a set of stairs hidden toward the back of the enormous home, near the servants' wing. I couldn't believe it; he'd managed to get the rock. That meant I'd soon have Justin back to my poor parents.

"Where do these stairs go?" I asked.

"My dungeon, where else?"

That explained it. The stairwell was scary as hell with violent colors dripping down the walls. Sometimes, I felt grateful for my Seer gift. Sometimes I wanted to turn the damned thing off.

"I'd hoped it was your laundry room," I replied.

He laughed. "That room is behind the kitchen."

"Nice to know." *Because I am going to be washing my underwear later.*

King chuckled at my little unspoken joke, but I wasn't exactly kidding. The further down we went, the more petrifying the energy. It reminded me of Vaughn's basement, actually.

As mentioned, Vaughn was a murderous psychopath and the world's most twisted fuck of a human being. Not only did he enjoy mutilating women, but he took their skins and put them on his dead lover. The monster had murdered hundreds of women and also ended my brother's life. Not a shock that he was the leader of 10 Club, too.

King stopped at the bottom of the stairs and punched a code into a keypad at the side of the door. When the door sprang open, the smell of dank seawater filled my lungs. A faint orange light glowed from inside.

"You weren't kidding, were you?" It really was a dungeon.

"No."

I held my position mid-stairs. "Who do you have down there?"

King smiled at me, a wicked gleam in his beautiful eyes. "Come see for yourself."

I was too afraid to move.

"You have nothing to fear," he said coolly.

"Then why do I see those color—"

King grabbed my wrist, his hand covering the "K" tattoo, which meant I couldn't easily resist doing what he told me. It was an instant override switch for my mind. *This* was why I frequently found myself hating the man. When he couldn't persuade or manipulate me into doing something, he forced me.

Not knowing what I was in for, my heart thumped wildly inside my chest. One step. Two. Before I knew it, I stood in a long corridor lined with empty cells. The black walls dripped with seawater and tiny cascades of slimy green algae.

"This way. I promise you will not be disappointed." He yanked me to the door at the end of the passage and punched in another code. This time, when the door popped, he shoved me past him and shut the door behind me.

What the hell? I turned and pounded on the door. "King! You son of a bitch! Let me the fuck out of here!"

I heard no reply. Instead, he shoved a thin blade underneath the door.

My hand froze mid-strike. "What the fuck, King?"

"That knife won't do you any good," said a familiar voice, a voice that made my heart turn into a lump of dread coated in corrosive acid.

"Vaughn?"

His beady, brown, cataract-covered eyes gleamed with joy from behind a set of rusty iron bars. "Yes, Miss Turner, it is I."

CHAPTER THREE

I felt Vaughn's eyes drilling into the back of my head as I pummeled the door with my fists and screamed. Of all the messed-up things King had ever done, this took the cake. *Bastard!*

What I couldn't begin to fathom was why? Why would he call this a gift? Why would he risk pissing me off when we were so close to breaking his curse?

"Aren't you going to say hello?" Vaughn chuckled with a slithery tone that reminded me of a snake who'd swallowed its own blackened heart, the pitch somewhere between a hiss and a cancerous cough.

I slowly turned to address the monster sitting in the cell behind me. He wore a brown sweater torn at the shoulder and brownish slacks. His stringy silver hair was caked with dried blood from what appeared to be a large festering gash on the side of his head.

"King do that to you?" I asked.

He dipped his head. "Who else?"

"With your philanthropic track record, the possibilities are endless."

His thin lips curled into a treacherous grin. "Yes, well. One doesn't enjoy life without acquiring a few foes."

"One of whom is standing right here, contemplating killing you." Was that what the knife was for? King thought I might enjoy a little revenge?

Christ, he probably did. King had a dark, ruthless side, one he didn't hesitate showing to his enemies.

"Kill me? You?" Vaughn crossed his legs, and that's when I noticed his hands were cuffed behind him, anchored to some sort of metal ring on the wall.

That's pretty messed up. The guy can't even scratch his nose or take a piss. Nice work, King.

He continued, "You may be my enemy, but you don't have the balls to pluck a hair from my head, let alone stick me with a knife."

"You sure about that?" I asked.

"Quite. You're weak, Miss Turner, just like that piece-of-shit brother of yours."

I turned to the bars and gripped them with enough force to strangle a man. "You don't know a thing about Justin."

"I know more than you." Smug satisfaction gleamed in his eyes.

"Such as?"

"Have you ever asked yourself how this whole thing got started? You, me, King?"

I knew Justin had somehow met Vaughn and Vaughn's significant other, Jamie. I knew Justin had made a deal with Vaughn to get funding for his archeological dig, and in exchange, Vaughn would get dibs on anything Justin unearthed. I knew Justin, at some point, fell in love with Jamie and got her pregnant, which is when they tried to run from Vaughn. Of course, it all ended badly for her, the baby, and Justin.

"I know all I need to know," I replied.

"Oh, but you don't. The little fucker thought he could take my woman and have me killed. He *thought* he could walk away with my money and power. The entire tragedy is his doing."

"I don't believe you; Justin wasn't that cunning."

Completely fucked up, yes. But cunning, no. Justin had once tried to cheat in a math test in middle school. The teacher told my parents that if it weren't for the guilty look on his face, she might never have noticed something was off. It was typical Justin—he couldn't be dishonest, even if he tried.

"Wrong, Miss Turner," Vaughn said. "He was treacherous and greedy. He tried to make it look like I killed his crew and had the Artifact, all to bait King into coming after me because he wanted me dead."

When this entire mess started, Justin had been working in Mexico managing his first dig near Palenque. It turned out the dig site was the resting place for the Artifact—that rock Hagne used to curse King. How it got there was a complete mystery, but the moment Justin found it, he knew the rock was something powerful and dangerous. He ran like hell. In retaliation for welshing on their deal, Vaughn killed Justin's men.

"Justin would never have harmed his crew. He didn't have a reason to." From what I could piece together, Justin had already started seeing Jamie—Vaughn's mistress slash "property"—and she had been helping him to disappear. Justin was trying to get away, not kill Vaughn.

"Think about it, Miss Turner. Why would I kill his men? I would simply take the Artifact from Justin if I wanted it—he couldn't hide from someone like me, nor did he. And truthfully, I didn't want the Artifact until much later, after I learned of its true value."

As he spoke, I tried reminding myself who this person was: a deviant, wealthy serial killer locked in a cage, who might do or say anything to get free. And he didn't know Justin the way I did. He didn't know how Justin volunteered every weekend for his full four years of high school at the Children's Hospital, reading stories about dinosaurs, showing the kids his collections of tiny fossils, and telling them that even the tiniest creatures leave their mark. Vaughn didn't know that Justin was the one guy in the world who would never kiss a girl on the first date because he never wanted them to feel cheap. Justin was as rare and unique as the ancient artifacts he loved to unearth. So anyone could say anything they liked, but I knew my brother.

"I won't listen to your bullshit, Vaughn."

He leaned forward as much as his restraints allowed. "Oh, but I'm telling the truth. Justin was ruthless. Who do you think gave Guzman the green light to have his men hurt you?" he whispered. "He didn't want you interfering in his plans."

Those men had intercepted me in Mexico City when I went looking for Justin. They were animals. Luckily, King had gotten to me before they'd had a chance to do any real damage. In any case..."Justin would never d—"

"Your brother was an evil man, Mia. True 10 Club material. You simply don't want to see it."

"Shutthefuckup!" More lies. It sickened me. But now was my opportunity to get the truth. I wanted to know what really happened to Justin. I needed to know. I picked up the knife and began scanning the wall for a key.

"It's unlocked," Vaughn said, as if daring me to come inside.

Oh, I was coming inside all right.

I gave the cell door a push, and it did, in fact, swing open. *Lucky day.*

"Vaughn." I held up the knife. "I want to know what really happened. And if I so much as hear a hint of another lie, I'll slice off your ear."

Ignoring my words, Vaughn said, "I will escape, Miss Turner, and when I do, I will go straight to your mother and father. I will peel the skin from their bodies. I will wear your mother and dance in front of your father before I fuck them both."

I staggered back, gagging as the bitter acid crawled up my throat. Suddenly, I saw the horrific acts he envisioned for the people I loved playing out in front of me. I didn't know if it was a product of my imagination or if I was witnessing his thoughts, but I didn't care. It looked real.

"No!" I screamed at Vaughn as he lifted a knife to my mother's throat.

I blinked and found myself standing right where I'd been all along. In that cell with Vaughn.

I stumbled back, panting, sweating, my head spinning. *What was that?* A glimpse of the future? My Seer mind at work in some strange way? I didn't know, but I would give anything to stop what I'd just witnessed. It reminded me of Justin's final moments when I'd been in the room, viewing everything, yet Justin couldn't see me. I remembered thinking how weak and pathetic I was. Why couldn't I make him hear me and stop Vaughn from hurting him? I'd thought.

"Oh yes," Vaughn said, unaware of what had just occurred. "I plan to videotape the entire thing so you can watch. Would you like that, Mia? I would. I have every detail planned in my mind, and it makes me hard merely thinking about it."

I looked down and saw a bulge in his pants. It sickened me beyond words.

I found my legs moving, heading straight toward that vile excuse of a human being. Hovering outside my own rage-filled body, I watched my arm lift and plunge the knife into Vaughn's chest near his heart. I felt a profound sense of joy and relief as his eyes lit with pain.

Holy Christ. I dropped the knife, and it clanked to the floor. I'd stabbed him. And…it felt good.

"Thank you, Miss Turner." He winced and grinned simultaneously as blood flowed freely from the wound.

That's when I realized…"Wait. You wanted me to kill you."

He breathed heavily now. Clearly the pain was intense, and clearly I gave no fucks.

Vaughn coughed up a bit of blood and continued grinning. "You have no idea who King truly is, do you?"

"Of course I do." I knew more than he did. That was certain.

He shook his head slowly and whispered, "No. Not who he was, but who he became—who he really is…" He gasped for air and began to chuckle. "And you think you're safe with him."

More head games. "I don't give a shit what you say. Your words are meaningless lies."

Determined to make some sort of point, Vaughn ignored me. "You do not know anything, Miss Turner. Otherwise, you wouldn't be attempting to ascertain why I prefer dying over," he hacked and spit out a mouthful of blood, "over…" he gasped for air, "being King's dungeon pet."

I could only assume that Vaughn referred to the fact that King had the ability to pop inside a person's body and evoke copious amounts of pain.

"And the Seer bitch thinks I am a monster…Me!" Vaughn chuckled.

The man actually believed he was a nice person compared to King? *Psycho!*

"Yes. I do think you're a monster," I spat.

"Perhaps I am, but you are blind. Blind about King, as you are about your fuck of a little brother. That's the beauty of it all. You sacrifice everything to save someone who would leave you to be violated and mutilated by a group of thugs."

"You're lying."

"I have no reason to lie."

Of course he did. He wanted to watch me suffer. I'm sure it wasn't anything personal; he simply got off on it. Even now as his body gave out and blood flowed from the wound, he enjoyed this. The sick bulge remained in his stained pants.

I couldn't take it anymore. This had to end.

I picked up the knife and stared into his eyes. Then I sliced his throat. "Who's getting off now?"

"Mia?"

My head turned toward King, who stood in the doorway behind me, shock covering his face. "What did you do?"

I looked at my bloody hand, having to think about it. Was this a dream? "I think I, uh, slit the bastard's throat." I dropped the bloody knife at King's feet as I passed him.

CHAPTER FOUR

Later that afternoon, after a long, long run to ward off an imminent mental breakdown—*yeah, Mia Turner is officially a murderer*—I strolled along the empty beach, focusing on the sensation of the warm white sand sifting between my toes. Sadly, it did little for me. Neither did the sound of crashing waves—something I normally found soothing.

Cold hands shoved deeply into my jeans' pockets, I stopped to gaze out across the endless stretch of blue ocean, the wind whipping my face. To be frank with myself, I wasn't sure what felt more disturbing about the morning's events: the weird and very real vision I'd had of Vaughn hurting my mother, the ease with which I'd killed him, or the relief and satisfaction I'd felt afterward.

Definitely, the lack of remorse. Because, holy hell, it felt goddamned euphoric knowing this world had been rid of Vaughn. Now, if I could only get my hands on the rest of 10 Club.

You're going to go on a killing spree, Mia? Really?

No. But I wanted to, and my mind didn't know what to make of it. These were not the emotions of a decent person, but of a ruthless criminal. And if it weren't for my confusion over that fact, I would be off looking for King. *Sadistic pig. I bet he got a kick out of locking me up with Vaughn.*

"You look like you had a rough day," said a deep male voice.

I turned my head to find Mack, King's right-hand man and personal pilot, staring with a warm, boyish grin. Mack's messy blond hair, big blue eyes, and unshaven face gave him the appearance of a rugged, sweet, all-American guy. Handsome as hell, too. On the inside, however, lived a deadly, ex-military-something, and a damned pit bull—as fiercely loyal as he was ferocious. There wasn't anything Mack wouldn't do for King. Anything. Including throwing me under the bus, lying to me, and placing me in danger. All because King had freed him from being the whipping boy of another 10 Club member—Vaughn's psycho wife—*Christ*—widow. In any case, I didn't trust Mack and never would.

"Hey, Mack." I jerked my head.

"You still mad?"

Mad? I assumed he referred to all of the lies—too many to count—he'd told me over the last few months.

"This isn't about being mad." I walked away from him and the ostentatious estate.

"Of course it is," he called out.

"Idiot," I grumbled under my breath, just as Mack caught up and stood in my way.

How dare he? "Move."

His blue eyes narrowed, and with the bright sun shining over us, I noticed the red highlights in his dark blond hair and a few white whiskers sprinkled throughout his stubbled jaw.

"We need to talk," he said in a cold voice that reminded me of King.

"No, we don't." I tried to step around him, but he pushed me back.

"What the hell is the matter with you?" I barked.

"I need to talk to you."

Feathers fully ruffled, I stared for several moments. A guy like him wasn't going to leave until he got what he wanted, and I desperately needed to be alone. "You have ten seconds."

His eyes focused on my white tee shirt, which I now noticed had splatters of blood on it, along with my jeans. "Christ, Mia, you did kill Vaughn."

I hissed, "That's what you want to talk about?"

"No, actually. I was only curious about that—it's not like you."

I shrugged. "Yes. I did the world a giant favor and ended him. Your point?"

"You really have become a cold-hearted bitch. I wouldn't have believed it if I hadn't heard you say it."

I lifted my brows. "Are we done now? Because this 'bitch' isn't in the mood for small talk."

"No. We're not done." He glanced over his shoulder back at the house. "I need to tell you something, but it's not safe to talk here. Someone might hear us."

I shook my head. Obviously, he wasn't worried about any Spiros sneaking up on us; we could see those "someones."

"You mean King," I stated.

"Yes."

"I don't have time for this, Mack." Anything he had to say would only serve to advance some twisted hidden agenda of King's. I turned to head back toward the house, only to be yanked by my arm.

"Mia," he growled, "I know you don't have a reason to trust me, but I swear on my life that I'm trying to help you."

I stared into his vivid blue eyes as he towered over me. "What are you up to?"

His gaze moved to my lips as if he were contemplating doing something he shouldn't. I instinctively stepped back.

"Fine," he said. "If you won't come with me so we can talk privately, then I'll tell you here. Just know that if he overhears, I'm dead."

Again, I didn't believe a word the man said, so I shrugged.

"You really have changed, haven't you?" He shook his head.

"You sound disappointed."

"I liked the old Mia. As annoying and whiny as she might've been, she genuinely cared."

"You'll get over it."

He scratched his chin, and the wind picked up, pushing his blond hair back. "Already am."

"Good. So what did you want to tell me?" I asked to hurry the chat along.

"Something is wrong with King."

I burst out laughing. "Yeah, no shit."

"Goddammit, Mia. I am serious. He's not himself."

My laughter trailed off, but I couldn't help still smile. "Really, now?"

"You need to be careful."

"Are you trying to warn me that King is dangerous?"

Hilarious. Tell me something new.

"No. Not like before. I mean…" He looked down at his leather sandals, searching for the right words. And, as off topic as it might be, I thought to myself how odd that was, Mack wearing sandals. Handmade, worn, brown leather sandals. So, so out of character for a lethal, ex-military assassin type who flew private jets and had his muscular arms covered in tattoos.

But what do you really know about this guy? Nothing.

"I don't know how to explain it," he said, frustrated, "but you need to be careful. Don't be alone with him."

"That's pretty impossible, given I'm supposed to marry the guy so that we once again avoid his property being seized by the 10 Club. And, might I remind you, *you* are considered his property, too."

"Mia," Mack leaned in and whispered, "he got Miranda put in charge of 10 Club."

"What?" Miranda was Vaughn's wife—*Christ...widow*—and Mack's ex-owner. She was just as cutthroat, demented, and vile as Vaughn had been.

Mack nodded. "He asked me to deliver this to her." He held out an envelope.

"What's inside?"

"I don't know," he said, "but I have a feeling I'm not just delivering a letter; I'm delivering myself."

King had saved Mack from Miranda. It was the reason Mack remained loyal to King from what I could tell. That, and King had once "found something" he needed. God only knew what that was.

"Are you sure?" I asked.

"It's a gut feeling."

If I were him, I'd open the damned thing and find out. But that was Mack: loyal to a fault even when his own neck was on the chopping block.

"As fucked up as King is, he would never do that," I argued.

"That's why I'm telling you. The King I know—*we* know—wouldn't do that."

Maybe this was a trick. Maybe this was simply paranoia. Frankly, I didn't care. Mack had made his bed, and I wasn't about to lie in it with him or get anywhere near those sheets. Not after everything he'd done, including pretending to be looking after me while really acting as King's pawn. He had made sure on several occasions that I moved myself across the chessboard in a direction behooving to King. The last straw, the *final* straw, had been when he'd allowed me to be taken by Vaughn. Later I'd discover that King was Vaughn's prisoner, too, only the bastard was there on purpose so he could get closer to the Artifact. King had hoped, erroneously, that Psycho-Britches had the cursed rock in his possession. Luckily, I'd gotten free, but not without paying a steep price. One I didn't care to relive.

"All right. You told me. What do you want me to do?" I asked.

"Nothing." He reached into his pocket and held out a silver cuff bracelet. "But I won't be back, no matter what, so I want to give you this."

"What is it?"

"Your freedom."

Huh?

"It's—it's..." Mack cleared his throat. "You have to run this time, Mia."

I'd heard that advice from him before and hadn't listened. Too much had been at stake to walk away. And, unfortunately, the same rang true in this very moment. "*Now* I know you're up to something, Mack, because you know I can't run."

"Forget your brother, Mia. He's gone, and frankly, your life is worth more than his, anyway."

Asshole. He didn't have the right to pass judgment on my dead brother. And why did everyone think this was only about Justin? My mother and father would be devastated without him, and that alone was worth trying to bring him back.

"You will move on eventually," Mack said, anticipating my argument.

"You've apparently never loved anyone, because if you had, you'd know that no one ever moves on. Not really."

His eyes narrowed. "Quite a bold statement for a woman who knows so little about me."

"I know everything I need to; you can't be trusted."

"Mia, I can be trust—"

"Why would I believe that? Because you say so?"

"No. Because I'm risking my life to save you. King won't hesitate to end me for telling you to run."

"You've told me to run before."

"This time is different," he said.

"Why?"

"Because before, it was *King* who wanted you to run. *He* wanted you to have every chance to leave, and I wanted you to stay."

His words shocked and confused me. "Why?"

"You think I've never loved anyone, but you're wrong. It's what got me into this fucked- up mess to begin with. It's why I'm standing here now."

Something itched in the back of my head, but I couldn't quite reach it. "I don't unders—"

"For fuck's sake," he barked, "you don't need to, Mia! Take the damned bracelet and run."

"Even if I wanted to, he'd find me." I held up my wrist and showed him the "K" tattoo. With it, King had not only staked his claim on me with the 10

Club, but he could find me, too. It connected us—permitted him to hear my thoughts, and allowed me to see him with little effort on his part. When he wanted to be seen, of course.

"Thus the bracelet." He shoved the silver cuff into my hand. "It's from King's arsenal. The catalog says it has the ability to 'hide' a person. It ensures there are no traces—physical or otherwise."

"Otherwise" meant whatever weird magic King used to track me down.

"Wear it over the tattoo and never take it off," he added.

I stared at the thing. Was it possible that this small, curved hunk of metal with odd symbols could prevent King from hunting me?

"Where would I go?" I asked purely out of curiosity. After all, it wasn't like I had money to travel because King had made me quit my job. Also, any friends or family I had were no secret to a man who knew every corner and crevice of my mind.

"If it were me," Mack said, "I would try thinking of someplace I'd never been before. Somewhere far away from this."

I had to admit, the idea of escaping for good sounded very tempting. "You really think it works?"

He nodded. "Yes. For fuck's sake, run, Mia."

I held the bracelet in my hands, thinking. I needed to get Justin back. No, I absolutely didn't believe a word anyone said about him. I knew my brother. They didn't. But more importantly, I needed to end my parents' suffering. "I can't."

He sighed and shook his head. "Stubborn, stubborn, Mia. Maybe you haven't changed."

I cocked my head. "Trust me, I have. Which is why I'm not trusting you." I held out the bracelet.

"No. You keep it. In case you change your mind." He turned to leave, and I watched his shoulders sag a bit as his strong frame strode away. I had to admit, a tiny part of me wanted to believe he cared, but he'd shown me differently.

Then why the hell is your stomach knotting up? The nausea was threatening to make me hurl.

"Where are you going?" I yelled out.

"Back to hell," Mack replied. "See you there."

He shot a smile over his shoulder, and in that very moment, an image flashed inside my head. It was of King standing over a body, a bloody sword in one hand and the head of his twin brother dangling from the other. It was the image I'd seen in my mind when King had made me read a translated copy of Hagne's journal. She had been his queen, but hated King with every fiber of her being. She loved his twin brother, Callias, though, and it destroyed them all. I suspected it was the cause of the Minoan civilization's downfall. No, I hadn't had time to do any heavy research, but archeologists said they mysteriously disappeared between 1500 and 1200 BC. Some say it was an earthquake, some say it might have been a volcanic eruption or foreign invasion, but I thought it was war. A civil war sparked by King's executions of his own traitorous brother and of Hagne.

I shoved the bracelet into my jeans pocket, planted myself down in the sand, and let my mind cull through the random bits and pieces it had gathered up over the past few months. So many questions, so few answers. And lucky *mio* had another one to add to the heap: *Is this another trap?*

"What do you think?" I heard King say.

My head whipped around, but I saw no one.

"Over here, Mia." The sound radiated from the deep blue waves. Like a mirage, King emerged from the water, completely nude.

My jaw dropped.

I hadn't really seen King naked since he'd lost his tattoos (compliments of Vaughn when King was *his* dungeon guest). One tattoo, in particular, was of a sundial that gave him a few hours each day to walk among the living with little effort. The other tattoo had been an elaborate Egyptian-looking collar that circled the base of his neck all the way down to his pectorals. I never did learn what it had been for, but now that his body was free of any ink, I more clearly saw every exquisite inch of the man.

Yes, I wanted to look away and be bigger than my physical feelings for him.

Yes, sometimes I failed. Miserably.

Like now.

I so don't get it.

Unable to pull my eyes away from the chiseled perfection of every muscle and his deep olive skin glistening with drops of water, I simply stared. His long thick cock hung low between his thighs as he ran his hands through his wet black hair.

He strolled up and stood before me, his penis dangling freely in front of my face. "Like what you see, Miss Turner?"

My eyes snapped up to meet his. Yes, I liked what I saw, but so what? Didn't mean anything. Of course, the bastard could read my mind.

"Mia," I corrected.

He dipped his head and sat beside me, stretching his long legs into the warm white sand.

"What did the infamous Mack have to say?" he inquired.

"Don't pretend you didn't hear."

"I did not. Otherwise, why would I ask? I'm not the sort of man to waste my time with games, Mia."

Yeah right. King was the master of games.

"Of course not," I said sarcastically. "That's why you threw me in that cell with Vaughn."

"Ah. Well." He scratched his chin. "I admit, I may have gotten carried away."

"You've turned me into a murderer."

"Perhaps, Miss Turner, I simply wanted to grant you the opportunity to confront your brother's killer."

"Confront," I repeated his word. "Is that why you slid a knife under the door?"

"No, but that was one hell of a confrontation."

He thought this was amusing. *Evil bastard.* I didn't feel regret over what I'd done, but it wasn't entertainment material.

"No, not entertaining," " he replied to my thoughts and spoke in a deep, slow voice. "Stimulating, however…"

I turned my body and scowled at him. "Why would you do something like that, King?"

"I've already answered your question; you simply don't care for the answer."

"Because you're lying." King always had a motive for everything he did, and they were never frivolous.

"Don't we all?"

"All what?" Sometimes I wasn't sure if he referred to something I said or to something I thought.

"Do we not all have our motives? You, for instance; what motivated you to end Vaughn when you know perfectly well, Miss Turner, I wouldn't have let him live?"

"I don't know."

"Ah, but you do. You merely don't wish to say it."

"I saw what he intended to do to my mom," I blurted out.

"Saw?"

"Like I was right there with him," I explained.

"Perhaps you were."

"That's not possible," I argued.

He shrugged. "You are a Seer. A very powerful one who's just beginning to comprehend her abilities."

"What are you saying?"

"I'm merely stating that Seers have unusual gifts which develop over time. Who knows what you are capable of?"

"Seers *had*," I corrected. "You killed them all. Remember?"

And thank you for that, because now I'll never know squat.

"We all have our pasts, Miss Turner. Even you."

I looked at him and scowled, knowing he referred to my incident with Vaughn.

Thanks to you.

"I did not make you kill him," he pointed out. "That was all you."

I sighed bitterly. As usual, King liked to focus on partial truths. "The weird part was Vaughn wanted me to kill him. He kept egging me on about Justin being a villain, and about wanting to hurt my parents. Any idea why?"

"Perhaps he feared I might torture him for a bit."

"Were you going to?" I asked.

"I hadn't decided."

"I wish you had—maybe you could've gotten him to tell me what happened with Justin." Not that I believed a word he'd said.

"The truth often lies somewhere in the middle," he said, commenting on my thoughts. "However, Miss Turner, I'm shocked."

"What?"

"You would have liked me to torture him? My, how you've changed."

"Don't look so pleased, King."

He chuckled quietly. "Well, I believe a little darkness is healthy in a person. Good for the soul."

I wasn't going to touch that one. "Whatever."

Looking out across the waves, we sat in silence for several moments.

"I think I will miss this after I move on," he said.

"Miss what? Torturing me?"

"The banter."

I half laughed, half huffed. "You would."

He grinned a bit. "And...perhaps throwing you in with Vaughn was not the best of ideas. However, the knife was merely a precaution for your defense as the man was dangerous—with or without chains—which is why I stayed close."

"Did you just apologize?" I could hardly believe it. The man never apologized for anything.

He shot a look meant to warn me.

"Just wanted to be sure," I said flippantly. *Not like you're one to make mistakes, let alone admit to it. Lying, on the other hand...*

"Very well, you were right; I had another motive for the gift. I acquired Vaughn because I planned to kill him after you had your words with the man."

"I thought you couldn't touch other 10 Club members?" Of course, it was a rule they followed superficially.

"I obtained clearance as part of the deal. I needed to know you would be safe after I am gone. Needless to say, I now know that I have nothing to fear; you are capable of doing whatever is necessary to survive. Even kill your foe. So, I suppose you might argue the gift was for me."

His "gift" had turned me into a cold-hearted killer that I didn't recognize. Bottom line, however, I didn't want to think about it anymore. I needed to focus on something else, or I might crack the rest of the way. Letting that happen when I was so close to the end would be a tragedy.

Next time you want to give me a gift, try some clothes.

"I am glad you mentioned that; I would like to take you somewhere special tonight. The dress is waiting in your room."

"I meant that *you* should wear clothes, not buy me some." Sitting next to his naked body made it hard to remember why I hated the man or why I couldn't trust him. "We're not going to an empty restaurant in San Francisco, are we?"

He flashed a wolfish smile. "I can arrange that, if you prefer."

"No."

"As I thought. Which is why I will take you somewhere special to me. From my childhood."

"We'll be alone?" I asked to confirm my suspicions.

"Someone must cook and serve the food. However, we will have the opportunity to talk privately so that you may ask me anything you like. I assumed this would be an adequate compromise to my earlier proposal."

My eyes wandered over to his lean muscular legs, up to his groin, where he'd left his legs open.

Crap. Don't look. Luckily my mind was quickly back in control, smothering those tingles concentrating in my core and between my legs. Seriously, there was no rational reason for the effect this man had on me.

"Then it is settled." King slowly rose from the sand and dusted off his hard bronzed ass. I tried not to look, but it was impossible.

"I'm going to take a soak in my tub. Care to join me?" he asked.

I blinked. It wasn't a tub, but a round, large sunken pool with tiles made of the same deep blues as the Aegean Sea and smack in the center of his room like some ancient Grecian spa. I'd literally dreamed about bathing with him in it a million times—our bodies wet and steaming as I rode his muscled frame and devoured his sensual lips with my mouth.

King lifted one dark, silky brow. "My, my, Miss Turner. You *do* have quite the dirty mind. I hope to sample the fruits of its labor before my time is up. Perhaps tonight?"

I shook my head, feeling ashamed. My imagination was out of control. "No."

"Such a shame, as I think we both might enjoy it." King shrugged and began walking toward the house, dissolving into thin air right before my eyes. "I hope you like the dress, Mia."

"I didn't agree to go with you."

"Do not be late," his disembodied voice called out. "It displeases me."

Pompous jerk. I hung my head and covered my face before blowing out a slow breath. I tried not to be excited about tonight, but I was. I tried not to hate myself for it, but I did.

But what about the thing Mack said?

Focus on something else. I needed to keep that to myself. If something really was wrong with King, it changed nothing. Not the fundamentals, anyway. *Eyes on the prize, Mia.* And his believing my ignorance over the matter would be my only defense should anything go wrong. *Think of something else, think of something else*, I chanted inside my head.

It wasn't hard to move my thoughts back to images of King's naked, rock-hard body, and to the unsettling mystery of what he planned for tonight.

CHAPTER FIVE

When I returned to the house after a few hours of deep contemplation interrupted by quiet fits of panic, I finally had my game plan figured out for the evening. The old Mia would have hummed and hawed, but King was right. Today I'd learned that this Mia wasn't simply colder and perhaps crazier, but she was stronger, too. This Mia could face her fears and do what had to be done. Which was exactly why I wouldn't allow my worries to get in the way of my goal: saving Justin, and, therefore, saving my parents' hearts. Everything else was noise.

So, if bringing Justin back required me to share an intimate dinner with King and force myself to feel something for the man, then that's what I would do. I would push myself to *see* him, really truly *see* him for who he was, without judgment or fear. Besides, I'd already met his bad side. Maybe if I did this, I'd get to see more of his soft underbelly.

I wearily climbed the stairs towards King's room, but found Stefanos Spiros, the head of the Spiros family and of King's mysterious Greek mafia, blocking my way. Stefanos was also the chief of police, which is why he wore an intimidating uniform.

"You are to go to your personal chamber to prepare for tonight," he said with a thick Greek accent. "To the left and at the end of the corridor."

I had stayed in King's suite during my handful of nights at the estate, upon King's request.

"Why the change?" Not that I minded, but King never did anything without a reason.

Stefanos shrugged. "Don't know. Don't care. When our king asks me to do something, I do it."

"And when I'm your queen, what then?" I asked just to torment him. "Will you follow me blindly, too?"

"No. You are not my king," he replied.

"And I'm a Seer of Light." The Spiros were not super-fans of my heritage—being related to Hagne—despite the fact she'd died over three thousand years ago. The strange part was that the Seer "gift" was passed on through bloodlines, but not everyone had it. How did I know? There were quite a few women in my family—cousins and aunts, yet I was the last living Seer. The end of the line.

"Yes." He narrowed his dark eyes, eyes that matched his thick brown hair.

"You do realize how ridiculous it is to hold a grudge that long."

"We have our reasons," he replied.

"Such as?"

He gestured toward the corridor to the left, meaning he wasn't going to answer. "Ypirétria awaits to assist you."

I sighed. "In what?"

"Dressing for your evening. The helicopter leaves in thirty minutes." He glanced at his watch. "Make that twenty-eight minutes."

There was no point in asking where I was going because King would have already told me if he wanted me to know. "Thank you, Stefanos." I nodded. "I'll be ready in forty."

The look in his eyes told me he was about to remind me of King's punctuality obsession but decided against it. After all, it was my ass that would be chewed out by King for being late, not his.

I passed Stefanos on the stairwell and was almost to the top when I stopped. "Stefanos?"

He gazed up at me from the bottom of the stairs.

"I'm sorry if my being here makes your family feel uncomfortable."

He gave me a cold look. "You won't live forever."

I assumed he thought I'd want to live here until my last dying breath, even after King departed this world. I had no such intentions. "I'll be out of your hair by next week, actually."

He gave me a peculiar look, then glanced at his watch. "Twenty-seven minutes."

I shook my head and continued on my way. When I got to the fairly large room with a balcony overlooking the side garden, Ypirétria, which was Greek for "maid," sat in the corner with a pair of knitting needles and pink yarn.

"Hi. I'm back," I said, knowing she didn't understand English (nor I her language), but saying nothing felt strange.

She blurted out an exclamation I imagined meant, "Where the hell have you been, young lady?" But who knew?

"I went for a long walk." I made my fingers walk across my palm to illustrate.

The elderly woman, who wore a black drapey dress and scarf, pointed to the bathroom and mimed that I needed to shave my legs.

Err. Okay...thanks for the concern? "I'll be ready in five minutes." I held up five fingers, expecting she'd get the cue to leave.

She mumbled something, shook her finger at me, and then pointed to my armpits, once again miming that I was to shave.

I'm twenty-six years old and have a mother, I thought, but didn't want to say something so rude, even if she couldn't understand.

She walked over to the enormous walk-in closet and emerged with a black satin strapless dress. She swept her hand over the front as if presenting me with a very nice gift, which I'm sure it was. King didn't buy dresses off the clearance rack at Macy's or Neiman's—my usual hunting grounds. But with its ultrashort hem and scandalously plunging neckline, it was the sort of dress a woman wore when she didn't intend to keep it on very long.

My body involuntarily reacted to the thought of King selecting something so seductive for me.

The woman then pointed right at my groin while making her other hand into scissors. "See-reez-ma," she said slowly.

I scratched my head. "You want me to groom the kitty?"

"You make di lobe tonight," she said in broken English. "Sex weet King."

My jaw dropped. Not because the woman could barely speak a lick of English and had managed to say something so shocking, but because it gave me a sick sort of sexual satisfaction imagining King telling her how he wanted me to look for him, right down to my naked body.

Get it together, Mia. This is a mind game. The guy was probably in the room right now, watching me and enjoying the hell out of my reaction. Well, I wasn't going to give him one.

I cleared the sticky, indecent thoughts from my throat. "No. You tell King, no sex. No sex tonight."

The woman repeated her instructions.

"Tell King if he wants sex, he can go fuck himself."

She stared.

"You don't understand me, do you?" I asked.

She slapped her palms together, symbolizing a man and woman lying together. "You make di sex tonight." She nodded happily as if she believed we'd come to some sort of understanding, and then walked from the room, leaving the dress laid out on the bed.

Lord, help me.

The entire time I showered—yes, and shaved—I kept thinking about the part of me that really did want him. He was a beast that oozed sexual desire. *More like a goddamned lion. And you're lunch.*

So why couldn't I make the feelings go away?

Mia. Stop. Just be on your guard and stay focused. We had the Artifact now and were so close to the end of this nightmare. Justin would be brought back. King's suffering would end.

And King will be gone from your life forever.

I drew in a deep breath, the hot water beating down mercilessly on my tense neck. "This is goodbye." The man who'd lived over three thousand years, who'd witnessed the world age and change, would soon cease to exist. And curse or no curse, this would be the end of something profoundly epic, the end of a king from a lost civilization.

My mind quickly began to wander. What had the world—his world—been like? What had King been like? I tried to imagine him before Hagne's evil had sunk its claws into his soul and turned his life into an unimaginable suffering, but I couldn't. I couldn't visualize King being…well, a king. Or just a man. With a heart and worries, with disappointments and triumphs, just like anyone else.

Whoever he once was and whatever he knew would soon be gone. Just like that. All to end his suffering and for "everything to be set right again, for everyone to get back what was taken," as he'd once said.

I finished rinsing my body and shut off the water, solemnly comprehending that there would be a sacrifice on his part. A big one. And just like that, I felt my heavy mental armor eroding.

King was going to die.

Feeling like the wind had been knocked out of me, I sat on the bed and held my hands over my mouth. Evil tendencies or not, the good in him triumphed. No, it wasn't love, but it was a start. A start to our end.

࿐

Forty minutes later on the dot, I made my way down the stairs—shaved, plucked, hair swept up into a twist, and a hint of red for my lips—in a dress that barely left room to sit, let alone breathe. My breasts nearly spilled from the top of the black satin scallops that formed the neckline, and only a centimeter of flesh stood between me and exposing my nipples to the world.

"You look very nice, Miss Turner," Stefanos held out his arm, "but you are late."

I carefully took the last step in my spiked black heels before latching on to him. "Sorry. But King ordered additional grooming for tonight."

Stefanos raised one dark brow but did not say a word.

He walked me through the spacious living room and a side door, where a gleaming black, very large and fast-looking helicopter awaited on the cement pad. With the sun almost completely set and the sky streaked with hot pink bolts, my ride looked more like an evil black beast waiting to whisk me away to the land of sin.

I shuddered and my skin erupted with goose bumps.

"Are you all right?" asked Stefanos, probably wondering why I'd stopped moving.

I had a very bad feeling all of a sudden. *It's your nerves, Mia. Suck it up.*

I flashed a glance at the sleek helicopter. The pilot wore a tux and stood at attention next to a set of small steps placed beneath the door. He quickly bowed, and it made me laugh. King wanted very badly to make me feel special tonight.

Maybe that's why you feel nervous.

"Miss Turner?" Stefanos said. "It's time to go."

I took a deep breath and made my way to the black beast.

"Good evening, Miss Turner. Right this way." The pilot gestured toward the cabin.

"Thank you." I flashed a polite smile.

Once inside, I paused for a moment to take in the extravagant decor. I'd never been inside a helicopter, but this looked more like the executive lounge at some swanky nightclub—black leather seats surrounding a table topped with a bottle of champagne chilling in a bucket. The recessed lights were slightly dimmed, and calming spa-like music piped in from the surround sound system. It actually felt larger and more spacious than King's private jet.

"Have a lovely evening, *my queen*." Stefanos dipped his head and shut the door after the pilot climbed in.

"Make yourself comfortable." The pilot proceeded to the front cabin and shut the door behind him. The engine cranked almost immediately, but instead of a roar like I'd seen in movies, the sound was a quiet purr.

I stood there staring at the empty chairs, wondering where the real alcohol was hidden.

"We are about to depart, Miss Turner," said the pilot over the intercom. "Please take your seat."

I felt the floor lift beneath me straight into the air, and my stomach lurched. *I definitely need whiskey.*

I sat patiently for a few minutes, twisting my body toward the window to watch us make our way over the ocean. But instead of going north as I thought we would, the helicopter headed east, away from the setting sun.

I kicked off my heels to make walking a bit safer and popped open the door to the cockpit. The noise was deafening.

"Hey!" I screamed. "Where are we going?"

The pilot, a thin man with gray hair, couldn't hear me with his headphones on, so I poked his shoulder.

He glanced at me with a startled expression.

"Sorry." I repeated my question, and he pointed to a headset hanging on the wall. I carefully slid it over my hair. "Where are we going?"

Looking ahead, the pilot responded, "I have been instructed not to speak to you or answer your questions."

"Seriously?"

"He does not want the surprise ruined. We'll be at our destination in an hour. I suggest you relax and make yourself comfortable."

Great. It was clear I wouldn't be getting any answers from this guy. I missed Mack already. At least he spoke to me.

My gaze momentarily set on my right wrist as I thought of him. Yes, I'd worn the bracelet. I'd told myself it was because I needed something to go with the outfit, that I would never run and leave my parents to deal with the loss of two children. But truth was, it gave me comfort knowing that if things got bad, really bad, I had an option. As an added precaution, I still wore the ring King had given me. Also from King's arsenal of powerful goodies, the giant solitaire did more than simply decorate one's finger. It could bring a person back to life if they wore it at the time of death. Yes, I'd already used it once. Not so fun, but very handy.

"Oh, and Miss Turner?" said the pilot, just as I was about to slip off the headset. "If you prefer, there is a nice bottle of scotch in the cupboard above the sink in the back. I had to secure it so it wouldn't break."

King's pulling out all the stops tonight.

"Thank you." I slipped off the headphones.

Back inside my soundproofed luxury cubbyhole in the sky, I found my prized elixir of the nerves and poured two fingers' worth. I couldn't make out the distillery on the old faded label, but the golden brown liquid tasted like velvety smoke and sweet toffee. This was an expensive treat, no doubt.

I took a seat and breathed it in, using the beverage as a way to keep my mind from feeling anxious. Wherever we were going, I imagined it would be interesting. *Someplace special*, he'd said. The man really wanted out of his curse, so it made sense he'd be making a special effort. Hell, maybe that was why Mack had seen a change in him—not that I had. But after three-thousand-something years, King had to be going crazy. He was so, so close to seeing his suffering end.

Of course, I needed to be on my guard. Not that King would ever welsh on our deal, but King was still King, which meant he always had some other agenda.

Getting into your pants, maybe? I smiled to myself. *Probably.*

An hour later, the helicopter set down in a field or something—I couldn't see—nestled in complete darkness. From the lack of lights, I knew we weren't near any cities or towns. The engine quieted and the pilot emerged from his cabin. "Right this way, Miss Turner." He opened the door and hopped out, waiting to help me down the small steps.

Standing in the doorway, the moist ocean air immediately hit me. "Where are we?" I asked. "Where is King?"

The pilot held out his hand, and I hesitantly took it. Complete darkness surrounded the helicopter's illuminated perimeter. The sound of waves crashing far off in the distance swept over me with a gentle breeze.

"King instructed me to bring you here," he said.

My heart started to pound. I didn't know where "here" was. "You are *not* dumping me in some dark field in the middle of goddamned—"

"Mia, I am here with you." I felt King's hot breath in my ear and his warm palm press against the small of my back. "There is nothing to fear."

I turned to find King towering over me. Even in my six-inch heels, I still felt meek compared to his size.

"He cannot see or hear me," King explained in that deep, confident voice which told me I was behaving like a child, "and I did not want to frighten the man. By the way, you're late for dinner."

Ugh. King and his punctuality.

I turned toward the pilot. "Thanks for the ride. See you later."

The pilot dipped his head and disappeared inside the helicopter.

"So now can you tell me where we are?" I asked.

King smiled and reached out, placing his large hand on my cheek. "You look beautiful tonight, Mia." He then rubbed his thumb across my lower lip, staring with intensity at my mouth. "I cannot wait to show you what I have planned for us."

His devilish smile almost brought me to my knees, half in fear, half due to the excitement I felt when he touched me. It was a rush. A drug. A sick addiction.

King took my hand and led me away from the field. It was difficult to see anything, but I tried my best to make out the hard texture of the ground to avoid falling in my heels.

"My apologies for the rustic accommodations," he said, "but cement has no place here." He pulled me along, and I heard the helicopter's engine start. A strong gust of wind whipped at my hair, blowing a few clumps loose.

"He's leaving?" I asked.

"He's needed elsewhere but will return shortly," King said. The wind whipped violently around us.

There goes the hair.

"I prefer your hair down, anyway," he commented.

My blonde locks generally resembled a wildebeest's chin unless I took care to trim it regularly and use anti-wildebeest products, but there'd been little time for any of that, so I'd worn it up.

"Just don't complain when it attacks you." I slipped the pin from my hair and let the rest fall loose.

King let out a deep chuckle, and I had to admit, it made my toes tingle. There was nothing like it in the world—sensual, unapologetically male, and completely seductive.

"Wait here one moment," he said.

Before I could protest, a torch burst with flames in his hand. "There. Now that the helicopter has departed, we can have light. Right this way."

He held out the torch, and I saw a long, narrow, sandy walkway ahead and a set of stone steps leading up. Up to what, I didn't know.

"This is my private island," King said. "I've had it since I was born. Handed down from my father."

"Seriously?"

"Yes," he replied. "I spent many summers here with my family. It brings good memories."

I followed him up the steps, and along the way, he lit various torches staked into the ground. "How did you keep it all this time?"

"It helps that it doesn't appear on any maps. And I have quite the security system."

"Dogs?" I asked.

"No. Any strangers who come near it spontaneously combust."

"That's a bit severe, don't you think?"

He laughed. "All right, they do not explode into flames, but they cannot enter. They then forget they ever saw it. As I said, the island is private, and I intend to keep it that way—hidden from the world."

I just hoped never to become shipwrecked in a place like this. It would make being rescued a bit...

Fuck.

I jerked my hand from his and stopped in my tracks, my stomach falling into my knees. I didn't speak, but I didn't have to; King knew exactly what was going through my head.

"Calm yourself, Miss Turner. Panicking at this point will not save you."

I sucked in a breath. I'd been hoping for some sort of reassurance that his intent was not to imprison me here. What I got instead was a confirmation.

"Why?" I asked.

King held the torch between us, allowing me to see the sinister glow in his eyes, eyes filled with red lights—pain; horrible, excruciating pain. "Because I know what you want, Mia. And I am going to give it to you." He smiled, and deep lines formed to the sides of his mouth.

"Wha-what is it you think I want?"

He leaned in a bit. "To scream as I break you."

෯෮෯

I savor the delightful sound of Mia's terror-filled cry and the exquisite horror in her blue eyes as she realizes the truth. Oh yes, her mind is working hard now, putting together those tiny, unsavory pieces, allowing her to finally see me for who I am: a monster who takes what he desires.

And I desire her.

I have never wanted to fuck a woman more than I want Mia. Her sweet little ass and plump tits make my cock harder than a slab of granite merely thinking of them. I keep a flock of Mia lookalikes—

wavy golden hair, tight asses, luscious lips meant for sucking—on call simply to keep my uncivilized urges at bay. But my wait is now over, and I will have it all: my life returned to me; my revenge; Mia's soft lips wrapped around my shaft, begging me to come in her mouth.

She has no fucking clue what lies ahead—the darkness, the pleasure.

She turns to run, but there is nowhere to hide on this island. *Oh, yes, fight, little Mia, fight. It will make tonight so much more exhilarating.* After I'm done with her—breaking her, hurting her, fucking her—she will realize how I have only given her what she truly desires, what she truly needs from me, but is too afraid to ask for. Yes, I am her king, and it is my blackened soul she longs for.

"Don't fucking touch her."

I laugh. It pleases me when the king's feathers ruffle. "I bet she'll enjoy the whip, too. I know you do."

The king says nothing at first. He is realizing he cannot win.

"If you do this, there is no going back. And the outcome will not be in your favor. Best to cut your losses and let her go."

"Let her go? And deny myself the pleasure I've waited so long for?" Yes, she wants me to tear away her clothes, to make her scream, to claim her.

"For fuck's sake, you are goddamned sick. Which is why your plan will not work."

He's doing it again. Trying to undermine me, make me doubt myself. But I will not fall for his tricks. I am the stronger one, the smarter one.

"Let her be, and end this. It is time for our suffering to be over. Time for us to move on."

I think it over. Part of me shares the old king's desire to stop our pain. But I want what I want. I want to finally take what's mine. I want to fuck her and hurt her and break her. I know she will love it.

And when the time comes, she will choose me.

"It will never work."

"Shut the fuck up. No one is asking you."

CHAPTER SIX

Red. I saw nothing but red light in King's eyes. And I knew without a doubt that he intended to harm me.

I screamed, struggling in his iron grip while we moved up the hill with a speed my brain could not process. When he stopped, he threw me to the ground, and I landed with a thump in the darkness onto a hard wooden surface.

Torches burst to life around us, and I quickly saw we were underneath some sort of large circular thatched roof structure. In the middle was an enormous bed with restraints. I sat up staring at it, my mind buzzing with adrenaline. "Why are you doing this, King?"

He stood next to the bed and began removing his white shirt, one leisurely button at a time. "I know you've dreamed of this, Mia. Of me fucking you like a savage, of me taking you hard. And I plan to make all of your dreams come true tonight."

"Those were my nightmares."

He walked over and crouched in front of me, the fire dancing in his eyes and the red light of his evil soul swirling all around him. "Come, come now, my sweet Miss Turner; there is no reason to hide the truth from me."

"What's happened to you, King?" I whispered, desperately trying not to think about the things Mack had said. Because he had been right: this was not the King we knew. This was not that same disciplined and calculating man. This King was out of control. Vicious. And he had the right aura to prove it.

No, I must keep my thoughts to myself.

He laughed. "There are no secrets between us, Mia. I can crawl inside your mind and take what you won't give me. Just as I can take from your body."

King's handsome face looked almost demonic.

"Did the 10 Club do something to you?" I whispered. "Did they put some sort of spell on you?" It was the only explanation I could think of.

"The 10 Club?" He roared with laughter. "I own those fucking clowns. They can't touch me!"

Was he serious?

He grabbed me by the hair and dragged me to the bed. I kicked and screamed, but it only seemed to amuse him, make him laugh.

He threw me onto the bed, face down, and I felt him harnessing my ankle and then the other. I looked up at my wrist and caught sight of the gleaming silver cuff. I only had a moment before he tied my arms. I slid the cuff over to my left wrist to cover my "K" tattoo and shut my eyes, hoping something might happen—him suddenly unable to see me or…something.

Instead, I felt my right wrist being bound. "King, please stop! Please, I don't want this. I won't ever love you if you do this." He tightened the restraint over my left wrist, and knowing that there was nothing I could do now, I started to pray for my life.

"You won't be needing this." He slid the diamond ring from my finger.

Oh fuck. He's going to kill me.

"Not yet." He laughed. I felt him rip my dress down the back and whip it from my body. "Oh yes, look at that fucking ass." He palmed my flesh and slapped it hard.

I sucked in a sharp breath from the pain and tried not to cry, because it only made him more excited.

No, must remain calm. Try to talk to him, make him see this is wrong.

"King, please stop," I said. "I know there's something inside you that understands what you're doing isn't right. I know a part of you cares." *I just don't know where it went. But please come back to me. Please.*

His sharp teeth bit into my back as he stripped away my panties and strapless bra, leaving me completely bare and face down. *This can't be happening. This can't be happening. I don't want this.*

He slid his hand between my legs from behind and stroked me hard.

I cried out.

"Yes. Scream, just like that, my little Seer bitch. Just like that."

I held my breath, bracing for what I knew would come next: a horrible nightmare coming to life.

Where had he gone? The King who'd saved my mother, who'd save me once, too. I thought of that man, and of how Mack tried to warn me. "Run, Mia. Fucking run." Why hadn't I listened this time?

The tears of desperation poured from my eyes as I felt King lay over my unwilling body, prodding me with his erection through his black jeans.

"This is what you want, isn't it?" he asked.

"No." *Dear God, no.*

"Yes, it is. That's the good little girl speaking. But I'm not giving you your prize just yet." He backed off, reaching for something. "First, a little foreplay. Then I will fuck you until that boring bitch is purged from your body." He leaned over to whisper in my ear. "We'll be together, Mia. You, me, and that black little heart of yours. Because I know you love me...I know I am what you really want." He straddled me, and from the corner of my eye, I saw his hand lift high into the air. In it he held a whip with multiple arms and knots on the ends, the kind that looked like it could take the skin clean off.

My heart isn't black. I'll never love you.

He roared with laughter. "Says the woman who slit a man's throat today and enjoyed it; just as I'd hoped. Now try not to move. This will only hurt a little," he said with a sinister tone that clearly meant it would hurt a lot.

My mind, perhaps to protect me from the horror, instantly focused on a place that was safe, a place where King couldn't go: my heart. He could never touch it. I would be safe there.

I felt a sharp pain and heard my cries fade into the distance.

᪥᪥᪥

The gentle sound of waves caressed my mind in a peaceful dream, a dream where my body lay resting on powdery sand, the warm sun cocooning me in a blanket woven from clouds and tropical air. I couldn't recall ever feeling so at peace or so comfortable. Was I dead? Was I somewhere inside my mind, hiding from King?

I rubbed my eyes and slowly sat up to take in the long stretch of sand and deep green forest skirting the pristine beach. The sun was high in the sky, about noonish, and I wasn't wearing a stitch of clothing.

No clothes. I winced and then closed my eyes, pushing away the dark images of King, of that horrible island. If this was a dream, I didn't want to wake. Not ever. I would rather die naked in a strange place than return to that nightmare.

How could he do that to me? How? It didn't make sense. Not when King needed me to free him from his torment.

Mack had been right, that's how. That had been a monster back on the island. And that monster wanted me to fall into some dark, delusional state where I'd learn to love him. *After he'd beaten and raped me.*

No. I shook my head slowly. That had to be another one of those strange visions like I'd had in Vaughn's cell, or like the time of Justin's death when my mind had been there but my body hadn't.

Maybe I'm having a vision now.

But as I surveyed my body, the burn marks on my wrists and ankles, which were red and raw, certainly felt real.

I blew out a heartbroken breath that hurt just as badly as my wounds. I suddenly felt the bile creep from my stomach and launch over my naked chest. "Oh God." I flipped over and heaved.

After a minute or so, the pain subsided. I stood and stumbled my way to the water. Dream or not, I didn't want to be covered in my own sick.

The warm ocean water simultaneously stung my fresh wounds but felt soothing on my trembling body. I walked out as far as I could and then dove head first into a cresting wave. Yes, the water felt real. The salt in my mouth tasted real, too. But how did I get here? This couldn't be right.

Another of King's tricks? After all, the man had powers I couldn't begin to comprehend, one of which was the ability to crawl inside my body and show me his memories. He'd done it once before.

Yes. That had to be what was happening. The only issue was that this felt real, not like a memory or watching a movie.

My head pounded and my stomach began to cramp again, but I held it together. And that's when it hit me. My nausea and headaches only came when my mind didn't want to accept reality. It'd happened on the day I'd learned about being a Seer and I'd felt my two conflicting realities collide.

Christ. It just happened when Mack tried to warn you about King.

But this can't be real. I felt my face turn hot and more bile creep up.

There was my proof: more resistance, more nausea.

I dove underneath the waves, allowing the ocean to pacify my angry, frayed nerves. When I brought my head up for a breath, I spotted a young woman with dark hair and skin, wearing a white dress, standing on the beach and staring at me.

I stared back but didn't speak. Besides, what would I say? "Hey! I'm naked. Got any idea where I am and how I got here?" Instead, I waded in the water for several moments and then hesitantly lifted my shaky hand to wave.

A look of surprise overtook her face, and she sprinted away, disappearing into the forest.

At that moment, something sharp jabbed my toe as I bounced along the bottom. "Shit!" The pain seared its way up my leg, and I paddled back to the shore where I crawled from the water.

"Oh no." Blood seeped from a small puncture wound. My vision blurred, and I tried to blink it away, but the burn traveled quickly into my chest, cramping every muscle I had.

I fell onto my back. *Real. Not a dream. Real, Mia.*

᷂᷈

Sharp-toned words, spoken in a loud hiss, were what woke me this second time around. I couldn't understand a single damned thing, but a woman and man argued over something.

Cautiously, I popped open one eye and found myself lying on a wooden table. The home looked to have three rooms without any doors. The walls were made of smooth white plaster and a thatched roof with wooden beams. Wherever we were, these were very simple people who lived without electricity or running water.

I slowly began to move the rest of my body, surveying the damage. Someone had draped a flimsy piece of fabric, too small to be called a sheet, over most of my torso. My leg throbbed, too, but my foot burned like a sonofabitch. Both had been bandaged.

Shit. What happened? I wasn't sure what to do or say because the situation had zero explanation. Not only that, but I didn't know where I was or how I'd gotten there. I only knew I didn't ever want to go back to the hell I'd run from. There would be no saving myself in that place, which meant there'd be no redemption for that evil bastard I'd trusted like a fool, which meant there'd be no saving Justin. What would happen to my poor parents now?

Simply put, everything was fucked. Fucked up beyond salvation.

And if I ever get the chance, I will hunt King down and end him. What King did to me, whatever the reason, there would be no forgiving. No amount of hate in this world could measure up to the rage I felt. *Evil bastard. I hope you burn in hell.*

The only questions now were: Where the hell was I? And how long would it take for King to find me?

I hope never.

I then realized I still wore the silver cuff on my left wrist. Was there some chance that the bracelet had worked and taken me somewhere "far, far away where King would never find me"?

I sat up slowly, and the young woman shrieked and jumped back, as did the man. It was the same woman who'd watched me on the beach.

"Anyone happen to speak English?" I ground out my words, my brain throbbing against the inner walls of my skull.

The man with deep brown skin, in his late forties perhaps, wearing a simple-looking, cream-colored tunic that hung down to his knees, pointed at me and barked a few angry words.

"I don't understand," I said.

He grabbed a clump of my blonde hair and shouted as if accusing me of some wrongdoing. Was I in a country where women showing hair was a crime? But no, the young woman in the room wore hers loose, and her dress, though long and unrevealing, showed plenty of shoulder and neck.

He looked at the young woman—also with dark skin and hair and perhaps in her late teens—and screamed at her again before storming outside.

"What was that about?" I asked.

The woman and I exchanged several awkward glances, but she didn't speak.

I carefully swung my feet to the dirt floor. "I'm Mia. Mia." I pointed to myself.

Her eyes lit up. "Kitane." She pointed to her chest.

"Kitane," I repeated. "I need to find a phone." I made a phone shape with my hand and held it up to my face. "Phone?"

She shook her head.

Crap. No phones. Well, there had to be one somewhere, maybe in the nearest town.

I tried to stand but staggered on my wobbly legs.

She protested and made me sit, quickly plucking a small twig from the dirt floor and drawing a picture of a snake.

Great. A snake bit me. I unbandaged my foot and leg, relieved to find them red and swollen but nothing more. I didn't know a lot about bites, but I knew that people generally got worse, not better.

She disappeared into the adjoining room and returned with a white tunic, very similar to the one she wore, only without the stains and dirt.

"Thank you." The fact that she didn't have much but was generous enough to clothe me meant a lot. She then handed me a scarf made of roughly woven burlap and placed it over my head.

"My hair. It worries you." I wondered why, of course.

She helped me to my feet, slid the tunic over my body, and then tied the cloth around my head, tucking in any loose strands.

She called out, and within seconds, the man—her father, I assumed—appeared and walked me outside. Their little home was surrounded by a stone wall with a few weird-looking chickens and three white goats running around the yard. I didn't see the ocean, but I smelled the salt air wafting through the trees that surrounded the clearing.

Just outside a small gate stood an old, scraggly-looking gray ox attached to a little cart. The man pointed for me to sit.

I hoped to God he was taking me to a town with a phone.

"She coming?" I asked and glanced at Kitane.

He pointed to the cart and then sort of pushed me into it. If I were in any better shape, I would have pushed him back, but as it was, I could barely walk.

I mentally said my goodbyes to Kitane and watched the little house fade through the trees—an orchard, I realized.

Olive trees. Where the hell am I?

Over the next hour, we passed several more primitive homes and rustic-looking farms along the narrow dirt road, where I still saw no signs of civilization. Seriously, no signs, no electricity, no telephone poles. Just lots of trees, animals, and curious people who stared as we passed, me facing backwards, sitting in the rickety little cart.

Jet helicopters to this. Well, I would take this, any day, over where I'd been.

When we approached a bustling market filled with merchants selling animals, grapes, and piles of olives, I was convinced that we were on some remote Greek island. Had King dumped me into the ocean, and I'd miraculously drifted to this place? Maybe. There were many islands in Greece, one of which was King's horrible house of pain. This place, however, had people. Lots of people, and I'd never been anywhere like it.

The man tied up his ox and pulled me up from the cart, mumbling at me.

"You know I don't understand you, right? I mean, you can keep talking, but I won't understand a single, frigging, goddamned word."

He gestured for me to follow him toward a high wall on the other side of the market.

"Phone?" I asked, again making the shape with my hand.

He shook his head and brought me to a thick wooden door, where two shirtless men, wearing blue and red skirts—yeah, skirts—stood with long frigging knives strapped around their waists.

Okay. This keeps getting stranger.

The man said something to them, but they didn't seem to want to let us in. That's when he snapped the scarf from my head, and the two guards gasped.

What the hell? What was the problem with my hair? Yes, I knew it looked like a curly blonde pile of turds, but this situation had crossed all lines in the sand where pretty hair seemed like a priority.

The guard slipped the man a coin, took hold of my arm, and thumped on the door.

"Wait. Did you just...*sell* me?" I said to the man who'd brought me.

The guard pushed me through the doorway, following closely behind, and quickly slammed it shut.

"You can't sell me! I'm a person! An Ameri—" *Wait, that might not win points.* "I want to go to the police. A phone!" Once again I held my hand to my ear, but the man just stood there looking at me as if I were some crazy animal from another planet. Then he shoved me and pointed for me to walk.

"Fuck you!" I spat, not that he could understand, which was why I probably didn't hold back with the swear words one little bit. At least they made me feel better.

Sorta.

The guard grabbed hold of my arm and dragged me up a set of stone steps toward a temple with large pillars and bright red and blue paint on the walls.

Once inside, the smell of incense and sage hit me. He threw me down, pushed my face into the floor, and began screaming at me.

"Get the fuck off!" I fought and dug my nails into his hand, but he held tight to a ball of my hair.

I imagined he was telling me to shut the hell up, but I was not about to let him or anyone treat me like this.

"I'll kill you!" I belted. "I swear I'll fucking—"

When I heard that voice—deep, commanding, and uniquely masculine—my flesh tightened around my quaking bones. I stilled.

Again the voice spoke, and I slowly lifted my gaze to the menacing man standing before me and glaring down.

"King?" I gasped.

His eyes narrowed as he took me in, scowling as if I were some despicable bug he might squash for entertainment.

"I take that back," I said to the guard. "I'll fucking kill *him*!" I broke free from my captor, leaving behind a clump of hair in his fist, and lunged for King. He fell back, and we both slammed into the floor. The crack of his skull hitting the ground was like music to my ears.

"You piece of shit!" I managed to get my hands around his neck as he stared at me, apparently shocked as hell. The moment lasted for only that—a moment—before two large men pulled me off.

King sat up, broodingly taking stock as he watched them drag me off.

"I'll kill you! Do you hear me? Do you fucking…" My voice trailed off as my brain began to register the bizarreness before me. *Green? His light…was that…?*

What my eyes saw couldn't have been real, which meant that I had cracked and King had successfully broken me. Because the man wasn't King. I mean, he was, but he wasn't *my* King. This one didn't glow red, blue or even purple, but green. Bright, vivid green.

Life.

This King was alive.

So the question quickly shifted from wondering where I was to when…

Holy shit.

CHAPTER SEVEN

Like an animal on exhibit at a zoo, a nearly endless stream of people visited my wooden cage over the next day. Most of them had the same deep dark skin, hair, and eyes, and wore toga-style dresses—the women, obviously—pleated or gathered at the waist with a leather or cloth belt. The men walked around shirtless with blue fabric, trimmed in gold or red, wrapped around their waists.

Without a doubt, as impossible as it was, I had to accept what I saw right in front of me: I was in King's time. This was goddamned crazy.

I'm in ancient frigging Minoa. Aka Crete, before it was Crete.

From the little I'd read, there wasn't much known about the Minoans, either. They were mainly peaceful, traded broadly with other cultures, and were fascinated by nature. Then one day—poof—they disappeared.

Just like I might any second now.

An entire day had passed, and no one had offered me food or water. The cage they'd placed me in was underneath a tree, and I supposed I should've felt lucky for that; however, because of the heat of the day, coupled with my recent snake bite, I could no longer stand.

On the second day, as the late morning sun began to warm the air, I lay there, sticky and dirty, eyes half-mast, dreading the sweltering heat to come, and wondering how much longer I'd last. The only thing for me to do was sleep and hope I wouldn't wake up.

But, of course, that's not what happened.

I awoke to being poked with a sharp stick.

"Go the fuck away," I grumbled.

The guard who stood at the mouth of the opened cage offered a small clay jar and gestured for me to drink. I toyed with the idea of lifting my head, but it just wasn't going to happen, so I opted for groaning instead.

He grumbled angrily—I imagined he was saying, "Get up, you lazy ass!"—but gave up on the verbal encouragements quickly and decided instead to get his hands dirty. He pulled me toward him, propping me against the rough branches that formed the sides of the cage before forcing the jar to my lips. The liquid tasted of water mixed with juice and olive brine, or some weird crap like that.

I took several sips and pushed it away. "It's missing the vodka."

He forcefully urged me to take another sip, but my stomach wasn't having it. I threw up right on his chest.

"Oops." I flashed a little smile. *Assholes.*

He called out, and two more men appeared to drag me from my "box of misery." They hurriedly hauled me by the arms through a garden filled with flowers and lush potted pomegranate trees, only to dump me in a small room. The little stone platform they laid me over felt like heaven compared to the hard, roughly-cut branches of my cage, but my horrible thirst and cramping stomach were torture.

King appeared almost immediately, looking down with a judgmental frown. He wore only a deep blue sarong that stopped just above the knees and some odd-looking sandals. His shoulder-length black hair was pulled back, giving him more of an untamed, fierce look compared to the elegant, clean-cut billionaire version I knew so well.

"Let me guess, this is why you're so into commando," I muttered deliriously, staring at his skirt.

He studied me with curiosity for a few moments until a woman, petite with wide black eyes and curly flowing hair, appeared and bowed. He instructed her to do something, and she pulled a sharp quill from a small leather bag, along with a few tiny seeds. She popped the seeds into her mouth, chewed, and then spat the mixture into her palm.

When she dipped the sharp quill into the spit concoction and then reached for my wrist, I began to understand that she intended to poke me with it.

"Uh-uh. No," I mumbled in protest.

King held down my left arm while the woman chanted and jabbed my skin. With each poke my brain heard a weird sort of static, like a radio station trying to break through the noise. She jabbed away for several moments, forming a figure-eight pattern on my wrist just above my "K." Then, suddenly, a sharp shrilling noise hissed in my ears. I yanked my hand from her and cupped my ears.

"Make it stop!" I screamed.

"There," said the woman. "Now she may speak our tongue and understand ours."

I blinked and looked at each of them. "How the fuck did you do that?"

King bent over me, snarling. It was then that I noticed the color of his eyes. Not gray, but a pristine sky blue. "You watch your tongue, or I will have it cut out."

I snapped my mouth shut, but struggled to accept that any of this was really happening. However, fact was, I'd seen stranger things: living heads in jars; a ghost manifest himself, run an empire, and drive around in expensive cars; and the color of people's souls, including their emotional imprints when they died. This situation really wasn't so far out there, given all that.

"King?" I whispered. "It's really you, isn't it?"

"Yes, I am the king. Who, by gods, are you? And why are you—a foreigner—roaming about our island without my permission?" he asked.

"I'm Mia. And…I have no clue."

His head whipped to the side toward the woman, who wore a pale blue, floor-length dress with elaborate gold embroidery on the hem. "Hagne, make her speak the truth."

Hagne? Oh shit.

The woman nodded and whipped out her quill again.

"Wait," I protested with as much strength as I could muster. "Please, no more spit tats. That's so unhygienic, it's not even funny." I tried to clear my scratchy throat, but I seemed to have run out of saliva. "Water. I need water."

King jerked his head at Hagne, who disappeared out the door. Meanwhile, he studied me with his intense electric blue gaze, the muscles of his bare arms and chest bursting with menacing, flexing strength.

I wanted to tell him to stop looking at me, but I felt too fascinated by what stood before me: King. Masculine. Powerful. Intimidating as hell. But not evil. The green aura around him was almost blinding, and I had to admit, seeing him like this— so alive and untainted—made me want to reach out and touch him.

Hagne reappeared with a ceramic jar and held it to my lips. This time, it was watered- down wine. I didn't think it would help my dehydration, but I felt too thirsty to argue. I took several small sips and then lay back down, unable to hold myself upright.

"Speak, woman," King said, "or I will take you outside and beat you."

What the hell?

"Touch me," I shot him a look, "and you'll never see your precious penis again." I snapped my teeth at him, and he burst out laughing. It was that same laugh I knew—deep, silky, deliciously male, and arrogant.

"Glad I amuse you," I grumbled. "To answer your question, I'm a Seer. From..." Oh hell, this was going to sound so corny, like some bad version of *Terminator*. "I'm from the future. I work for you." *And I'm running from you, you evil bastard-rapist-asshole.*

Yes, I was running from him, but still somehow ended up here with him? Goddamned weird.

My eyes flashed to the cuff still on my wrist. If it was, in fact, the reason for my being here, I had to wonder what would happen if it were removed.

"Is this true, Hagne?" King asked.

Shocking. King actually entertained the idea that I was not from their time.

"Yes, my king." Hagne kept her eyes to the ground like a submissive pet when she spoke. "I mean to say, she is a Seer; I sense it. However, I cannot say if the rest of her story has merit. I can only tell you that I have never seen a Seer with golden hair. Or anyone, for that matter."

"But she is of your blood?" he asked.

Hagne nodded but did not lift her eyes. "Yes."

"Then you will look after her and make her feel at home. Place her in the ocean-side guest quarters."

"The one next to the orchard?" Hagne asked, appearing alarmed.

He pinned her with his fierce gaze. "Did you not hear me, woman?"

Hagne immediately dropped her eyes back to the floor and nodded. "Yes, my king."

"Good. Have her presentable for dining this evening." He turned to leave.

"Where are you going?" I asked.

As if I'd punched him in the back of the head, he swiveled on his heel and shot me a stern look. "I am king; you do not ask me such questions." He strode off, shoulders square and proud.

Fucking King. Some things never change.

After King's departure from the cramped windowless room, Hagne brought several servants to rehydrate me. They gave me water and fed me a sweet fig jam—not generally my favorite unless accompanied by a ripe brie—but I immediately felt better. That also meant my mind played a little game of, "Oh shit. Really?" As in, "Oh shit. I'm really here? Really? Oh shit. Did I really travel through time to escape King?" And, "Oh shit. Am I here for good, or will I be flung back at any second?"

Answer to question number one: yes.

Answer to number two: yes.

Answer to number three: I had no damned clue.

Sure, I was safe from evil King, but for how long? And being in Minoa didn't mean I was completely out of danger. I knew nothing about the rules of this society, its etiquette, their enemies, and…well, everything was foreign. Not all bad, of course. For example, no one had tried to violate or whip me. That was nice. And these people seemed peaceful and fairly calm. At least what I'd seen of them during my countryside tour.

Everyone except King. He carried the authority and arrogance of a man with little patience and all the power. A dangerous combination.

"You will follow me," said Hagne, appearing in the doorway, addressing me like a lowly piece of algae stuck to a rock in her favorite swimming hole.

"Not until we talk." I stayed put, sitting on the little stone platform I'd been using as my bed.

She smiled, but her eyes filled with a serpent-like vibe. Whatever she had planned for me didn't involve making me "feel at home."

Game on, bitch. After all, she'd destroyed King. She'd taken a man who'd been devout, loving, and genuine, and reduced him to a vile sadistic demon of sorts. She'd mutilated him.

Maybe that's why you're really here, Mia. Revenge. Not likely, but my insides jumped up and down, cheering frantically. I hated Hagne. I hated the impact her choices had on my life three-thousand-something years later.

Oh. My. God. Could every shitty hand I'd been dealt be leading to this? A chance to change everyone's fate?

Didn't matter. I'd do it anyway. I simply had to act quickly before I found myself snapped back to where I came from. Not that I knew for sure it would happen, but seizing the moment was an absolute must.

I smiled sweetly. "Hagne, I really am from the future. But the gods brought me here, so that I may help you procure your true love, Callias."

She blinked rapidly. "The gods?"

"Oh yes," I lied, playing my cards for every dime they were worth, because she needed to believe I was powerful. "How else would I know about your dark little secret?"

"I know not of what you speak. Draco, our king, is my betrothed. He is my intended—"

"Cut the crap." I rose to my feet and pointed my finger in her face. "I know everything. I know the evil bullshit you're planning and how you hate Draco because you suffer from delusions that he is not as manly or deadly as his twin brother. I know that you'd rather die than marry him, but because of the oppressive time you live in, you feel like you have to do as you are told," I snarled at her. "But we always have a choice. Always. And yours fucks up endless multitudes of lives for thousands of years, including mine. All because you didn't have the balls to call off the wedding." I clenched my fist. "But make no mistake, the gods have granted my wish to come here and stop you."

Her jaw hung open, and then she snapped it shut.

The fury and sense of purpose pulsing through my veins revived me. I stepped in closer, placing us nose to nose. "You understand me?"

She nodded cautiously.

"Good. Because if you cross me, I'll kill you." That was something that I learned from the Spiros: never make idle threats.

"Wha-what do you want?"

"You'll call it off with King...Draco. Whateverthefuck. You'll tell him that you love Callias."

"He'd kill me before accepting that."

"Then I'll tell him."

"He will kill you," she argued. "He will kill us both. And he will never believe you."

"No. He'll thank us. And he'll believe me, because you will tell the truth when he asks."

She stared demurely at the floor for a moment, but I knew the timid act was a sham. A viper in a woman's skin stood before me.

"How do I know what you say is true?" she asked.

"You don't. But the way I see it, you have no choice, because I'll kill you if you don't do what I say. Either way, I win."

She nodded, as if trying to swallow the bitter pill named Mia that had been shoved down her throat.

"I'm glad we understand each other," I said. "Now, would you be so kind as to take me to my quarters and summon Callias for me?"

Her eyes burst open. "Why?"

KING (OF) ME
97

"That's my business. Just do it."

"May I ask one question, Mia?"

I shrugged.

"Why?" she asked.

"Why what?"

"Why do you care so much about our king? It seems your demands are founded upon other motivations, aside from circumventing events that have yet to pass."

She was right. My rage was more than simply avoiding this shit-storm called my life. Now that I'd caught a glimpse of the man—unspeakably beautiful and unsoiled by her damned curse—part of me mourned for that piece of him. Trapped, suffering and tortured for three thousand years, buried underneath layers of evil. If I could keep him from ever becoming cursed, it would not only change my fate, but his, too.

"It's none of your damned business," I said.

"You love him, don't you?" Her words were spoken as an accusation, as if to say any acknowledgement on my part would confirm her suspicions of my insanity.

"Love is not a word I would use to describe how I feel about that man." A man who sent me fleeing for my life. That said, I really didn't know how I felt. It was complicated. "My motives and feelings are none of your business. Just do as you are told, Hagne."

Dammit. I sound like King now.

Sinister intentions twinkled in her deep brown eyes, but her lips curled up into a polite smile. "Let us be on our way, then."

Outside the temple waited five burly guards, their already dark skin deeply tanned, and their black hair pulled into tight braids. They each wore an embossed leather chest plate over plain blue tunics that reached mid-thigh. These guards also wore little leather headbands with bright red and blue feathers.

How festive.

"These are Spiros, the king's personal guards," Hagne said.

Spiros? These were Arno's and Stefanos's ancestors. My mind quickly toyed with the notion of undoing yet another unfortunate turn of events. The future Spiros didn't seem too pleased about being eternally bound to King. On the other hand, it would be a moot point if I prevented King from becoming cursed.

Hagne added, "These men are to see to your safety, per the king's orders."

She really meant they'd make sure I didn't go anywhere.

"What's new?" I said. "Lead the way."

With the escorts on our heels, Hagne walked me through several corridors, outside through another courtyard with bright red, overflowing flowers in giant clay pots. Every building and structure seemed made of the same pale stone painted with murals of sea creatures or goddesses.

As we neared a small fruit orchard overlooking the ocean, another large structure—with soaring pillars, large doorways, and more flowers—came into view. I realized it had to be King's "wing of the palace," because every room had more. More elaborate paintings. More ornate carvings on the stone pillars. More space. It had a grand palatial feel.

I stopped and looked at Hagne, pointing at the temple. "I'm staying…here?"

She nodded with a toxic glare. "You will stay in the chamber adjacent to his."

I stepped back.

"Something the matter?" she asked, holding back a snicker.

I shook my head. "No. I just—"

"You said you would handle the beast. Are you not capable?" Her words made me take another step back. I was treading in unknown waters. This King wasn't cursed or evil, but was he some other breed of savage? A man who took what he wanted, no questions asked?

We're still talking about King. What the hell do you think?

Okay, but this is a much less complex and tainted version of King. This King is just a man.

I had to admit, a part of me secretly felt intrigued. This King was the one who still had all of the singularly seductive qualities—the raw male strength and the frigging hot as hell body—but without the curse. This version of King was human and alive, which meant the depths of his fucked-upness were limited to one lifetime. In fact, I'd bet if we compared notes, my past would out-shady him at this stage.

"I can handle your king," I replied.

When I entered the lavish chamber, I immediately noticed a few things. One: no doors. Two: adjoining balcony to King's chamber, overlooking the ocean. Three: indoor plumbing.

Yes! Steam drifted from the sunken stone tub, and floral scented soaps were piled into painted dishes beside neatly folded stacks of soft cloths. I turned and savored the view from the glassless window overlooking a never-ending stretch of turquoise and deep blue ocean. In fact...

Holy shit. This was exactly where King would build his new home. Right on this very spot. The position against the setting sun and the shape of the shoreline—sort of a small inlet between two rolling hills—were almost the same. I noted to myself how even cursed kings can be sentimental creatures.

"I will have a fresh gown brought to you," said Hagne, "and the girl will do your hair after you have bathed." She pointed to a young woman, about fifteen or so, wearing a plain brown tunic, standing with a rigid posture in the corner of the room. Four more awaited instructions near the doorway.

"Does she have a name?" I asked.

"Why do you care? She is a slave," responded Hagne.

"She's a person. With a name. Just like you."

"Ypirétria," Hagne responded impatiently.

I hated that they called them maids and not by their proper names.

"And what are their names?" I jerked my head toward the other four.

"Ypirétria," Hagne replied again.

I shook my head. "So, what? I'm supposed to call them out numerically, like Thing One and Thing Two?"

Hagne blinked at me.

"Never mind." Now was not the time to school them in the value of civil liberties, but I did take comfort in knowing that this problem would eventually improve, though not soon enough in my book. In the meantime, it didn't mean I had to follow their rules.

Hagne dipped her head and took her leave. One of the girls closed off a curtain over the doorway and approached me.

"I can undress myself." I held out my hands. "Thank you, umm…what's your name?"

The young woman didn't want to answer.

"I insist on knowing your name."

"Mela," she replied.

"Thank you, Mela. If you don't mind, I'd appreciate it if you'd wait outside."

The five women exchanged glances.

"It's okay," I assured them. "I've been washing my body for a few years now. I promise not to miss any strategic spots." I seriously needed a few minutes alone.

Reservedly, they nodded and left me to soak in the amazing tub that smelled of fresh rosemary and sage. I couldn't believe such luxury existed in ancient Minoa, but there it was, and I felt damned grateful for it.

I closed my eyes and my mind drifted for a moment. An image of my parents popped up. *Oh God. By now, they have to be a mess.* Only, they didn't know I was gone, did they? Because they hadn't been born yet.

I mentally scratched my head. *So that means if I die here, my parents won't ever know what became of me.* On the other side of the coin, if I went back, King would be waiting to kill me and do God-only-knew.

Not if you stop him from becoming cursed. He'll die a natural death, and life will go on. That was, after all, the way it was meant to be. We all had our time, and then we went. And that was the only way to stop the horrific tragedies still to come. I could only hope I'd get the chance to go home and see the new future with my own eyes.

CHAPTER EIGHT

"Mia, wake up."

My eyes snapped open to find Hagne standing over me. Still feeling a bit weak, I'd drifted off in the tub.

"The meal will be served shortly, and you are not ready," she said. "This will displease our king."

I cocked one brow. As if I gave a flying Minoan fig leaf about pleasing him. "He'll just have to wait, then."

Her eyes nearly exploded from her skull, but then she smiled and nodded. "As you wish."

Translated to mean, "It's your ass, not mine."

"See you at dinner," she said.

After she left, I dried myself off and slipped on the dress left for me on the "bed" (a hay mat over a stone platform). My vivid blue frock was pretty damned impressive for folks who didn't own sewing machines. It was a pleated toga style, belted at the waist, that hung over the right shoulder and flowed to the floor. Luckily, it hid the fact I wore no undergarments.

"Ready!" I called out. The posse of young women stormed inside and made me sit. They frantically began putting my hair up, using little copper pins with rounded jewels on the ends. Then they wrapped a little headband made of pearls and other polished stones of various colors to hold everything up, with the exception of the curls in the back, which they left hanging down. They quickly rubbed my underarms with oil that smelled like lavender mixed with roses, and then held up a small polished plate.

"Wow. I look beautiful," I said. "Thank you."

The women stared at the floor, and Mela gestured toward the door to where that battalion of guards awaited. "I hope he is pleased," she said.

"I'm sure he will be," I said, "thank you." I felt so incredibly guilty about the way these women lived. Maybe I could talk to King later.

I followed the men outside down a set of stairs that skirted the edge of the building and through another courtyard illuminated by torches. I entered the open-aired hall with vaulted ceilings and noticed a shirtless King sitting at the head of a long table lit with oil lamps, a look of utter outrage shooting from his eyes. Hagne sat to his side, smothering a glib expression, and the other eight guests, all men, were motionless.

I cleared my throat and smiled. "Good evening."

"You are late," growled King. The muscles in his neck and shoulders flexed with irritation.

"And you never change," I scowled.

The room collectively gasped.

Okay, I get that at this point some might accuse me of insanity for behaving so rudely toward this man, especially given my current predicament; however, this was no time to start second-guessing the facts. Curse or no curse, King was not a man who respected weakness. Nor was he the type to trust easily. If I was going to change his fate, and thus all our fates, he needed to see that I was there without hidden agendas. What you saw was what you got. That also meant cowering to anyone, especially him, would be the kiss of death.

That said, I prepared for his wrath. Because the other thing I knew? He hated to be disobeyed. "Do as you are told, Miss Turner," he'd say.

King's stunning blue eyes drilled me for several nerve-racking moments, and then he exploded with laughter, his head full tilt toward the aquatic-themed, mural-covered ceiling. The guests chuckled along nervously as well, exchanging glances. They didn't have a clue as to why their king laughed like a madman, but I sure as hell did: my insolence amused him. It would three-thousand-something years from now, too. I equated it to how one might feel if they were hiking through the woods and came across an ornery chipmunk. It could squeak and squeal all day long, but you'd never feel threatened. You'd simply say, "Look at the balls on that furry little bastard. He knows I could squish him, right?" You might even feel a bit of respect for the creature's standing up to you, even if you weren't quite sure what its damned problem was.

That was how King thought of me.

King's laughter died, and he gestured toward an empty little stool made from carved wood, opposite Hagne. "You look very beautiful tonight," he said.

I self-consciously reached for my hair. "Thank you. Mela did a nice job."

King frowned. He had no clue who Mela was.

A few servants appeared out of nowhere and poured wine into my metal chalice. On the table was quite a spread of almonds, fresh figs, more olives, and some lentils mixed with herbs and...stuff. Hell, I had no clue.

What I wouldn't give for a glass of whiskey right now.

The servants began placing small portions of food on the beautiful, hand-painted ceramic plate in front of me, depicting a blue octopus eating a fish. A scoop of barley, topped with some cooked snails and little sardines, was placed in the center. *Eesh...*

I smiled, knowing it could've been worse. At least I recognized most everything. "Looks delicious," I said.

"Eat. You will need your strength tonight, Seer," said King.

I held in a gasp. He'd said similar words to me in a dream that had spiraled into a nightmare and turned out not to be so farfetched. King tying me up, tearing off my clothes...The reminder sent a cold spike through me.

My pulse sped up, and I felt the new Mia—cold, hard, ready for anything—evaporate into thin air.

"Excuse me. I need a little fresh air." I stood and headed for the door before I lost my composure. A few simple moments were all I needed to stomp out the freaking-out flames.

I headed to the balcony overlooking the ocean and braced myself, allowing the cool breeze to fill my nostrils. The full moon was high in the sky, its light bouncing off the rippling waves.

"What is the meaning of your retreat, woman? Get back inside this instant," King commanded.

Great.

I swiveled on my heel and faced him. His shirtless magnificence was not lost on me one bit, and neither was his long dark hair. His unshaven angular jaw remained just as wickedly handsome as ever, too. Without a doubt, he took my breath away.

"Did you hear me, woman, or shall I carry you back to the table?"

Be strong. He won't respect a coward. "Stop calling me 'woman.' My name is Mia."

"Get back inside, *Mia.*"

I scoffed. "I'm not hungry and, frankly, the company does not please me." I referred to Hagne, of course.

He blinked. "You dare insult my council? You, a lowly Seer who claims to be from another time?"

I held up my finger. "Lowly? What makes you think that?"

He looked me over, his eyes momentarily sticking hungrily on my breasts. He caught himself, cleared his throat, then threw back his shoulders a bit. "All Seers are lowly."

"Don't you mean that everyone who isn't you is lowly?"

"I am the king."

"Well, this lowly Seer is your fiancée."

"Hagne is my betrothed." He frowned at me. "You are mad. I suspected as much, but now you have confirmed it."

I'd been impressed so far by how well Hagne's little tattoo translated everything, but I wondered how it would do with what I had to say next.

"I'm not crazy. I am the only one capable of preventing an utterly hellish situation—"

"Prove it. Prove that you are not mad and that I should believe any words coming from your mouth."

Crap. I had no cell phone, laptop, or Internet to show him the place I came from, and anything I said would sound like insane tales of an insane person. I had only one thing, and it was a huge risk.

I showed him my "K" tattoo. "You put this on me. It allows you to feel me, my presence, and"— *Hell, I am so going to regret this*—"control me."

He laughed. "Control you?"

I nodded. "You place your palm over it, and I'll do anything you say."

He burst out laughing, and it was a deep, hearty laugh. "Well, woman—"

"Mia," I corrected.

"Mia," he said condescendingly, "if you speak the truth, I can see why such a device might be necessary. You are like a wild animal, frothing at the mouth, seeking to sink its teeth into anything that moves."

I growled.

"You see?" he said smugly.

"Very funny."

"Show me," he commanded.

"I can't."

"Why not?" he asked.

"I'd have to take off the bracelet."

"And this signifies...?"

I shrugged. "I don't know, actually."

"You obviously have some sort of assumption that has sparked your concern."

I had to show strength. I had to speak with conviction. Otherwise, he'd blow me off, and this would all be for nothing. "This is a bracelet from your collection of powerful relics. It supposedly prevents your mark from working, and...I believe it's what brought me here."

He leaned in and stared deeply into my eyes. "Exactly why *are* you here?"

"Don't change subjects. You wanted to know why I can't demonstrate how your tattoo works. That's the reason."

He stepped back and folded his arms over his sculpted bare chest. "Remove the bracelet, or I will hold you down and remove it myself."

I had to think this through. If I took the thing off, there were two outcomes I feared: getting snapped back to the horrific situation I'd come from, or that removing the cuff would allow King, the future one, to come and find me.

Mia, if he had the ability to travel back in time, don't you think he would have done it by now? He would've undone his curse and changed his fate on his own.

All right. So perhaps I only had one thing to fear: going back. But not trying my damnedest wasn't an option. This could be my only shot to make everything right again.

"I'll remove the bracelet on one condition," I said.

His mouth formed a snide grin. "You mean to negotiate with *me*?"

"Give me your word you won't command me to do anything sexual." King's one saving grace: he was a man of his word. *Except when something goes horribly wrong with the man's curse and he turns into an evil bastard who should be destroyed.*

But that was not this man. He was the kernel of goodness inside the demon. That said, he was still King.

He laughed. "What you must think of me."

"I know you better than anyone, King." I stared him down. "You're fierce, calculating, and determined."

His smile melted away. "You forgot impatient."

"I was getting to that. Do you agree or not?"

He stared, not amused by my flippancy, but then gave me a nod.

"All right. Here goes." I slipped the bracelet off and held it in my palm, bracing for the worst. The moment I realized that nothing happened, I released a breath. "I'm still here."

"Obviously," King said.

I slid the cuff onto my right wrist for safekeeping and then held out my left arm. "Okay."

He placed his hand over my tattoo. "How will I know you are not simply pretending?"

"Ask me to do something you know I can't fake. How about putting me to sleep? You can give me a poke with that pin." My eyes flashed to a small circular broach stuck to the front of his wrap-skirt thing.

His lips formed a wolfish smile. "You wish me to poke you? I am more than willing to appease the wish; however, I assure you it is not a pin."

I frowned. "You gave me your word."

"So I did." His eyes flickered for a moment over my shoulder toward the ocean. "Jump."

"What?"

"I command you to jump."

Holy shit. I'd seen over that balcony, and it was a straight drop down to the rocky cliffs below.

My feet began to move toward the stone bannister, my eyes tearing. "Don't make me do this."

But King simply stood inches away, a cold, heartless expression on his face as he watched me climb onto the bannister, my back to the ocean.

"My king! What is happening?" I heard a woman scream.

I turned my head toward the sound of the voice, my heart and lungs pumping frantically, wanting to override the desire to jump to my death. In that moment, everything seemed to move in slow motion. King's head swiveled away from me to see who'd called out. As I too looked, I felt my body falling back over the ledge. King's head whipped towards the sound of my scream, his beautiful face filling with horror, realizing I'd gone over. He lunged his powerful body and caught my ankle. My body slammed hard into the wall below, knocking the wind right out of me.

"By the gods of insanity, woman!" he roared.

I was in shock, dangling precariously by one foot, my dress completely covering the upper half of my body while the rest of me, everything normally below the belt, blew in the wind. Tears of pain and horror streamed from my face.

I heard the voices of several other men and a flurry of gods-related exclamations.

"Help me get her back up," King commanded.

Another set of hands gripped my ankle and heaved my body back over the bannister to the terrace.

With my dress now falling into place around my nether regions, I leaned forward to catch my breath.

"What is happening, my king?" I heard Hagne's voice ask.

"She slipped," King said. "She is fine now. Go back and enjoy your meal."

The crowd of guests and guards exchanged hesitant glances and returned to the dining hall.

"Jesus Christ," I panted and then stood. Immediately my feet began moving again to climb the railing. "Dammit! Tell me to stop!"

With panic-stricken eyes, King quickly grabbed hold of my arm and flung me over his broad shoulder. "Cursed crazy woman."

As we strode off back toward his chamber, he grumbled antiquated profanities, again targeted at the gods. I had to admit, hearing him make references to deities of fire, war, death, and destruction was almost comical. Almost.

When we reached his quarters overlooking the ocean, the room glowed softly with dozens of oil lamps. Murals coated the walls with scenes depicting warriors gripping spears and animals being sacrificed.

He flung me down on his bed—also a raised cement platform with a fluffy mat and pillows. I sat up and held back an epic tongue lashing. I wanted to throttle him. I could've died.

He hovered over me, fuming.

"What?" I growled.

He suddenly crouched down in front of me and grabbed my "K" tattoo. "Do not ever think to do that again," he commanded.

I snapped my arm back. "Thank you. So now you believe me?" I stood, placing us belly to belly. "After you nearly killed me!"

"I did not believe you would jump."

"Well." I poked his chest. "Now ya know!"

He took a sharp angry breath that caused his nostrils to flare. "Now you will tell me why you are here."

I was about to snarl and scream, but he surprised me by grabbing my wrist and repeating his question.

I glowered at him for a moment before my mouth began to move. "I don't know why I'm here."

"A person is not granted such a power," he pointed to my cuff, "without having a divine purpose."

Oh God. This is so weird.

"Tell me what you want from me." The muscles in his square, bristly jaw pulsed with tension.

"I don't *want* anything." I snapped my arm away. "I-I…" I sat back down. "Jesus." I sighed. This was going to break the man's heart.

"What is Jesus?" he asked.

I glanced at him. "He's a who, not a what, and never mind; it's a long story."

"I command you to cease these riddles and tell me what you are hiding. You say that you know me, that you are my woman—my betrothed many, many days into the future. Am I old? Am I dying?"

I shook my head.

"I'm"—*going to sound crazy*—"from three thousand or so years ahead." I didn't know what calendar they followed in these times, so I did some quick math. "About a million days."

"I don't know this million."

I scratched my head. "Well, say you have one revolution of the sun, winter, spring, summer, and fall."

He stared.

"Okay," I said. "Cold weather followed by planting, growing, harvest?"

He nodded.

"Good. That's one cycle. One year. If you had ten of those," I held up my fingers to show ten, "that would be a decade. If you had ten decades," I flashed my fingers ten times, "a century. If you had ten of those, that would be a millennium. So try three millennium."

He frowned. I think he got the picture. "This is impossible. People do not live that long."

I nodded. "You're right."

"Get to the point, woman."

Mia. Why is it so hard for him to call me "Mia"?

I took a deep breath. "Sit." I patted the bed next to me. Hesitantly, he did as I asked.

His big body next to mine made me feel like a fly sitting next to a Venus flytrap. I could be gobbled up at any moment.

"Hagne doesn't love you," I said.

His straight black brows pulled together. "Of course she does not."

"Then why are you marrying her?"

"Her lineage is powerful and her family is feared and well respected by our commoners. Our union will ensure peace for many generations to come."

Okay. That was good. He didn't expect love from her. On the other hand, I clearly remembered

Hagne's journal. King had it translated and made me read it so I'd understand how he'd become cursed and why he did the things he did. I admit, his story had made me see him in a different light. I understood his pain. But he'd written his thoughts in that journal (I supposed he wanted the last word), and I sensed he'd cared for her at one point. Therefore, I could leave no doubt in his mind about Hagne. She was a psycho, backstabbing bitch. He had to believe it.

"But she does love your brother, Callias," I said.

"This is impossible."

"No, it's not. She loves him, and sometime after your wedding, she turns him against you. He challenges you publically to a fight and you kill him."

King stood. "You lie."

I held up my wrist. "Ask me if I'm lying."

He glanced at my tattoo. He got the point, and a wounded look appeared in his hypnotic blue eyes.

"I'm sorry," I said. "Really, really sorry. But maybe that's why I'm here; to change your fate."

"What happens to me?"

"Hagne happens to you," I replied.

"I become aware of her betrayal?"

I nodded. "She's pregnant with Callias's baby—I think—so you spare her at first, but not her family. After she loses the baby, you kill her, too, but not before she curses you to walk the earth for eternity."

He stared coldly ahead at the wall, his broad, bare shoulders perfectly square like a proud soldier taking a beating.

"And this is when you meet me, a cursed man?" he asked.

"Yes. But..."

"But what?" he snapped.

"You're not a man."

"What am I?"

"You're a ghost, a spirit."

"I do not understand."

"Neither do I. But you have the ability to make yourself real. You talk and walk and eat and drink, but you're dead."

He nodded. "And I was not the one to send you here?"

I shook my head. "No. I was running from you. You were going to"—I couldn't say the real words aloud. I just couldn't—"*hurt* me."

He looked like he'd just been punched in the gut. "And my people? What becomes of them?"

"No one knows for sure," I said quietly. "They disappear."

He stared at the floor for a moment, scratching his thick black whiskers.

"What are you going to do now?" I asked.

"I must think on what you have said—it does not seem believable nor possible." He turned toward the door.

"So you don't believe me?"

"I do not know." He was almost out the door and then stopped. "You said I behave cruelly towards you. Do you despise me, then?"

I wasn't expecting him to ask that question, but I answered honestly. "Yes. It's why I attacked you a few days ago."

"Then why tell me any of this?"

"Hagne is the one who creates the monster. And her decision destroys a lot of people. Including someone very important to me."

"I see." He turned away.

"But I think—I *know*—that you're still in there somewhere, inside that monster, trying to get out." Otherwise, why would he have saved my mother? Or attempted to save Justin at one point? There had to be someone good living inside.

Without another word, King disappeared into the night. I hoped he might return in a few hours and declare that he believed me and had a solution. Because I sure as hell didn't see one. Not one without any pain and suffering, anyway. If one sat down and moved the pieces around the chessboard, the outcome didn't look so drastically different from the original version of this story. King could preemptively incarcerate Hagne, or even kill her, but this might incite a civil war if her family was in fact powerful and respected among the working class. Another option might be to let her run away with Callias, but that might undermine his position if the people saw him as weak.

I simply didn't see any good solutions aside from warning Callias, which I intended to do at the first chance.

I lay back and closed my eyes, hoping that when I woke, I might see a clean way out of this.

CHAPTER NINE

At sunrise, I was woken by a very insistent Mela, who shook me by the shoulders. "You are late, mistress. You must rise and get to the temple immediately."

I groaned and rubbed my face. "What does King want?" I asked, assuming that he'd summoned me.

"Today is the ceremony of the harvest."

I cracked one eye open. "I'm sorry. I don't know what that is."

Mela had her dark eyes outlined with thick black charcoal, making them appear exaggeratedly large. "The non-slave women must make an offering of grain, fruit, and wine to the gods so they will bless our crops in the next planting season."

"Oh. Sounds lovely," I mumbled and rolled over. My body felt like it had been through a blender. Twice.

"You are a Seer and must be there. It will anger the gods if you are not."

Ai-yai-yai. I was pretty sure that boat had already sailed. Case in point, my crazy, fucked-up life.

"The gods hate me," I grumbled. "I should stay here out of sight."

"Please, mistress, you cannot shame the king like this. You are his guest and a Seer. If you do not attend, it will cause a horrible uproar."

"If it was so important, why didn't he mention it last night?" I muttered.

"I'm sure our king was quite...*occupied* with other thoughts."

Oh hell. I sighed. Yes, I understood that Mela meant "occupied" in the sexual sense. I had, after all, woken up in the king's bed. Nevertheless, her comment wasn't so far off. King's mind had been engaged with some very, very troubling news.

"Please, mistress," she begged.

Oh...dammit. The poor man already had enough on his plate, and I didn't need to be the cause of any more heartburn.

I sat up. "Fine. I'll go, but someone will have to tell me what to do."

Relief twinkled in her big brown eyes. "Of course. I will tell you everything you need to know, but first you must dress."

She held up an odd-looking orange dress. The only way to describe it was chestless—like the neckline was intended to be a belly line.

"I think someone forgot to sew in the front," I said.

She looked at it. "No. This is what the women must wear to the ceremony."

"But…"

"The bosom is the symbol of fertility and life. It is blasphemous to offer a gift to the gods with your chest covered."

My head sagged in disbelief. This absolutely had to be some male-contrived bull-crap designed specifically for getting a free peek at all the women's boobs.

"I'll come to the ceremony," I said, "but I'm not going topless."

Fear washed over her face. "Please, mistress. You must. Or I will be punished. It is my responsibility to have you appropriately dressed."

She couldn't be serious. "Don't you mean undressed?"

The young woman looked like she was about to faint from a nervous attack.

I tilted my head. "All this fuss because I refuse to show my breasts to a bunch of horny men?"

"I do not know this word 'horny,' but your body is a gift from the gods. There is no shame in showing it to anyone. And this is the way we have performed the ceremony for generations." She pointed to a large painted vase standing in the corner, depicting several topless women holding wine jugs.

Ugh. Dammit. I knew my modesty was a product of my times, but…"Are you sure everyone is going to be naked from the waist up?"

She nodded.

"Fine. Give me the dress."

❧❧

After I took the world's fastest sponge bath and Mela did my hair, we were out the door and speed-walking our way through a labyrinth of temples and lush gardens toward the opposite side of the compound. Yes, I wore the dress, but I'd strategically wrapped a festive-looking piece of red and orange fabric I'd found in King's room around my shoulders like a shawl. Mela, too happy to have me wearing the dress and attending at all, said nothing.

When we arrived to a football-field-sized, overly crowded plaza situated in front of an elevated temple—about twenty feet up—I spotted King almost immediately. He sat on a stone carved throne at the top of the steps, underneath a red and orange sail.

I glanced down at my shawl. *Great. I'm wearing his backup sunshade.* I could only hope no one noticed.

Mela ushered me over to a long line of bare-chested women amidst the crowd, holding everything from baskets of grapes to stacks of flatbread. No one seemed to give a hoot about their state of dress.

"What do I do?" I asked Mela.

She shoved a basket of mixed grains into my hands. "It is simple. When it is your turn, you raise your basket to the sky, wait for the king's nod to confirm the gods have seen your offering, and then you lay it at the foot of the temple."

I tried to see through the crowd, but the bodies were dense with men of every age, even children.

Okay, Mia. This is not a porn festival. No big deal. I nodded politely and took my place in line. The crowd, almost exclusively men—with long black hair tied back, deep brown skin, and brightly colored fabric around their waists—watched each "donation" with a seriousness that indicated the importance of this ritual. They really, truly believed that the offerings would bring them good luck the following year.

After almost half an hour, I was one body away from making my very innocent, topless offering to the gods.

The woman ahead of me offered a pastry of sorts, raised her arms, got the nod from King, and laid it on the giant, growing heap of food.

When I stepped up, I was sure my face matched the red in my "shawl," and I froze up.

"Well?" King said. "What are you waiting for, Seer?" His face held a hint of a wicked smile I recognized to mean he enjoyed watching me squirm.

All eyes were on me, and the silence in the air was palpable as King and I stared at each other. I tried not to react to the strange feeling in my stomach and much lower down, but it was impossible. The thought of showing him my breasts combined with the lustful, hungry look in his eyes triggered an unexpected arousal. He wanted to see me, and I wanted to show him.

Oh Lord, what's wrong with me? But even as I thought those words, my mind couldn't help focusing on those hypnotic, fierce blue eyes sinfully drilling into me. Then there were those wide, strong shoulders, his chiseled tan chest, and a set of abs so perfectly defined that I could easily count eight little squares even from my distance. The man was just as sinfully tempting now as he he'd ever been. Even without the fine Italian suits or expensive cars. Even without radiating that seductive, supernatural power that seemed to ooze from his every pore.

Get a hold of yourself, Mia. Seriously.

I was about to get on with it and bare myself when a man to my side—older, hairy, with a bitter scowl—reached for my shawl. "Make your offering properly, bitch. Before you bring down the wrath of the gods upon our heads."

Instinctively, I tugged back my shawl. "Get your hands off me."

The man slapped me hard.

I blinked away the pain, and before I could react, King marched down the steps of his temple, sword unsheathed. The crowd drew a breath, and the man instantly fell to his knees.

"You strike my guest?" King growled, raising his sword into the air.

I reached up and gripped his arm, knowing that I would not and could not watch this man lose his head. Yes, he deserved an ass whooping, but losing his head?

"Please, King." I begged with my eyes. "It's okay." No it wasn't, but we had much bigger issues to deal with, versus some asshole chauvinist from 1500 BC.

King's eyes drifted down to my chest. Yes, I'd let go of the shawl. A look of brazen lust washed over his face.

"Get a good look? 'Cause it's your last," I whispered.

King dipped his head, amusement flickering in his wickedly handsome face. "We shall see."

He lowered his sword and bent down to retrieve my "shawl." He inspected it for a moment with a confused face—*Yes, it's your sunshade*, I thought before wrapping it around me.

He turned and marched up the steps of his temple with defiant, confident strides. At the top, he turned and sheathed his sword while looking out across the shocked, silent crowd. "This woman," he pointed to me, "is my guest. She is not from our lands, yet she has decided to make an offering to our gods today. I consider this a very great honor, as do they. If anyone should lay a hand on her, *anyone,* the gods would surely see it as an insult, one that I will be forced to address."

The nervous crowd dropped to their hands and knees, the looks on their faces telling me they feared him as much as they trusted him.

It nearly took my breath away. I had never seen that sort of power before—one that came from deep inside a person's soul, from sheer conviction, but it was more hypnotic than anything I'd ever witnessed.

He took his seat, turned his vivid blue eyes back to me, and then gave me a nod and a smile. I stood there for a moment in awe before Mela appeared and poked me in the arm. "Mistress, put the basket down."

"Oh. Sorry." I did my part and quickly turned to hightail it out of there before I provoked any more incidents. Almost to the furthest edge of the plaza, I flashed a glance over my shoulder at King. His fierce gaze was still on me, and my body instantly reacted—weak knees, sensual heat and tingles—the whole sinful nine yards. I felt more in danger with this King than I ever had with the other. This man had the power to get inside my heart.

෧ೞ෨

I spent the rest of the day hiding out in my chamber, waiting for King to return and fully expecting him to give me a tongue-lashing of epic proportions for messing up his harvest ceremony.

Instead, just after sunset, Mela appeared with three other ladies, holding a new clean blue dress and a multitude of hairpins.

"Please don't tell me I have to go bottomless to a dinner party," I said.

"No, mistress," she said, not getting my joke, "the king has requested you dine in his chamber tonight."

"Alone?" I swallowed.

"Yes." She flashed a confused look at me. Clearly she thought we'd already slept together. "This is his request."

I nodded slowly. "Oh. Okay." This couldn't be avoided, anyway. He'd had almost an entire day to digest the bad news and think up some sort of a solution. If there was one.

Yes, I'm sure that's what he wants. To talk. Nothing more.

Within the hour, I was once again bathed, coiffed, and my teeth were scrubbed to a pristine shine, but I procrastinated leaving the room.

"You are ready, mistress," Mela said.

I sat at the edge of the bed. "I think I need to scrub my teeth again."

"No. I assure you, three times is more than sufficient, and the king does not appreciate being kept waiting."

I blew out a breath and nodded.

"Are you all right, mistress?"

My body felt like it had been wound up in giant knots, and my heart raced at a million miles per hour. Images of King staring at my bare breasts, that sinful pleased look in his eyes, made me feel heated up all over again. I wanted him, and I wanted to continue the nonverbal conversation we'd started earlier. The problem? My liking him in any way, shape or form would not be a smart idea. There was no future in it. Especially if I prevented him from becoming cursed. The man would hopefully live out his life, grow old, and die in this time as he should.

I, on the other hand, hoped to get back home to a new, evil-King-free life.

"Yes. I'm good. Just a little tired, I guess." I stood and walked as slowly as I could out the door to his chamber.

When I entered, there were only a few oil lamps lit. King lay with eyes closed in his steaming tub of water, his bare, muscular chest gleaming with drops of water.

I was about to turn and leave when he spoke. "Come in and sit."

He hadn't opened his eyes or looked at me.

"Okay." I looked around the room. Against the wall, there was a table with enough food to feed ten men. I sat and waited, trying to keep calm. If I'd found it hard to keep my wits around the evil King, this version of him was proving impossible.

"So," I said. "Did you have time to think?"

King remained still and quiet, his muscular arms extended across the edges of the tub.

I waited for a response, but he said nothing.

"King?"

"You sound nervous. Why don't you join me?" he said.

I blinked. "Thank you, but I already had a bath today."

He slowly opened his blue eyes and smiled. "Ah yes. You do not like baring your naked flesh. Exactly why is that?"

I shrugged. "It's just not something I generally do unless I'm intimate with a person."

He suddenly stood up and removed himself from the tub in all his naked glory. It wasn't the first time I'd seen him nude, but my feelings for him at the time felt infinitely different.

My eyes drank in every towering, lean, chiseled inch.

"Like what you see, Mia?"

My eyes snapped up to his face. This time, I didn't want to deny it. "Yes."

He smiled. "Good. At least you are honest." He reached for piece of white cloth and wrapped it around his waist. "Care for some wine?" He strolled toward me, poured a glass, and offered it to me.

"Thanks."

"So." He sat in front of me and poured his own chalice. "I have some questions for you."

"All right."

He gulped down his wine and set down the empty cup. "You say you do not know how you came here to me."

"I think it was the bracelet. But I'm not sure."

"You also say you were running from me," he said sharply.

"Yes," I replied.

"But you are here to help me."

"Yes." I nodded.

"Why?" His gaze was steady and harsh.

"I already told you that." I didn't think it was fair what had been done to him.

"Yes. But there is more to our story, isn't there?"

I nodded but stared at my glass.

"What are you not telling me?" he asked.

"It's hard to explain."

"Try."

I lifted my eyes. "I can't."

"Cannot or will not?"

"Can't. I don't know how."

"But you are my woman, yes?"

"Yes. I mean—you claimed me as yours, but we've never…"

"I have never lain with you," he said, completing my sentence.

"Why are you asking me all of these questions?"

"I am not certain I believe your story."

"Which part?" I asked. "The part about my being from the future, being yours, or your fate?"

"All three. Who is to say this is not a ploy to win me, to be my queen in Hagne's place?"

Dammit. So stubborn. If he didn't buy my story, then we were all screwed. History would repeat. *Unless you do something to stop Hagne on your own.* Which I was fully prepared to do, but wouldn't get the chance if King thought I was bonkers and had me thrown back in a cage.

"Then ask me anything." I lifted my arm to remind him of the "K" tattoo.

"You could pretend your words."

"You saw me jump with your own eyes," I pointed out.

"Perhaps you knew I would catch you."

"That's ridiculous; I almost died." I took a moment to catch my breath. This conversation felt useless. "You know what? Fine." I stood up. "Don't believe me. Go ahead and marry Hagne. Kill your brother. Enjoy your cursed life."

"Where do you think you are going?" he asked.

I'm going to find Hagne and take care of this mess on my own.

"I thought you were stronger than this," I said, "but I was wrong."

"You think me weak because I do not believe your wild story?"

"I'm saying that there is nothing I can say to convince a man who refuses to accept the truth."

He rose from the table, fury pouring from his eyes. "You will sit, Seer. Or I will have my guards tie you to that chair."

I hesitantly sat back down. "What do you want from me?"

He poured himself another cup of wine, drank it down, and then returned his sharp gaze to me. "The truth."

"About what?"

"Prove that you are not trying to manipulate me."

"What do you want?" I barked.

"The truth!" He slammed his fist onto the table, causing the plates of food to jump.

"I don't know what that is," I yelled. "That's the truth. I go to you for help. You claim me as your property. I find out you're cursed and looking for a way out. You manipulate me, use me, and try to hurt me. Then poof, I'm here."

"So you are saying you fear me. Completely."

"Yes."

He reached across the table and grabbed my
wrist with the tattoo. "Remove your clothes."

"What?" I said.

"Silence. Do it."

Without giving my body permission, I rose from
the table, fearing why he would ask this. Sheer
panic took over as my brain began recalling the
horrible memories of the future.

King's intense blue gaze focused on my angry
horrified face as I slipped the dress off my shoulder
and allowed it to fall to the floor.

His eyes looked me over hungrily for several
moments before he stood, gripped my wrist and
leaned in. At first, I thought he might kiss my neck
or touch me, but he didn't. Instead he placed his
nose at my nape and smelled me.

What the hell?

Still gripping my wrist, he whispered, "Tell me
you love me. Tell me to make love to you."

The nightmares of his private island came
crashing down. I could taste the fear on my tongue.

"I love you. I want you to make love to me," I
said unwillingly.

King released my wrist and stared deeply into
my eyes. I could feel his wine-scented breath on my
face and hear my own heart pounding away.

I began to pray I'd find the strength to release
myself from his command as I'd done once before
in a state of panic.

"I believe you." He turned and sat back down at
the table. "You may get dressed."

I blinked and then reached for my dress. The moment I was covered, my eyes became glued to a sharp knife on the table. *I'm going to kill him.*

"Go ahead," he said, also staring at the knife. "If it will make you feel better."

"What the hell was that?" I fumed.

He poured another glass with a cool, calm, and steady hand. "I smelled the fear on you, saw it in your eyes. You really do hate me."

"Your fucking point?"

"Emotions like that cannot be faked. You truly believed I would hurt you, which means I've hurt you before."

He rose from the table and glanced at the food. "Enjoy your meal."

He was leaving? Before I had the chance to stab him? How ungentlemanly.

"Where are you going?" I seethed, expecting him to say it was none of my goddamned business.

"I do not wish you any further distress this evening, and I have some difficult decisions to make. I will return later. Rest. You will be safe here."

He stopped halfway out the door. "By the way, Mia. I would never take a woman against her will. But I did enjoy seeing your body. The gods will surely give the people a plentiful harvest next season."

Completely shocked, my mouth hung open. *Who is this guy?*

I sat at the table for the next hour pondering that question. More precisely, I pondered how he made me feel. Angry, overwhelmed, crazy.

I couldn't deny that being around him was like a highly addictive narcotic I couldn't get enough of.

And that little move of his hadn't been simply about proving I feared him. It was also about making me trust him. He'd put me in a position where I felt exposed, where he could do anything he liked. Yet he hadn't, and made a point of it as if he felt the need to win my trust.

Staring at the food and unable to eat, the cool breeze drifting through the open doorway finally got the best of me. I nestled into King's bed and covered myself with the soft silky red blanket. His delicious masculine scent—a sort of citrus and musk—enveloped me, and I closed my eyes, thinking of him. This King was seductively strong and fearless. He was human, yet somehow bigger than life—utterly powerful, but kind, too. He was that part of future-King who left me breathless and speechless with his brutal honesty and beauty. That was the man who'd saved my mother. He'd held me when I felt like my life was ending. Yes, now my mind clearly saw two completely different people living inside that future version. One I hated and wanted to kill. The other was this man…

Goose bumps broke out over my body thinking of him—shirtless with that long black hair—and those vivid blue eyes. And that body. Holy Christ, did that man have abs. And thick muscled arms and legs. And…

The tension pooled between my legs, and I shook my head. *How fucked up am I?* There was no possible scenario resulting in a happy ending for me. Regardless, I couldn't help wanting this untainted version of him. He was the entire package without the baggage.

Except...he lives in 1500 BC, give or take a few centuries as I wasn't sure about the exact year. *Care to think these feelings over?*

*I won't fall for him. I just...*I sighed. He was magnetic, that was the best way to describe him.

Unable to resist the numbing oasis of sleep, I closed my eyes and tried to think of something else. An image of a perfect future popped into my mind: everyone gathered at my parents' Victorian home on Knob Hill in San Francisco. Justin and his girlfriend, Jamie, holding their beautiful baby while sitting on that floral, overstuffed couch in the living room. Becca and her mother squabbling over some random fact about an actor they both loved. "No, he's dating that model," one would say. "No. They broke up," the other would respond. Then there would be my parents sneaking kisses in the kitchen while they prepared the finishing touches on the meal. Me, well, I was there, too. Somewhere. Although, I couldn't see any details. Maybe because I was still in ancient Minoa, beginning to wonder if I ever wanted to leave.

Could I do that to my poor parents? Because their losing a daughter would be just as bad as losing my brother. And losing us both? I shuddered. I couldn't begin to imagine the grief.

Nevertheless, even if I wanted to go home, it might not happen. So then what? What would become of my parents?

Jesus, we're all so screwed.

CHAPTER TEN

I didn't know the hour, but when my eyes opened, it was because my subconscious had been poking my conscious mind in a petulant, little sister kind of way until I couldn't ignore it.

I sat up in King's bed. All but one oil lamp had burnt out, enough to spot King's well-constructed frame sitting on a chair in the corner, his eyes intense and focused like an animal. All too reminiscent of the man I knew many years from now, his posture—stiff with hands clasped and elbows resting on his knees—meant he was deep in thought and not at all happy.

"You're back," I said.

King continued staring with a dark gaze, irate and feral. That was another familiar King move. No, not a good one.

My heart began to gallop inside my chest. "King?"

"What?" he responded coldly.

"Are you okay?"

"What do you think, woman?"

"No."

"Any manner I choose to examine the puzzle results in death."

"I'm sorry. I'm really sorry," I said remorsefully.

"I did not ask for your pity."

"I don't pity you," I said calmly, sitting up, "but my wagon is hitched to yours."

"What the Hades does that mean?"

"My fate is heavily dependent on yours. And I want"—*what do I want?*—"you. I mean, you to live a happy, full life."

I looked away for a moment because the gaze of his sky blue eyes was too intense. They made my skin break out in erotic shivers and my body heat with need every single goddamned time.

When I gathered the gumption to look at him again, he stood, crossed the room, stared for one uncomfortable moment, and then sat on the edge of the bed, facing me.

"Have you put a spell on me?" he asked.

"What? No. Why would you say that?"

"I cannot think when I am near you," he said sorely. "The moment I saw you, I felt an odd joining. As if you and I had lived several lifetimes together."

His words shocked me. Maybe because I felt the same way.

"And last evening, when I dozed off under the stars," he said quietly, "I saw you in my dreams, a look of pain in your eyes while you watched me drown in an ocean of red light. Each attempt I made to open my mouth only filled my throat with blood. I awoke tasting it on my tongue." He looked down at my hand and began absentmindedly tracing a tiny circle over my skin. The sensation of his touch, the intimacy of it, instantly triggered a gnawing, heart-wrenching, carnal hunger. I found this real live version of him mesmerizing. I wanted more. More touching. More of his smell. More of his warmth. But I knew I shouldn't.

"The red is pain," I said. "It's your curse." I knew this, because I'd seen his light with my gift. It was red—pain—and blue—sorrow—mixed so violently together that it turned into a deep purple. "And it's a tragedy what happens to you."

"How is it possible that you fear me, but do not despise me?"

"Because your curse isn't who you are." I realized that now. I couldn't blame *this* man. I couldn't hate him. And I couldn't deny that I felt something profoundly emotional between us.

How the hell that was possible, I didn't know. But I couldn't stop it.

His gaze intense and fixed on my eyes, he leaned down and pressed his soft lips to mine. It didn't feel like a kiss meant to lead anywhere. Instead, it felt more like a test or a validation, to see if what he felt was real, despite the improbability.

It was.

The sensation surged through my lips' sensitive nerve endings, down my throat, and into my heart. It took my breath away.

He pulled back and stared with those luminescent blue eyes. "I'm sorry for what I have done to you, Mia. I'm sorry for hurting you."

I hadn't been expecting that. "It wasn't you. I mean—it wasn't your fault."

He tilted his head. "No. It was not. But you needed to hear that from me. I can see it in your eyes."

I teared up, but held back from crying. "Thank you."

King suddenly cleared his throat and threw a giant wall between us. "I have thought this through. All outcomes lead to a civil war and, therefore, a collapse of my people and the destruction of everything I have built. All except one."

"What are you going to do?"

"I will be gone for several days and leave my guards to watch over you."

"Where are you going?" I blinked rapidly.

His large chest puffed out with a deep breath. "Callias is on the other side of the island seeing to several disputes between the farmers. I will go and attempt to reason with him, give him a choice to discontinue his pursuit of Hagne—something I doubt he will do."

"Why do you think that?" I asked, because it was exactly what I had planned to do.

"Callias is stubborn and wild. But I owe it to him to try. And I owe it to myself to die with a clear conscience."

Die? Clear conscience? "I don't follow."

"You say that he challenges me for the throne."

I nodded.

"And that he fights to keep Hagne."

I nodded.

"Then to change our fates, I will fight him and allow him to win."

No. No. Fuck no. Their fights were not boxing matches; they fought to the death.

"You can't fucking do that!" I protested.

He frowned with a smugness befitting a king. "I do not know this word 'fuck,' but I can do anything I damned well choose; I am king." He stood and left, leaving me utterly speechless. This King wanted to give everything to save the people he loved. Even if it meant his demise.

In that moment, my tears came hard, and my heart fell even harder. Yes, for him. He was that little piece of something strong, noble, and good hiding inside the monster I'd seen from the beginning. And the connection I felt, the deep-seated lust and inexplicable loyalty, had always been for him. This man. Which is why I couldn't allow him to die.

That's when my earlier thought hit me again. Maybe, just maybe, I really was there to make everything right. But what options did I have?

Hagne. She was my only option. I could either get her to see reason or kill her. That would almost certainly mean my death, too, because if Hagne's family was powerful, they would demand justice.

But if I died, then so be it. This alternative path would stop her from cursing King, and prevent my brother from digging up the Artifact in Palenque. It

might even prevent him from ever getting mixed up
with the 10 Club, if King in fact "owned those
clowns."

I smiled to myself as the twisted little pieces slid
effortlessly into place, and that gnawing uneasiness
deep inside my gut lifted. This was right…

As soon as the sun rose, I asked one of the guards—
a shirtless behemoth with mocha-brown skin, long
black hair, wearing a sword and a manly—yes,
manly—little blue and red pleated skirt (not much
different than a kilt but made for warm weather) if
he could tell me where I might find Hagne.

"I do not know, but I will send someone to look
for her," he replied.

"Or point me in the right direction, and I'll go
find her."

He eyeballed me cautiously as if conflicted. "I
am sorry, but our king has forbidden you to leave.
You are to remain in his or your chamber, or in his
private courtyard."

Of course. King would know not to trust me to
follow his command and stay put.

I looked at the guard and smiled. "Thanks. I'll
wait here, then."

He whistled for another guard before scurrying
off promptly. In the meantime, I looked around the
room for something sharp or blunt, unfazed by my
new hard shell and utter lack of remorse or concern

over wanting to end Hagne. If I couldn't get her to see reason—a serious long shot—I would get her away from here, where the guards couldn't intervene.

I riffled through a few large woven baskets in a little cove that looked like King's closet. There were piles of finely woven fabric—golds, blues, and reds—neatly folded and scented with dried flowers. In another basket, I found a jeweled dagger sheathed inside a suede holster. I plucked my finger over the tip. It was sharp as hell.

I lifted my dress and strapped the dagger to my thigh, hoping the pleats would conceal the bulky handle. I went outside to wait, and ten or so minutes later, Hagne appeared in the courtyard, her face flushed as if she'd run the entire way.

"Mia, are you all right?" she panted with false concern.

"Hunky-dory."

"I know not what that means, but the guards said it was urgent."

"I told the king he has to let you be with Callias."

"What did he say?" she half gasped.

"He wasn't upset. In fact, he fully understands. He really isn't a bad guy, Hagne."

Bitterness flickered in her spiteful eyes, and I knew what she was thinking: she'd said several times in her journal how she despised the king for being so weak. And right now, I'd bet she was congratulating herself for being right. Because only a weak man would roll over and give his betrothed to his brother.

"How did you convince him?" she asked.

"I offered to take your place," I lied.

Her face was bright red with anger, but she said nothing.

"I didn't tell you this, Hagne, but I am his betrothed in the future. Your marriage to him ends in a tragedy for everyone, including him. My proposal was simple: he lets you be with Callias. You live, your family lives, and your baby lives."

"But I am not with child."

"You will be."

This was the point where any rational, decent human being would simply thank their lucky stars and feel happy that they'd been given a chance to get what they wanted. But not Hagne. Nope. She did exactly what any psycho-bitch would do.

"He is casting me aside," she whispered in disbelief. "Everyone will see me as his rubbish."

I wanted to roll my eyes. I really did. But this was too important. "You get out of marrying a man you despise and get to be with the one you've loved since childhood. Does it really matter what people think?"

Pure unfiltered hatred sizzled in her brown eyes, and I knew that any shot at a peaceful resolution would be impossible. *Shit. I have to kill her.*

But then, like a switch had flipped, her gaze fell into a neutral state. "No." She bobbed her head frantically. "Of course, you are right. Callias is the love of my life. Nothing else matters."

Her words sounded as fake as she was, so I wasn't at all tempted to let down my guard. The woman was dangerous, and I had to assume powerful. Hell, her spit gave me the ability to speak ancient Minoan.

"So you will marry the king instead?" she asked.

Not that he'd asked, but part of me really wanted to make him mine forever. The man was seduction, power, and sexiness wrapped up in a manly, ancient Minoan package that left no woman unaffected in this time or in the future. Truth be told, however, there were structural issues with my situation. Such as…I was going to kill Hagne, and King would likely have to execute me, among just a few.

I replied, "You focus on Callias."

She lowered her head with the grace of a lady. "As you wish."

So damned fake. "And now, I have a favor to ask," I said.

"Yes?"

Let your guard down so I can kill you. "I'd like to go to the market and look for a few items for when the king returns. Can you get me out of here? The guards won't let me leave."

She grinned. "I can take care of them. It's the least I can do. After all, you have saved me." She held up her small hand. "Wait here. I shall return."

Hagne disappeared for several minutes and then returned, waving for me to follow her down the stairs that led to the right of the building.

"This way," she whispered, giggling like a girl. *Psycho.*

She added, "There is a secret tunnel leading beneath the palace and to the hill just north of the market."

This was perfect. I could follow behind her and then…

Be strong? Save King? Save your brother, too?

Yes. I could do that. I just had to remember who Hagne really was.

I followed along, and when we did, in fact, reach a small cave, about five feet tall and four feet wide, she stopped. "It is dark inside, but the tunnel goes for several passes to the right and then you will see the light. Simply follow me."

I didn't trust Hagne, but when I looked inside, there really wasn't anything there: a muddy floor, muddy walls, and a lot of darkness. And, hell, she was going first. And…hell, I had the dagger, which I was about to get out and use.

She rushed inside, and I followed along for almost forty or so yards until all light faded away.

"It's really dark in here." I began reaching for my dagger, trying to keep pace with her.

"Yes, but fear not. Just a few more steps…"

In that instant, she grabbed my arm and pulled me forward. I whipped forward and stumbled, but instead of falling onto firm ground, I kept on falling. Down, down, down, screaming every inch of the way until I landed with a splash.

The water was ice cold and deep.

I fought my way to the surface only to find that it offered little more than air. No light. No warmth.

Just the faint snicker of Hagne's voice off in the distance.

"Psycho bitch! He'll know it was you!" I screamed, but she was long gone. There was just me, the water, and the darkness now. "Who the fuck puts a well in the middle of a dark, goddamned fucking cave!" I yelled. "Really! Jesus H. fucking Christ. You. Have. Got. To. Be. Kidding. Me!"

Gah! But all the blasphemous cuss words in the world wouldn't change what was. Me. At the bottom of a well in a goddamned cave.

Treading water, I threw back my head and closed my eyes. The water was cold, but not hypothermia-chilling. I'd drown from exhaustion before anything else. *Think, Mia. Think.* But my heart raced at a million miles per second. *Don't panic. Panicked people die much faster.*

I began to hum "Yellow Submarine" by the Beatles—a nervous habit I'd picked up as a kid. To be clear, any Beatles song would generally do, but the aquatic theme felt appropriate.

Ten verses later, my heart rate lowered and my mind began to sort through the options.

There were none.

I wasn't about to develop super-Spidey abilities and scale the fifty-foot drop. And no one except for psycho-Seer knew where I was.

I'm screwed.

After an hour or so, I came to two conclusions: I would die here like a complete chump, but Hagne would still lose. King knew my secrets, and he would do everything in his power to alter his destiny. But goddammit, why did he and I have to be the ones to die? We only wanted to make things right. King loved his people. I loved my family.

And I love him… There was no use trying to deny it anymore. What was the point? I would be dead in a few hours, and there was no one left to impress or fool.

Not even myself.

Taking this journey had finally allowed me to reconcile the conflicting emotions I'd lived with these last few months. Yes, it was possible to simultaneously hate and want a person. Yes, I'd felt compassion and remorse for that man's plight and suffering, even when I feared him. Yes, my life with him felt like a sick and twisted merry-go-round of epic proportions.

Until now.

Now I knew. King wasn't one man; he was layers. Light surrounded by a thick layer of darkness. Life encased by death. Scar tissue over a soul that was noble and good.

I felt a deep sense of relief and gratitude. *I got to meet the real man.* And he was beyond anything I could've ever imagined.

So what now?

I took a breath and swayed my arms from side to side as there wasn't much else to do. I had no magical transportation or…

Wait. Yes, I do. I had the damned bracelet. I could go back.

But what if…what if I returned to that horror I'd left? That monster's hands all over my body, my wrists burning as I tried to break free, the absolute nightmare of knowing I'd once again miscalculated King and his aptitude for cruelty.

You have to choose.

I still wore the bracelet on my right wrist; it might lead me home. But would I return to a scene of unspeakable violence, or find that King had changed all our fates and so return to a completely different future? And if different, would I lose those memories most precious to me? Surprisingly, those moments weren't the big events—graduation, first kiss, or landing the dream job. They were the small breaths in between the noise: Justin crying in my arms when he was five with a split knee on the playground, the tears pouring from his little red face because he thought he'd die from the cut. It was the first moment in my life I remembered feeling that I mattered. I was this person's big sister. I could make it all better with a simple hug and a few reassurances. I had wiped away his tears with the back of my hand and told him what he needed to hear. Within a few minutes, the bleeding stopped and Justin was swinging without a care in the world. Then he became a man, one with a heart bigger than anyone I'd ever met. I was his sister, his to protect and pick back up when she got knocked down.

Once again, though, I mattered. To him, anyway. I was the piece of the puzzle in his life that made him feel like *he* mattered. It was why he'd once ended up in the hospital when we were in high school. All because I'd had a bad day and decided to blow off a bunch of steam at a party. Tequila.

More tequila. And…them—a bunch of fucking idiots who weren't going to take no for an answer. Justin was there for me, and they beat him within an inch of his life.

I swore in that moment that I'd never again put the people I loved in danger, because my only worth in this world was when I did the saving. Perhaps Justin, too, felt that way. Perhaps…I really didn't know, but maybe that was why he'd gone to such horrible lengths to free Jamie from her prison with Vaughn. In my heart, that didn't make up for the things people say he did to me, but in some messed-up way, I could understand how his need to be the hero was his Achilles' heel.

Because that was mine. I was the idiot who would do anything to save her baby brother. And now King. It was the only goddamned thing on this planet that I ever felt good at.

Yet, here you are…needing to be saved. Great job, Mia.

After days or hours passed, I didn't know, I finally arrived to the point where my body burned from the chill. My legs and feet cramped, and my shoulders ached from swaying my arms. I wouldn't last much longer.

Dagger or bracelet?

I'd rather die than get sent back and let King hurt me. It was the God's honest truth.

I slipped the dagger free from the sheath tied to my thigh and gripped it in my hand. Could I do this, could I drive it into my chest?

I'd died once before, when King had stopped my heart, and it wasn't like people say. The anticipation, the body's will to fight, is far more traumatizing than the actual event. The actual dying felt like drifting off to sleep. And when the ring I'd worn—that giant solitaire diamond given to me by King—brought me back to life, it felt like waking right back up. Point was, I wasn't afraid of dying.

This is the only sane choice, Mia. The only one. All other options left me to either drown or go back to where I came from—maybe.

I lifted the dagger, but suddenly saw an image of King, his electric blue eyes filled with disapproval and a scowl on those beautiful, strong lips. I could practically hear him yelling at me for giving up.

Fuck. He was right. And more than anything I wanted to see him just one last time. I promised myself that if I did, I wouldn't hold back. A life where you didn't follow your heart wasn't a life. And sometimes you just had to make the leap and trust in something that didn't make sense.

Hang on, Mia. Hang on. He'll come for you.

CHAPTER ELEVEN

No two deaths are alike. That was my conclusion. How were they different? It was hard to articulate. When I'd died the first time, King had literally gone inside my body and stopped my heart. It was an eerie frightening feeling, the terror diluted by the knowledge that he was doing it out of concern for my well-being—so I'd thought—and that I, barring any unforeseen snags with the ring, would come back. Fully intact. Fully me. There was also a tiny part of my brain that quietly rejoiced in the sensation of his soul or light, or whateverthehell you call it, moving around inside my shell. Yes, it also hurt like a sonofabitch, too, because of his curse. However, there was an undeniable tickle of erotic delight from being so intimate with such a wicked sexy bastard. Call me sick, I know. Of course, that was before…he hurt me.

This death, though, was so very, very different. Drowning was lonely. It hurt. And there was no secret pleasure or intimacy of a man's touch. It felt like being ripped from my skin while my insides pulsed with life, every nerve ending scorching with nonexistent fire. My bleeding soul and oxygen-deprived muscles screamed in agony. Had I been sent to hell?

Shit. Shit, I thought. *This can't be happening.*

"Mia, wake the *fuck* up, woman." I heard a deep masculine voice plunge through my misery and a sharp sting on my cheek. "Do you hear me? You wake the hell up this instant, or by gods I will…"

Slowly, I peeled open my eyes.

Blue. Blue…so much blue. There was the bright heavenly sky above and the sanctuary of cobalt orbs staring down.

"King?" I whispered.

"Yes, it is I. Your king."

I blinked. "Did you say 'fuck'?"

He growled. "Foolish Seer. Why did you attempt to kill Hagne?"

I wiggled my toes and fingers. The cool air and warm sand on my back felt real.

"Where are we?" I asked.

Inches above my face, King brushed the wet hair back from my forehead and beamed. "I thought I'd lost you."

"But…I drowned. I…"

"No. You nearly drowned." Deep conflict shimmered in his eyes.

I coughed violently for a few moments and then flung my head back, panting. "Who the hell put a well there?"

"Who the Hades knows? But what were you thinking?"

"I couldn't let her ruin you."

"So you meant to stab her with this?" He reached to my side and plucked a shiny object from the sand.

"Something like that."

"This is the dagger of Potnia. If left inside the body, it is said to mimic the appearance of death, but merely puts a person to sleep."

Oh, great. Nap, Hagne? "It was the only weapon I could find. So it was either that or claw her to death. But I would've done it. I'm not letting her win."

He stared affectionately into my eyes for several long moments. "You are mad, Mia. Mad and beautiful."

Slowly, I brought myself to my elbows and looked around. We were alone on the quiet beach just outside of the cave's mouth. "How did you find me?"

He slid his large, rough hand over my "K" tattoo. "I believe this drew me to you. I felt your anguish, as if you were calling to me." His eyes filled with distress. "The moment I returned, I confronted Hagne, but she would not disclose where you were. However, by the grace of the gods, I felt the pull. I followed, and it led me straight to you." He cupped the side of my cheek. "I cannot remove you from my thoughts, Mia. Awake or asleep, I see only you." He unexpectedly slammed his lips to mine and plunged his tongue between my lips, thrusting in and sliding out at a slow, sensual pace.

My body, already wet and now growing warm from the sun, instantly grew hotter and wetter. His mouth felt like everything to me. Life, love, and need. I slid my hand behind his neck and urged him to deepen the kiss. Perhaps it was a signal, too, of what my body really wanted: him, me, as close as we could get.

I wasn't going to let this chance go. Not for anything.

Arched over me, King's large body hovered, as if reluctant to take what it wanted.

I moved my hand to the small of his bare back and pulled him in toward my hips. I hoped he wouldn't hesitate to accept my offer.

He didn't.

Within the space of a breath, he moved on top, our tongues colliding and lashing, our teeth bumping. Our bodies ignited and hands clawed to get closer to each other. He tore away the top of my wet dress as I clumsily broke the small metal clasp at his waist and freed his lower torso.

Within seconds, our bodies were naked, and he slid his muscled lean frame between my legs. Needing to touch him, I reached down and found his insanely thick long shaft. A groan emanating from deep within his chest erupted from his parted full lips when I gripped him firmly and began stroking. I wanted to drive him so close to the edge that he'd be begging me for it, that there'd be no chance of him turning back.

I reached for his sensual lips with mine and found that hot, wet tongue ready, just like his magnificent cock, the heat spurring me on.

I ran my thumb over his tip, finding a delicious drop of moisture, which I spread over his silky head in little circles.

King tilted his face toward the sky. "Damn, woman, what you do to me."

I reached with my free hand and snaked it behind his neck to pull his salacious lips back to my mouth. But instead of delivering those sweet, wet, and sinful kisses I longed for, his head moved down to my chest.

Staring at me with those piercing blue eyes, his mouth opened and covered the erect tip of my breast. He began to suck hard, and I began to pant harder. Watching him take my nipple into his mouth, his tongue swirling rapidly over that sensitive skin, nearly brought me over the edge.

I couldn't take it anymore. I just couldn't. Foreplay was for people who needed to warm up, who didn't feel comfortable acknowledging their sexual hunger, or who had all the time in the world. We fit none of these.

I firmly gripped his shoulders. "Please?"

A carnal smile spread across his lips, but he didn't obey. Instead, his hand slid down between my thighs and began stroking. The moment his fingers penetrated me, I flung my head back and gripped handfuls of sand.

"I must ensure you are ready. I do not wish to hurt you."

"I'm ready," I panted. "I'm ready." In fact, I was about to orgasm. "Please…"

"If you insist." He kissed his way up my torso, and the moment his hard cock was within reach, I had it in my hand, guiding it toward my entrance.

He quickly gripped my wrists and pinned them above my head. "I do not require any encouragement." Hips slightly raised, he laid the massive bulk of his body over mine and kissed me deeply for several long moments. The anticipation was torture.

He broke from my mouth and kissed the side of my neck, still pinning my arms over my head.

"Oh my God, please. Please…"

He lifted his head and stared into my eyes. "Please what?" he said with a husky voice saturated with sex.

I wanted to say, "Fuck me hard with your thick long cock," but I didn't want to shock the poor man with my modern ask-for-what-you-really-want ways. So instead, I simply said, "Fuck me."

"Is this what you want?" He released my arms, gripped himself in his hand, and began circling the tip of his shaft over my moist entrance teasingly, as if priming his cock for penetration.

"Yes," I breathed, bringing my hips forward.

He backed off, denying me the end to the sexual torment.

"Don't do this to me. Please, King, I'm begging you…"

"If you are begging…" He slowly thrust his hard shaft between my legs and gazed deeply into my eyes. Everything became so damned clear. There was no separation of time when it came to love; it saw the past and future in one blinding light. And I'd never let go of that light. Not ever.

"Yes," I panted.

King thrust himself inside me once more, his hypnotic blue gaze never leaving me. I cupped his face and opened myself as far as I could, wanting to savor the feeling of his thick rigid flesh driving into me, of his body inside mine.

"Harder," I panted, knowing this might be our one and only chance. "Fuck me harder."

He smiled with that wickedly wolfish grin I now knew like the back of my hand. "I'd never fuck you, Mia." He thrust himself so deeply that it stole my breath. "Only love."

Tears filled my eyes, forcing me to close them from the intensity of the emotion and pleasure while King pounded away, pushing us toward a brilliant light filled with ecstasy. Again and again, he moved his large cock in and out until my body couldn't help release that erotic tension in one giant rapturous explosion.

I drove my fingertips into his taut tanned back and cried out. He slid his large hands beneath me and cupped my ass, allowing him to drive his cock deeper, to hit that special spot head-on, igniting me once more. I moaned for him while he slid and grunted, coming hard inside me.

Moments passed before I even remembered we were lying there in broad daylight, the sun scorching my face, and our bodies covered in slippery, sensual sweat.

"Holy shit, King," I panted.

"Yes," his chest heaved with exertion, "I am your king. And don't you ever forget it, woman."

I smiled and brushed the sweat-soaked strands of long black hair from his beautifully bronzed face. "Yes. You are."

Still inside me and still rock hard, he dropped his head to my chest and slowly began moving.

"I need more," he said.

"Take all you want." I sighed, gazing up at the beautiful blue sky, three thousand years in the past, knowing that all the pain and suffering had led me to this moment.

And it was…beautiful. Breathtaking. It was everything.

∽∽

"Mia, we have to talk." King hopped from the steaming tub and wrapped his large, lean, and muscled frame in a piece of white cloth.

I sat still, glowing and weak from hours of ravenous lovemaking. The man was insatiable. In fact, at one point, I had begun to wonder if he'd taken some sort of ancient herbal supplement because I'd never heard of a man coming twice in a row, then being ready for another round thirty minutes later. But he did. And he had. And after a sensual swim in the ocean—our bodies and lips glued together the entire time—to rinse the sand from our sticky skin, we'd dressed and returned to his chamber. He ordered a day's worth of food—wine, fruit, bread, and cheese—my favorite meal of all time—and instructed the guards to ensure we wouldn't be bothered until further notice.

We ate, we drank, we shared stories. He told me about growing up on the island, and of the pressure knowing he'd someday be responsible for so many. He didn't talk much about his parents or how they died, but I had the impression they'd been loving people who'd instilled the importance of loyalty and duty in their children. When I told King about my family and snippets of the life I'd had before everything changed, he listened with such intensity that I knew he was visualizing every detail. He asked questions about what that part of the world looked like, how many people lived in my "village," and why I hadn't married at the age of sixteen.

Yeah, that was kind of cute. But cuter still was the look on his face when I told him lots of women never married, choosing to focus on their careers instead. The open mouth and blinking blue eyes told me that King didn't get it.

"You are saying that they refuse the protection of a husband?"

"Yep," I responded.

"And…they are not whores?"

Like I said, it was cute. But cute quickly turned into wicked and sexy the moment his body was ready for more. This last round, though, when he'd bent me over the edge of the tub, his hand bringing me to orgasm three times in quick succession as he pounded his cock into me, was by far the best. It was as if our bodies were so attuned to one another that every touch, lick, and thrust was perfectly calibrated. I couldn't imagine ever living without him now—not because the sex was more amazing than anything on earth, but because it was proof we were connected in a way that literally defied...everything. Absolutely everything. Which is also why his desire to talk and the serious tone scared the hell out of me.

"There's nothing to talk about." I looked away, knowing that was a huge lie. There were a ton of things to say, like he needed to abandon—forever—any thoughts of sacrificing himself.

"Do not pretend that the situation has changed," he said.

I looked at the murals of fish and octopi on the wall. "Can't we just pretend for a few more hours?"

"No."

I took a hollow breath.

"I have killed Hagne," he said.

My head whipped toward him. "What?"

He lifted his chin. "I killed her."

My spit stuck in my throat, but there were no words.

"I went to her home, and she told me that she killed you. Admitted it in front of her entire family. Out of anger, I drew my sword and executed her on the spot."

"Oh no. No..."

"Even though she defied my orders not to harm you and my actions were justified, her family demands justice or there will be a civil war," he said.

I cupped my hands over my mouth. I couldn't believe this.

He continued, "Callias will fight in her honor to settle the dispute."

"But...but...why?"

"Because I will ask him to," he replied. "He will understand that if there is no justice, many more lives will be lost."

"Then kill him with the dagger." That way he'd be brought back.

"No." King's head hung low. "There must be a beheading. The dagger will not work for that."

I stood, and King's eyes focused on my naked breasts. I grabbed a cloth and covered myself, not wanting to feel like I did. So...angry. "What the hell are you saying?"

He looked at the floor. "That nothing has changed. I will die."

I shoved my nails into my palms. "Like fucking hell you will."

"Silence, Mia." He held up his palm. "This is the only way. My people, those women and children, are more important than us."

I knew that. I really did. "I would never ask you to give up. Never. You're loyal to them, and there is nothing in the world more important than that. I'm asking you to consider other options." For Christ's sake, I'd just found him. I couldn't stand the thought of losing him now. It was just too painful.

"There are none." He looked away.

"There are always other options, King. We can leave—"

"No. I have reviewed every angle many times over, and this is the only solution that will maintain the peace. There must be blood. *My* blood."

Fucking Hagne! Why did it seem like this situation was on a path we couldn't change?

Then another thought struck me. "But Hagne hasn't cursed you. You'll die. Really die." I'd never see him again.

He nodded, clearly thinking about what that really meant.

Shit. Shit. Shit. I tightened the piece of cloth around my body and tucked the ends into my cleavage.

"Where, by gods, are you going, woman?"

"I can't be here right now. I can't breathe. I can't think." *A life without him. Really, truly without him.* After making love, a glimmer of hope in the back of my mind had begun to spark—that we might find a way through all this and come out the other side as two, whole, living people. But it just wasn't going to happen.

My body halfway out the door, he spoke. "Wait."

I stopped in my tracks.

"You. Are. A. Seer," he said.

I looked at him. "I-I don't understand." But what I really meant was: "Are you out of your *mind?*"

He stepped forward, his skin and hair still dripping with bathwater. "You will curse me to roam this earth, Mia, for however long it takes. And then you will be the one to free me."

I walked over to his bed and fell on my ass. Not sat, but fell.

"This is the solution." King sat beside me and brushed the wet strands from my face, tucking them behind my ear. "Callias will end me. *You* will bring me back."

I stared into the depths of his luminescent blue eyes. "You are asking me to sentence you to years of horrible pain. I can't do that." So many things could go wrong. I had no clue how to do a curse. And even if someone told me how, I could get the curse wrong, and he'd end up dead. *Dead* dead. Or I could be snapped back to my time before freeing him, and he'd be left to suffer for about three thousand years.

"I see no other solution, Mia."

I hissed out a breath. "I promise that in the future you would rather die than live like you do. The pain is…a living hell."

He looked at his hands for several moments. "It will be my burden to bear. Not yours."

"You have no idea what you're asking—"

"It is my decision and mine alone. You will not deprive me of my last wish." He sliced through me with those blue eyes. "I want to do this, Mia. For us."

His words made my stomach do sick little twists—joy mixed with a sense of deep guilt. It meant I'd see him again, but he really, really didn't understand what he was asking. And to condemn someone to this sort of agony, a torture so cruel and horrid that even in my darkest moment, even when I despised the man, I'd still felt sorry for him...I couldn't do it. Not if I really loved him.

"No," I said sharply. "We have to find another way. I don't know how to curse you. And how will I bring you back? What if you're wrong and—"

He pressed his lips to mine, silencing me for several long moments. My body immediately reacted to him—calm, hot, crazy.

He pulled away. "Has anyone ever told you that you ask too many questions?"

I nodded. "It's a sign of intelligence."

"I thought it meant the opposite." He grinned.

I smiled. "Funny, King."

"Yes. I do have my moments; however, today I believe it is because I am in love."

Once again, I resisted the tears. He'd said a word I couldn't have ever imagined coming from his lips: love. But there it was, the truth. I loved him, and he loved me. How it had happened, I didn't know. But it had. Despite the absolute impossibility, we'd found each other. Which is why he needed to fight for us instead of fighting his brother.

"Cursing you," I said, "means...it could mean..." I couldn't begin to comprehend. "If, for whatever reason, I can't bring you back right away and things play out like they did originally, you're going to do terrible things. Horrid, ugly, heinous things. You are *not* a good man, King." King had murdered off the bloodline of the Seers, except for me. Then there was his role with the 10 Club, heads in fucking jars, and God only knew what else. The man had been alive—or dead—for three thousand something years.

He squared his broad shoulders and stared with that glare I knew well. The man was about to lose his temper. "I do not wish to discuss this further, Mia. I am telling you—"

"Why can't we find a way to just...have you travel forward with me now?"

"Do you have one?" he growled.

"I have the bracelet. No, I don't know how it works, but you could try to use it, and I could—"

He suddenly grabbed me and kissed me deeply, with every ounce of emotion his body dared to expose.

I melted into him, wishing for this to never end, hoping that he'd change his mind and run. Run with me. Maybe we'd have another week together. Maybe we'd have twenty years. I didn't know or care. I just wanted more time.

"I know you are worried for me," he said, "however, I am the one volunteering for this fate. There is no other way."

I winced. He didn't understand who he would become and the terrible things he would do. Yes, I'd told him he became a monster, but clearly he didn't get it.

"What if," I said, "history repeats? Because if it does, you *have* to believe me, you don't want that future." I swallowed back the tears.

"What is it that I do? What are you not saying?" he asked coolly.

"You are not good to me. That's why us leaving is the only option."

"Mia, we are moving forward with this plan. And everything you hide only lessens our chance of seeing this through successfully. So whatever is it you are concealing—"

I'd already told him he'd hurt me, but I never gave him the explicit details. "I can't tell you. It's…"

"You will tell me!" he yelled.

I glared at him. "No."

"I will place you over my lap and hit your ass until you are black and blue if I must, but you will tell me."

I was speechless. Completely and utterly speechless with rage. "How dare you threaten me."

"I do not believe in threats." He grabbed me and pulled me towards his bed, throwing me over his lap with his hand raised. "Tell me! I am your king, and you *will* tell me!"

"How dare you!"

His hand came down hard with a sting on my ass. "I dare! I am the king. And I love you enough to fear nothing. You, however—"

"You whip me and rape me!" I screamed.

His body fell limp, like he'd been hit with a thousand bricks, and he tossed me off him onto the bed. "This cannot be." He suddenly looked at his hand in disgust, as if frightened by his roughness with me.

I looked away. "I escaped right before you…"

"I do not know what to say," he whispered.

The tears flowed down my face. "It wasn't you. Not really."

He stared at the floor. "And yet you allowed me to…" he whispered, "be with you. Without grudges." He was about to say something else, but closed his mouth, stood, and turned for the door.

"*You* are not that same man," I said. "And you can't feel guilty for something that hasn't happened yet."

"But there is no denying that I have the seeds of evil inside me. It must be there."

"Where are you going?" I asked.

His chest heaving, he swallowed. "I-I-I will fight Callias at sunrise."

He was almost out the door when I realized that it wasn't long before the sun came up.

"King?" I said, my voice trembling, the tone begging him to tell me what was going on inside his head.

He didn't face me, perhaps because he couldn't. "I must place the well-being of my people first." He took a breath. "And if what you say is true, then you are correct. You cannot curse me."

"What are you saying?"

His large shoulders lifted and fell. "I will die."

"No. Let's think this through and find another solution."

His beautiful eyes were as cold as two blocks of ice. "There are no other options."

King left, and I broke. Broke.

I'd lived through so much pain, but this...*this* was the wall. "I will break you, Mia," King had said on that horrible night. And he'd been goddamned right: I was utterly and completely broken.

CHAPTER TWELVE

Just after sunrise, I followed the massive flow of people outside the palace walls to an open-aired auditorium that reminded me of a scene straight from *Gladiator*. Present had to be the entire population of Minoa, their skin colors ranging from deep dark brown to light olive. Some had long straight black hair and others curly. The men, most anyway, wore only simple sarongs made from linen and kept their hair in braids or ponytails, while the women wore tunics or togas made from rough, hand-dyed fabric. Had I been in any other situation, I would have been talking to everyone and asking questions for posterity's sake. But my heart was too heavy to care that someday this civilization would cease to exist, and likely, I was about to witness the beginning of the end.

Unsure if I'd be able to observe the horrific event about to pass, but unable to walk away or stop myself from praying for a miracle, I sat high up in the last row of stone benches next to a group of women wearing white head scarves. They were much older than me and among the few spectators who looked dismayed. The rest behaved like a wild mob, ready for a boxing match between champions. I couldn't believe it.

Barbarians.

I sat on the edge of the bench and wiped away a tear, my mind still searching for a way to stop this.

"It is all right, dear," said the silver-haired woman to my side. Her eyes were dark brown and her skin worn by the sun.

I made a polite smile, but said nothing.

"You are the one Hagne spoke of, aren't you?" she asked.

I looked over, and all four women stared. "I'm not sure."

"You are Mia, the Seer."

I stood up. "I think you have me confused."

"This is Hagne's work." The woman grabbed my wrist and pointed to my tattoo. Not the one that King had placed on me, but Hagne's. "Sit," she commanded, "do not force my hand." Her touch sent static through my arm.

I didn't have the energy to fight, so I sat. "What do you want?"

"Is it true that Hagne tried to kill you?" she asked.

Of course, I tried to kill her first, but that wasn't the question.

I nodded.

"Is it true she had eyes for Callias?"

I nodded.

The woman turned to her companions, and the ladies mumbled frantically. With the roar of the crowd, I couldn't hear a damned thing.

The woman faced me once again. "So the king killed her with just cause."

"Yes, I believe so."

She nodded solemnly. "I am ashamed that we did not deal with Hagne in time."

"What do you mean?" I asked.

"We knew she'd been…let us say, using her gifts in unsanctioned ways. She was tainted, as are all Seers who betray their oaths."

"I'm not following you," I said.

"Those of our kind who use their gifts to gain power or wealth are defying the gods and the natural order. They become crazed animals who must be put down."

"You're all Seers?" I asked.

"We are the elders."

I had so many questions for them about Seers and how our gifts worked, but there was no time. "Then you can stop this," I pleaded.

She shook her head no.

"Why not? They haven't fought yet." I pointed toward the arena.

"The challenge was issued by Callias."

"Yes, because Hagne's family threatened to rally the people into a civil war. The king thinks this is the only way to avoid massive bloodshed."

"I'm sorry, my dear, but it is too late. The wheels have been set in motion."

"But you just said—"

She held up her hand. "Our people are unhappy that the king ended Hagne's life, one of our own, without consulting us first."

"But you're saying her death was inevitable."

"Yes," she said, "however the king has violated an agreement with our people, and there must be a fight to set things straight, or there will never be peace again."

This was ridiculous.

"Besides," she grinned, "everyone knows that our king is the better swordsmen. He will prevail. And Callias has been a thorn in his side, a jealous fool—"

"And a thief!" chimed in one of the other women.

"And a womanizer!" barked another. "He has three unclaimed children that we know of. We will all be far better off with him gone."

"But the king isn't going to win," I said, panicked.

The four women stared, clearly not understanding.

"King will let Callias kill him," I clarified.

"Why would he relinquish his divine right?" one of the women asked.

"It's a long story," I answered. "But you have to—"

"It is a shame, then, because our people will not stand to be ruled by Callias. They would rather burn the island and everyone on it to the ground."

I blinked as her words dangled in the air. If Callias ruling would cause civil war...and the Seers knew that Hagne was nuts and...My head hurt from spinning so hard.

I had to stop this. I had to. The only way to really change course was for King to live.

But Callias died in the first version, and that didn't work out either. King had been married to Hagne and then challenged for the throne by Callias. King won the fight but discovered that his wife had been behind everything and cheating on him. In retribution, or perhaps to smother any flames of civil war, he executed Hagne's entire family and then took her out, too.

But if King dies, it changes nothing. I had to stop him so we could rethink this. We had to. Because clearly King had no idea his brother was loathed by the people.

"I have to stop the fight." I ran down the steps of the coliseum, but arrived to a high railing that separated the first tier from the second. "Shit! Where is it?" I turned and spotted the stairwell and darted down, slamming into a brawny man with thick black curly hair, holding a spear. He looked just like future King's driver.

"Arno?" I said.

"I am called Sama." With his large size, he easily forced me back.

"Let me through; I have to speak with the king."

"Only the Minos family and the council are permitted to pass."

Dammit! "You're a Spiros, right?"

He nodded.

"I know you're supposed to protect the king. He's about to die—I swear it—and if he does, it all goes to shit."

He glared at me.

"I'm not crazy. I'm a Seer. And I see the future!" I lied.

"I cannot let you pass."

The crowd roared with deafening screams—the same sounds I'd heard when a football team enters their home stadium.

I covered my mouth. "Oh dear God, no."

I turned and ran upstairs to the balcony overlooking the arena. The male members of the crowd had already pushed their way forward.

I wiggled through a mass of sweaty, smelly, shirtless male bodies. "Move!" I barked repeatedly until I reached the front.

There, to my horror, was King. His shirtless, muscled torso glistened in the early morning sun. He wore only a simple blue sarong. No helmet. No body armor. Just a big bronze sword.

"King!" I screamed, waving my hands in the air like a madwoman. "King!" But he couldn't hear me let alone see me in the midst of an ocean of onlookers.

My mind buzzed. If I couldn't reach him, I couldn't tell him that he wasn't saving his people or anyone and history was going to repeat—the Minoans would disappear if he left Callias in charge.

"King!" I screamed again, just as Callias entered the stadium. The bastard wore a dark brown leather breast plate and a bronzed helmet as he strutted in like the hero of the day, waving his arms and sword. The crowd booed him.

"Fuck. Fuck. Think, Mia. Think." If they were all going down, then I had to do something to save King. Anything.

I glanced up at the row of silver-haired Seers looking on with emotionless expressions.

I pushed my way back through the wall of cheering subjects and leapt up the steps two at a time.

"You have to help me!" I screamed at them.

The women stared.

"Please. Please don't let him die," I begged.

"But he must, my dear girl. This is his fate."

Fate. Fate. What did that even mean?

Nothing to a woman who'd seen the laws of the universe broken as easily as a child might pull apart his or her favorite Lego set.

"Curse him!" I screamed. "Curse him to walk the earth until he finds a Seer who loves him." Meaning me. Facing him in the future would be my cross to bear.

The woman closest to me frowned. "Why in the world would we do that?"

"Because he is *my* fate."

"What you ask is impossible. To cast such a curse, you must have rage and hate for the person. We do not."

I thought about it for a moment. "I do." I had enough loathing and anger toward King, the evil version, to last a lifetime. Maybe an eternity.

The woman gave me an odd look, then glanced at the other three Seers and got the nods. When she looked back at me, she simply smiled, bent over, grabbed a small chunk of stone that had cracked off the corner of the bench, and then handed it to me.

"What am I supposed to do with this?" I asked.

"You must use an object that is from the earth, something that will endure the test of time as the anchor for the curse."

Shit. I felt my blood pressure drop. *This is the Artifact.* History was repeating.

It doesn't matter!

"Then what?" I glanced over my shoulder as the crowd roared wildly. King and Callias now fought, their swords clashing as they danced around each other like well-seasoned boxers waiting for the perfect punch.

The old woman shrugged. "You use your gifts to channel all of your pain, hate, and rage toward this man. Whatever injustice he has done to you, push it back to him. Then you cast your punishment."

"You mean I just wish it? Are you sure?" I asked.

"The gods will decide the rest," she said.

The crowd roared, and I glanced over my shoulder. King was on the ground.

No! Stone in hand, I rushed down the steps back toward the mass of bodies who'd now silenced. A pin could drop and be heard.

Now to the front and with a clear view, I watched in horror as Callias raised his sword to strike the blow.

I thought of the monster, of how his deceits and lies had changed me into someone I loathed. I thought about his disgusting hands on my body and the way he laughed so cruelly when I screamed. I thought of my rage over how he'd not saved Justin when I'd come to him for help. Then there was the pain I felt for my parents. I poured every ounce of anguish and despair into my words, willing them to make their home inside of King. "I curse you!" I screamed, the tears pouring from my raw face, momentarily halting Callias's victory. "I curse you, King, to walk this earth in search of my forgiveness and love!"

King's blue eyes met mine, and in that moment, I felt so hollow, yet so wholly connected to him. A gentle smile flickered across those beautiful, sensual lips, and time, once again, stood still.

"I'll see you on the other side," I whispered, not knowing if I spoke the truth, but knowing that this was my wish.

The sword came down, and I looked away. I didn't need to see what came next. Instead, I looked up at the old Seer woman, my eyes pleading for her to tell me if I'd succeeded.

The woman's dark eyes filled with pity, and she shook her head as if to say that she didn't know.

I released the air in my lungs and sank to my knees, sobbing. The crowd howled with horror and disbelief. Their king was dead. And so was I, as far as I was concerned.

CHAPTER THIRTEEN

Unlike the time I'd spent with King—the man who felt more real to me than my own existence—the two days following his death were a strange surreal blur of utter agony. Random people came by and left flowers outside King's chamber. Some came inside and laid them at the foot of his bed, where I stayed clutching that damned rock to my chest, weeping and praying he would appear before me, materializing from some dark shadow in the corner of the room.

He didn't.

And every time my eyes searched for him in vain, the crack in my soul widened further. There wasn't a place big enough on earth to hold the amount of heartache I felt.

Would he come back?

The only thought that brought me hope was knowing his absence didn't necessarily indicate I'd failed. Once, King had explained how showing himself required a tremendous amount of energy and power—thus the reason for his sundial tattoo. But that fact didn't guaranteed I would see King again, which is why I tried to make the bracelet work by channeling all of my energy into having it take me back to the hours before King's death.

Nothing.

Maybe I needed strength to make it work, but my heart felt too broken to lift even a finger. I couldn't stop crying.

On the third day, however, King's sublime face, with those exquisite dark features, appeared like a mirage, luring me to sit up and climb out of my deep dark hole.

"You're here," I gasped. I jumped from the bed, threw my arms around his warm body, and pressed my mouth over his.

King quickly gripped my shoulders and pushed me away. "So you are the infamous Seer: Mia," said the voice that sounded heavy, male, and melodic. But different somehow.

"King?"

His eyes, a familiar vibrant blue, were filled with sadness. "Callias," he corrected.

I wanted to claw his face and rip out his heart. The man looked exactly like King, but he wasn't.

"Leave," I growled.

"I see that you miss him, too."

"Miss him? Miss him?" I yelled. "You have no clue what I feel."

Callias raised his palms. "I know what you must think of me."

I pushed him hard, and likely not expecting it, he stumbled back despite his large size. "I think you are disgusting, evil, and a self-serving coward."

For a moment, Callias appeared angry, but his rage quickly defused into amusement. He laughed into the air.

"What the *hell* is so funny?" I scowled.

"My brother said you were a wildcat in a woman's skin, but I didn't believe him."

"King called me a cat?"

"Draco meant it as a compliment, I assure you."

Hearing King called by his real name startled me. Maybe because it made him feel even more real to me.

"Why are you here?" I asked.

"I really don't know, to be honest."

"Maybe because your world is falling apart and everyone hates you for killing their beloved king?"

Rage filled his eyes. "I loved my brother. And think what you will, but executing him is the only thing he ever asked of me—begged of me. So yes, I did it. For him."

"You should've said no."

"Have you ever said no to him?" he seethed.

Yes, I had. "He didn't listen to me." I sat down and cupped my face.

"So you understand what I say."

I nodded.

"And you understand he has left me all alone to pick up the pieces, but I am helpless to stop the destruction that comes."

Again I nodded and looked into Callias's distraught eyes. Why did he have to look exactly like King? Why? "This is so screwed up."

He smiled. "I am glad someone understands." He sat next to me. "This outcome was never my desire. But now the people cry out for my head. My brother is a martyr, and there is nothing I can do to win them or restore peace."

Dammit. I didn't want to feel sorry for him.

I drew a breath. "I'm sorry. I wish I could help you."

"As do I."

"So, why are you here?" I asked.

He shrugged. "Because tomorrow we will lay my brother's body into the ground, and my guards will kill me in vengeance."

My head whipped up. "What?"

"I realize it is hard to believe, but I do have friends. And they have warned me in hopes that I will run and save myself."

"What are you going to do?" I asked.

"Tomorrow I will die and join my brother."

"He wouldn't have wanted that," I argued.

"I know. However, that is the way it will end, and I cannot live with the guilt of killing him, so it is for the best."

So everyone dies for nothing. Holy frigging Greek tragedy from hell!

On the other hand…"Well, you killed him, Callias. You ended your brother's life, and you *should* hate yourself. Because you should've known the situation was fucked up. I mean, didn't it cross your mind to tell him that you've got a lot of enemies?"

"I did not know the people despised me as much as they do."

I still wanted to claw his face. He didn't deserve to wear something so beautiful. "You know what? It doesn't matter now. Just leave." Because, frankly, I had my own troubles to deal with, meaning if I ever wanted to see the man I loved, I had to make that bracelet work. I also had to mentally sort through what the recent turn of events meant for my family.

"I feel worse than you could ever imagine," Callias said.

"Why are you still here?"

His face bright red, he said, "Because I was there when you cursed him. I saw the look in your eyes, and I wished to spend my last night on earth with someone who understands my pain. I wanted," he said bitterly, "to remember my brother and share it with someone who loved him as much as I did."

"Oh." Feeling the despair and sincerity in his words, I shrank back. *Goddammit!* I couldn't win. Even if I wanted to blame him for everything, I couldn't.

Staring down at my feet, I sighed. "I'm sorry. I shouldn't have said what I did. I'm just…angry. And I miss him."

"So I was right; you did love him."

"Do," I corrected. "That's why I cursed him—to keep him alive." I realized how strange that sounded, but there was no other way to explain it. "But now I don't know if I've done the right thing."

Had I condemned everyone to relive the fate I so desperately wanted to change? I didn't know.

"You did what you had to," he said. "As did I."

"This is so damned awful."

"Does this mean you will grant a dying man his last wish?"

"You want me to keep you company?" I asked.

"Yes."

Insanity. Who would want to be near me? I was a mess.

"I promise," he said, "it is what Draco would have wanted."

What a guilt trip. And it worked. "Okay," I whispered.

"Thank you." Callias hugged me tightly like a big dopey kid. "Draco was right about you. You have a merciful heart."

Unable to breathe, I wiggled loose. "Not really."

Callias gripped my shoulders. "If I had been in your shoes, I would have killed me on the spot. Trust me, you are quite merciful."

Except for the mind-blowing, sexy-as-hell body just like King's, Callias was nothing like his brother. Callias liked to play and goof around with his guy friends, mainly drinking watered- down wine (they all seemed to be lightweights) and picking up women. He had zero interest in ruling or taking on responsibilities. I'd heard about twins being opposites, but now I'd finally seen it with my own eyes.

After safely depositing the Artifact in the bottom of King's treasure basket and instructing the guards not to let anyone in for any reason, Callias and I made our way to a quiet beach east of the palace, away from any crowds. All Callias wanted to do was talk about Draco, as if holding his own private memorial with me. It was sad and touching the way Callias looked up to his brother.

"Draco was the one my father groomed to rule," he said. "Not me."

"Did that make you mad?" I asked, holding down my blue flowing dress around my hips as the wind picked up. Callias, on the other hand, didn't seem at all bothered when his little man skirt flipped up, putting his penis on full display. I tried not to peek, but they were twins and...well, my curiosity got the best of me.

Yep, identical.

Anyway, the Minoan attitude toward nudity was pretty different than my own.

"No. I never felt envious of my brother," Callias answered. "Quite the opposite. No one cared about how I spent my time, so I enjoyed the fruits of life—played with other children growing up, spent time with my mother, fished, drank, hunted...I did whatever pleased me. I felt sorry for Draco."

It was so ironic. Draco was the one saddled with the future of their people, so Callias got to be the reckless wild child. Little did anyone know how things would turn out.

"So what was King—I mean, *Draco,* like?"

Callias shrugged his broad bare shoulders. Funny, even the way he frowned was exactly like King. It only made me miss him more, but I willed myself to keep it together. I desperately wanted to be there for Callias and take care of him like I would my own brother.

"Draco was always serious, always tough, never like a child. My cousins and I feared him. Even when we were little, I remember wanting to hide when I saw Draco."

I laughed. "I can completely imagine him being a little tyrant. It suits him."

"I think his attitude was a product of my father's grooming. He was extremely hard on Draco, shunning any signs of weakness. He wanted my brother to be a fair man and understand compassion, but not be controlled by it."

"He didn't hurt him, did he?" I guessed it wasn't unusual for people to beat their kids in these times. Hell, people still beat their kids. *A-holes.*

"He did not need to. One look from my father's stern face, and you'd feel the trickle of warm piss down your leg. Then, he'd say, 'Leave the compassion for the gods. We are here to rule.' To him that meant keeping the peace, ensuring there was a well-prepared army, and food for the masses."

"Doesn't sound like he had a fun childhood."

"Well, he got to have his own army, had first pick of all the horses, and owned about twenty islands." He smiled. "But yes, I had all the fun. I think Draco hated me for it, but as we grew older, I became his only true friend. Probably because I understood him best—what my father and mother were like, the pressures of the council, the constant endeavor to please the gods. He always looked to me for advice, especially when the issue at hand pertained to things more sensitive in nature."

That was sweet, really.

"Then," Callias said, "when my father died, I had to go to my brother's side to assist him. Of course, now I regret not trying harder. I did as little as possible."

"And Hagne? How did you meet her?"

"Her family serves ours and has for generations. I've known her since I can remember."

"Did you love her?" I asked.

"No," he spat. "I spend most of my time on the other side of the island, overseeing trade with visitors. I had not laid eyes on her for years."

"What visitors?"

He pointed beyond the horizon. "Everyone from the mainland. Of course, most are barbarians. We're lucky to be here, sheltered and isolated from them, with the exception of trade merchants who come for our olives, wine, and metal."

"Too bad you couldn't have traded Hagne away."

"I understand she tried to kill you."

"Yes," I replied. "She claimed to be in love with you, but hated your brother. I offered to take Draco off her hands." He was mine, anyway.

"In love with me?" He scratched his rough jaw, and it almost cracked me. It was exactly the way King did it. "The woman was mad. We've spoken barely a handful of words since we were children."

Knowing that Callias had not had eyes for Hagne gave me a bit of peace. Perhaps, in the first version of events, Hagne had used her "gifts" to make Callias think he loved her and wanted the throne. Because *this* Callias didn't seem to care about either. One thing was for certain, though, he did seem like the sort of man to be easily led astray. There was a definite boyish innocence to him.

"I am glad she's dead," he added. "Better world without her."

"Unfortunately, her death's put us all in this position." I paused, thinking for a moment. "So why not hop on a boat and leave?"

"I am many things, but a coward I am not. This is my home. I want to die here."

I shook my head. "But there's a big world out there. You might find another home."

Sure, I had zero clue of what the rest of the world looked like—Egyptians, I knew they were well established, and I knew that Europe wasn't Europe yet. More like a collection of barbaric tribes. Then there were the Mayans and…

Hell. Again, I found myself wishing I'd paid closer attention to world history, specifically the Bronze Age. Which, clearly, we were in, given the men toted bronze swords. Not a lick of steel or silver to be found.

"I will not leave my brother," Callias said. "I am certain he awaits me on the other side." Callias had stopped walking and decided to sit on a large washed-up log.

I sat beside him, thinking about the two brothers running amuck in this "other side," whatever that was.

"Well," I said, "if you find him, can you tell him I miss him? And I need to see him again, to break his curse."

"You truly believe you can bring him back?"

I shook my head. "I honestly don't know what's going to happen."

"Such is life." Several long, silent moments passed. "I need a drink. Might you join me?"

I gazed into those big blue eyes and imagined for a moment they were King's. I knew they weren't, but they gave me comfort nonetheless.

"Wouldn't you rather go find some women with your friends and live it up?" I asked.

He shook his head. "No. I prefer to watch the sun set over my favorite ocean while drinking my favorite wine."

I nodded. "Just please don't give me any of that watered-down stuff. It's disgusting."

He laughed. "Do not tell me that you drink your wine full strength. What would my brother say?"

"What's wrong with that?" I laughed, too.

"Only barbarians drink such potent spirits."

"Potent?" I chuckled. "From where I come, full-strength wine is considered a frou-frou drink."

"What is the meaning of 'frou-frou'?"

"You mean Hagne's tattoo couldn't translate that?"

He shook his head no.

"It means it's not very manly," I said just to mess with him.

His mouth fell open. "Are you saying I am not manly because I drink my wine with water?"

I burst out laughing.

"What?" He puffed out his chest.

"You are manly. A big dopy dude, just like your brother."

"You dare insult me? I may not be the king, but I am still deadly—very good with a sword and my fists, I might add."

It was strange, but in that moment, he really reminded me of someone. "Mack!"

Callias seemed to want to roll his eyes. "Another one of your insults, I presume?"

"No, no. Mack is…" How could I explain this? "Mack is your brother's most loyal and trusted friend. He's like a brother. You remind me of him, that's all." And now it made sense why King had him around; Mack must've reminded him of Callias.

"I was afraid to ask, but now I must," Callias said.

"Yes?" I said.

"Is it true that you come from another time, a time far into the future?"

"So he told you."

"Yes," he replied. "I thought him mad at first, but I saw in his eyes that he spoke the truth—or believed he spoke the truth."

"What else did he tell you?"

Callias rubbed his unshaven jaw. "That he would move the heavens and earth to be with you."

I suddenly felt my despair bubbling to the surface. I was going to lose it.

Callias noticed. He quickly stood and held out his hand. "Let us find wine and celebrate my final hours in this body."

"You're really not afraid to die?" I said in a quiet voice.

"Of course not. What is there to fear?"

"Everything." Like being cursed to walk the earth forever or staying dead and not coming back at all. *Christ, King. Where are you? I need you.*

CHAPTER FOURTEEN

"Are you sure the things in Draco's chamber are safe?" I asked, growing nervous about leaving the Artifact for such a long time.

Callias had procured a few "bottles" (ceramic jars, really) of wine and ordered the servants to build a fire on the private beach below the palace where we now sat.

"The guards may secretly wish to take my head," he said, "but they dare not defile my brother's belongings."

"Good, because I bound your brother's curse to a rock and hid it in his room."

He jerked his head in shock.

"Without it," I said, "the curse can't be undone. And if you ask me why, I couldn't explain it. I only know that it's the most valuable thing I own."

"Do you wish me to retrieve it?" he asked.

Considering that Callias intended on getting smashed tonight, not such a good idea. Also, there was a shocking lack of personal, portable storage in this age, i.e., no pockets. It was too easy to lose it.

"No. Just as long as you are absolutely sure no one will touch it." *Damn. What I wouldn't give for a fanny sack right now.*

"I assure you." He smiled, and I almost swooned. I couldn't help but look at Callias and fantasize he was King with those dark features, olive skin, and light eyes.

His happy expression melted away. He noticed me staring at his face, longing for his brother. "If only I were so lucky," he said.

I frowned with a smile, feeling awkward. I think he sensed it because he quickly offered a comfort-branch: "But of course, I only view women as objects of pleasure—nothing more. I sense this would not sit well with you."

I laughed. "No."

"Then let us be friends. Even if for only one night."

My smile disappeared. It was hard thinking about an exact replica of the man I loved being murdered tomorrow.

But that's not your choice, is it?

No. It's not.

Callias cleared his throat. "Forgive me. I did not wish to sour the evening."

"Not ruined." I looked into his eyes. "I lost my brother recently, and now Draco and—I just wish everything was different. Even for you."

He jerked his head and offered a sad little smile, but didn't say anything.

Changing subjects and not wanting to be a downer, I asked Callias more about his brother, about him, his parents, and his people. We drank wine—yes, full strength—*oh my*—and gazed at the stars. There were several moments when I had to admit that the wine made my head foggy and my body yearn to reach over and kiss Callias, to hold him and smell him. Not because I wanted him, but because I wanted King so badly it hurt. It would be easy to lie to myself for a few moments and pretend. Especially because I had no clue how long it would take for King to build the strength to show up. If he showed up.

Instead, I settled for lying on the beach, gazing up at the dark sky filled with millions of twinkling stars, imagining King there with us, watching and laughing along. I imagined him being grateful that I'd stayed at Callias's side during his last night on earth.

After a while, the fire died down, and Callias and I were too drunk to move. I closed my eyes and sighed, grateful for the chance to get to know this person who was a part of King's life.

Callias reached out and grabbed my hand. "If I ever get the chance to love in my next life, I hope it is a woman like you, Mia."

I didn't know what to say other than, "Thank you. I hope you do get the chance." *But with someone more extraverted*, I thought. He was a man who needed a fun-loving, vibrant woman without any baggage.

I closed my eyes and allowed myself to drift off, thinking of King, of my future, and of Callias finding his own peace.

"Cut the bitch's throat!" were the words that jolted me from an alcohol-induced sleep in the middle of the night.

"No!" I heard Callias cry out. "You tempt the fury of the gods if you touch her! She is a Seer."

Whoever had me by the throat dropped me in the sand like a cockroach-infested sack of shit.

"You want me, not her," Callias grunted, the men shoving him face down in the sand.

"Don't!" I yelled, getting to my knees. "He's the king!"

The man who had him by the neck grinned proudly. "Why do you think we are here?"

Callias didn't struggle, but instead asked them to take his head swiftly.

Kneeling on the other side of the fire, I stared in utter horror. How many people did I have to watch die?

"Please," I begged, my head still saturated with wine. "Don't kill him. Draco wouldn't have wanted you to do this!"

The man who'd been holding me reached down and slapped me hard. I felt the blunt pain in my nose and warm blood trickle from my nostril.

"You piece of shit." I glared up and felt the breath leave my lungs. "Sama?"

Motherfucking Spiros. The people who had sworn to protect the king.

I looked at Sama and felt the earth move beneath me, remembering what the old Seer woman had told me. All I had to do was use my anger and wish it. Nothing more.

I need an anchor.

I reached down and grabbed a handful of sand. "If you won't honor your oath to the king, then I will make you."

Sama's face, illuminated by the waning fire, turned ghostly white. "No. You cannot do this."

"Oh, but I can," I panted. And it felt so, so good. "You, your children, and every human being who holds a drop of your Spiro blood will loyally serve the king until he finds peace. You will protect him with your own flesh and place his life and happiness above your own." The power inside felt intense, like a heat raging through my veins.

"Mia, no! I want to die!" roared Callias while being held by two extremely confused-looking men, one with a knife to his throat.

"Shut up, Callias!" I barked.

The men stood still, and I waited for a moment, wondering if it had really worked. Then Sama looked at the men. "Let him up."

Callias sprang to his feet. "What have you done, woman?"

"I saved your life. And now Sama, here, and his men are going to put you on a boat and get you far, far from this island. You'll see the world, you'll live, and you'll die when nature or the gods or whatever are goddamned good and ready to take you."

"This is my home, my people," he argued.

"Not anymore." I looked at Sama. "Gather up anything you need, and then get the hell out of here before sunrise."

Sama dipped his head.

"You can't take me away from here!" Callias roared. "I must bury my brother."

"Where your brother is, he won't mind your missing the funeral." And I hoped that someday, Callias would thank me.

I watched the six men haul Callias down the beach, toward the palace. "And find a good woman to fall in love with! No more whoring around!"

They faded off into the darkness, and for a split second, I felt good. At peace. I had changed, I hoped, at least one person's fate. Then I began to wonder if anything had changed in my old life, especially that evil bastard version of King.

Not likely.

If only I could understand what had triggered the change in King to begin with.

Everything fell silent for several soul-chilling moments. No crashing waves. No small crackle of embers from the dying fire. No wind. Everything just...turned black and cold.

The air filled with the scent of mold and a stench of rotting...rotting something. I didn't know.

I held my breath, wondering what had just happened.

Suddenly, I heard the sound of heavy footsteps, like a man running.

"Who's there?" I screamed.

A clanking of metal keys followed by a scraping sound ricocheted all around me.

Suddenly, a door flew open and light poured in. A tall, dark shadow with broad shoulders stood in the doorway.

I squinted and held my hand up to block the light. I could barely see.

"What the fuck are you doing down here?" said that deep, disapproving, male voice that accelerated my pulse and lit up every nerve ending.

"King?"

"Yes. It is I. Your king." A burst of red light flooded my vision, radiating directly from his body.

Oh shit. This was not *my* King. This was not the good King.

CHAPTER FIFTEEN

Kicking and screaming, King pulled me from the dark room and dragged me up a flight of rough stone stairs into a dimly lit, cavernous hall. He threw me to the hard cold stone floor. "What. Are. You?" he seethed.

Afraid for my life, I slowly lifted my eyes and took in the wickedly powerful, menacing form standing over me. He wore black, odd-looking sandals with leather straps that wound up his insanely muscular calves and thick light gray fabric around his waist, the excess thrown back over one shoulder. His muscular chest and biceps were wrought with the menacing strength of a fierce gladiator.

"Speak, bitch. Or I will rip out your heart." His dark eyes filled with deadly rage, and the sharp angles of his unshaven masculine face glowed with an otherworldly vibe.

Shit. I need to get out of here. But where are we? Small windows, high up where the walls met the domed ceilings, were the only source of light aside from the low-burning fire in a pit toward the center of the room.

I resisted allowing my mouth to flap. "I don't know what you mean. It's me. Mia."

He dipped his head and stared with dark—*Fuck. So, so dark*—eyes. Not blue or steely gray, but black. "You…" he growled, "have a death wish, witch."

Witch? "I-I'm not a witch."

"You," he pointed, "cursed me."

I drew back my head several inches and began scanning for an exit. *Right behind him. Crap.*

I held up my palms. "King, please calm down."

He stepped toward me, the red light from within practically drowning out his form. "You, you vile witch, fucking tell me to calm down? Do you have any understanding of the hell I have endured because of your evil magic?" His head shook and his thick black unkempt hair fell in front of his eyes. He looked like a savage beast. Not a man.

"No," I whispered. "I don't."

He leapt forward and slammed me into the cold, hard floor. "I am going to kill you." His large hand tightened around my neck.

I clawed at his face, fighting for my life. His dark eyes bored into mine, pure hatred raining down. *Die*, they said. *Die…*

"Please," I croaked, my vision blinking out, "I love you…"

He paused for a fraction of a second, perhaps stunned that I would say something like that while he choked the life from me. But whatever, whoever he was, fighting and suffering were what he wanted.

I seized the moment. "I would do anything to save you."

He snapped back his hand. Horror displaced the rage on his face. "You're real. You're really here?"

I don't know. I don't know...Regardless, I nodded slowly and tried to hold his hands away in case he decided that strangulation was still a good choice. "It's me. I'm real." Tears filled my eyes.

His broad chest pumped with several quick breaths. "I thought you were another ghost come to torment me." He stood and stepped back.

Trying not to alarm him, I slowly rose to my elbows. "I'm not a dream. And to me, it's only been a few days since you died. Look at my clothes." It was the same dress he'd given me. "And would you dream this up?" I pointed to my nose. I knew it was covered with fresh blood from when Sama hit me.

He clenched his fists. "Who hurt you?"

"It doesn't matter. They paid. It's over."

He blew out a long breath and ran his shaking hands through his hair.

Dear God, the man screamed, "Crazy!"

"Can you tell me where I am?" I asked.

He shook his head at his feet. "Too long. It has been too long. I thought I had dreamed you. I thought you never happened. She does not exist. She is not real." He scratched his head so hard that I thought he might draw blood. "She told me she loved me. Why do this?" he mumbled, flicking his fingertips over his chest. "Why would she hurt me like this? Curse me. A witch. A witch...she is a witch."

"King," I said quietly, "I'm not a witch. I'm Mia. I love you. I cursed you because it was the only way to see you again."

His head snapped up. "I am not mad?"

"No, you're not mad. You're..." *just lost. And a ghost again,* I presumed. He now had the infamous sundial tattoo on his left arm. And the tattoo on his collarbone, the one that looked like an elaborate Egyptian collar in the shape of a semicircle, was partially filled in.

"How long has it been since you..." I swallowed, "died?"

"A thousand years. A thousand years of hell, waiting for you." He rushed toward me and dropped to the floor, grabbing the nape of my neck to pull my lips to his. His tongue plunged inside my mouth with desperation, like a man dying of thirst and running from death.

His warmth and hardness, his sweet smell and chilling coldness, the sinful burn of his madness, exploded in that one kiss. I didn't know where I was or why, but good God, I needed him as much as he seemed to need me. When he'd died, I'd missed him so much that every cell in my body cried out. So maybe, just maybe, that was why I didn't care if the man before me was shattered, dark, and utterly mad. In that moment, the wounds of his death were so raw and fresh, I would take anything I could get.

He pulled up my dress and ripped himself free of his clothes. His cock was large, hard, and veined with that pulsing tension I'd longed for from the second he'd left me in the tub. Only a moment of acknowledgement flickered between us as we stared into each other's eyes. Then he lowered his hips and thrust sharply. I closed my eyes and cried out. It didn't matter that it hurt; he was there. In me. He felt real, and that was all I could ask for. The wait for my drug was over.

He moved hard and fast, nuzzling his warm stubbled face into the nape of my neck while he groaned and fucked away his anguish like an angry beast. I gripped a handful of his dark hair and held him to me. I would never be able to come like this, but I didn't care. I just wanted his suffering to end. I just wanted him close. That would be enough.

"Mia, Mia, Mia..." he repeated underneath his breath, over and over again.

I willed myself not to fight against the ravenous pace of his animalistic-like pounding, hoping to God that whatever I could give would bring some semblance of sanity.

His one arm reached under my body and lifted my hips. He pushed his thick cock in a deep, brutal stroke that stole my breath, then came hard, shuddering against me.

His chest contracted with each rapid breath while he lay on top of me, and my mind rolled with conflict. Even in his broken state, it was euphoric to feel this man in my arms again, tangled against my body.

I gently petted the back of his head. "I missed you. I really missed you."

He lifted his head, looked into my eyes, and withdrew. Before I knew it, he stood over me, redressing. "Get up."

I blinked, sat up, and straightened myself out, nervous as hell that he was going to flip out on me. This was not the cool, calm, collected King I knew from the past or the future.

No. I didn't fucking care. I'd missed him so much it nearly killed me.

"You will leave immediately. You can't stay here," he said.

"What's the matter?" Not that I knew where "here" was, or if "here" was safe, but I didn't care. I wasn't going to leave him. Not for anything.

"It is far too dangerous for you to stay."

I stood up. "Where are we?"

"Athens."

"Are you at war?" *Dammit, dammit, dammit. Why didn't I pay attention in World History?*

"No. However…" His voice faded away. "You cannot stay. I am not—you are not safe."

He was afraid he'd hurt me. That had to be it. "I am *not* leaving."

He started mumbling to himself as if slipping away inside his head again.

"King?"

He looked at me with angry, dark eyes, and my heart jolted inside my chest.

"What happened to you?" I whispered.

Just then, two men entered: one blond and the other with red hair, both wearing similar garb—gray wool cloaks embroidered around the edges and belted tunics. They held an unconscious man who'd been beaten.

I stilled.

King looked at the men, unfazed. "Throw him down in the room."

"The room"?

"What's going on?" I asked.

King's eyes warned me not to speak. He then instructed the two men to take me away, to make sure it was somewhere safe and where he could never find me.

The men had a coldness in their eyes, like they were the sort a woman should never be left alone with.

"I'm not leaving with them," I said. "I am *not* leaving you."

King was on me faster than I could blink, his trembling hands gripped tightly on my shoulders and his face filled with rage. "You will do as you are told, woman."

"Or what?" I growled.

"Or you will die." He released me with a sharp push, and I stumbled back. "Take her. Now."

The two men rushed over and grabbed my arms so tightly, I felt their dirty nails digging into my skin.

I twisted away. "I'll go. Just don't touch me."

The blond man didn't speak, but I had the distinct impression he was about to slap me. I glowered, daring him to do it.

He looked away.

Good choice.

As we headed toward the large, arched doorway leading outside, I heard King repeat to himself, "Somewhere I cannot find her. Ever."

Had he forgotten about his "K" tattoo? He could find me anywhere.

The man is mad.

Partially in shock, I went quietly with the two men, hoping that they might explain what the hell happened back there. To be clear, though, I had no intention of leaving for good. I wasn't about to lose King again.

Passing several men in cloaks and women wearing pristine white dresses, with elaborately braided hair, we made our way down the cobblestone street stacked with perfectly square whitewashed temples. The sun was just setting, filling the sky with ominous reds, and when I looked back over my shoulder, toward the massive structure we'd just come from—King's home, I presumed—it glared back with empty dark doorways that reminded me of his eyes. The massive white pillars surrounding the palace looked like giant wicked teeth that wanted to chew me up and spit me out.

"Who is he?" I wondered aloud.

The blond man glanced at me, but kept quiet.

"Do you not know who he is?" said the man with red hair.

"No," I answered. Of course, that wasn't entirely true.

"He is the most powerful man in all of Greece, appointed by the gods themselves."

Okay. King is a representative of the gods. Or at least that's what they believed. Honestly, given what I knew about him, it would be an easy assumption for people to make. He was, after all, not exactly human.

"Why is he sending you away?" the redhead asked.

"I don't know." Not entirely true, either. King was mad, and he knew it. He wanted me to be as far away from him as possible.

"Did he not tell you?" said the blond.

I shook my head no.

"Perhaps she is a thief, and he likes her," said the other guy. "She is very pretty."

"I'm not a thief. But if I were, why would that matter?" I asked.

"He would not send you away; he would have you executed."

"For stealing?" I asked.

"You really have not heard of Draco, have you? He is not kind," said the blond.

"He is not meant to be," argued the other. "He is meant to serve justice."

"He's an executioner?" I asked.

"He is the law."

Jesus. King was some Ancient Greek purveyor of justice. *Damn.* I could envision him really getting off on that. It would appeal to his domineering maleness in a big way. That said, I needed to help him, not go "far, far away." I needed to break the…

Fuck. That's when I realized I'd traveled forward without the Artifact. *No, no, no.* I let out a heavy breath. *Don't panic, Mia. Think.*

All right. Maybe I could find a way to go back and retrieve it. But how? I didn't know how I'd managed to leave Minoa in the first place.

I hit rewind and recalled the moment I'd landed in that dark room. I'd been sitting next to the dying fire on the beach, thinking about King, wondering what had happened to turn him so violent that night on the island.

Maybe that was the real reason I was here; this was another chance to change things. *I need to go back and talk to King.*

"Wait," I said to the two men. "I have to—"

Blondie whipped out a dagger and pushed me forward. "Keep going."

I stopped walking to test if he really intended to use the knife or simply wanted to intimidate me. "I'm not going anywhere."

Blondie nodded at the other guy, who picked me up and threw me over his shoulder. I fought, and people didn't seem to care one bit as I yelled and clawed at his back.

We made our way into a crowded square, where I was deposited in front of a large man with white hair who had a crowd of filthy-looking thugs gathered around. The moment the white-haired man saw me, he immediately stopped what he was doing. "Well, well. What have we here?"

Blondie proudly said, "I want my debts wiped clean."

The man smiled and flashed a mouth full of rotting teeth. "Chain her up over there."

"Asshole. You're selling me?" I couldn't believe I had to go through this again. Only this time, I was being sold away from King.

"Sorry," said Blondie. "If our master does not want you, then I cannot let a good opportunity like this pass by." He faced the man. "Make sure she gets sold elsewhere."

The man nodded, clearly understanding that I was stolen goods.

"You were supposed to take me somewhere far away, somewhere safe," I protested.

"Trust me," said Blondie. "You will be taken far. As for 'safe,' that will be up to you keeping your mouth shut." Knife in hand, he pushed me up onto a cart with five other women and then shackled my wrist to a thick chain running along the side. I barely had enough room to sit. From the elevated vantage point, however, I truly registered where I was: in the midst of an ocean of slaves as far as the eye could see. Some in cages, some chained together in long lines. It was a time in history when humanity lacked the utter definition of the word.

After nightfall, the caravan of horses and carts headed out of the city. I couldn't see much on the dark road, but it felt like being on a movie set for *Spartacus*. Every man I saw was dirty, smelly, and armed, including the battalion of soldiers—some on horses, but most on foot—accompanying this particular shipment as we made our way inland. With every passing hour, the air grew colder, and I knew I needed to get the hell out of there before I became someone's property.

What a goddamned nightmare. *I bet Justin, aka the history nut, would love being here, though.*

My mind hit a brick wall. *Justin.* With everything that had happened, I'd briefly forgotten about him and my parents. And now I realized that I'd done nothing to change the bleakness of their future. Nothing. All of the major pieces remained intact: King's people ending in war because of Hagne, King becoming cursed, the Artifact...

I wanted to scream. It felt like no matter what any of us did, fate was determined to see things play out in a certain way.

I don't care. I still have to try. As long as I still breathed, I would not give up. Not on my family. Not on King. As soon as the caravan stopped, I would break free and make my way back to him. I needed to make sure he knew about the Artifact, that there was a way to break his curse.

It felt like six hours had passed before the caravan halted to allow the men to rest. They built small fires and brought out what I assumed was their wine. They didn't offer any of us "chattels" water or food, and needless to say, there were no bathrooms. That meant when you had to go, you went over the side of the cart if you could manage it. The conditions were horrible, despicable, and beyond imaginable.

I'd seriously had enough.

"Hey!" I screamed at the group of six soldiers gathered around the fire closest to me. "Are you assholes seriously going to sit there? Give these people some water. Let us stretch our legs."

They didn't bother to turn their heads in my direction.

"Helloooo. I'm talking to you." They continued eating and drinking.

"You're all a bunch of disgusting, immoral pigs. I just want you to know that. Seriously, I've met piles of horse shit with more attractive qualities. Although, I admit you all smell just as lovely. Haven't you heard of a bath?"

I heard the other women in the cart snicker under their breath.

One of the men, a lean tall guy with brown hair and a long beard, stood slowly and approached. I expected him to tell me to shut the hell up, but that's not what happened. He simply stood there and looked me over, his expression cool and calculating.

"I need to stretch my legs," I said.

"You have an odd speech for a slave."

I realized just then that Hagne's tattoo had been translating for me all along. These people spoke ancient Greek.

I lifted my brows. "Whooptie-fucking-doo. I need to stretch. Unchain me."

He shook his head. "I am not a fool. You will run, and I cannot risk it. You are worth too much money."

"To whom?"

His lustful eyes washed over me. "Anyone with a cock." He then adjusted himself.

Afraid he might start getting some ideas of his own, I blurted out, "I don't think Draco will appreciate my being taken against my will to become your whore."

"Draco? The Lawgiver?"

I nodded. "I am his..." I didn't know what, so I had to be creative. "I'm a friend."

The man crossed his arms. "Then how did you end up here?"

"Two of his men took me to that market and sold me to pay off their debts. Trust me; Draco has no clue."

His eyes washed over me. "I think you are lying."

"Why would I lie when you can take me to him and find out the truth?"

"Very well, if you are telling the truth..." He called for one of the other men, who came running. "Remove her from the cart."

"Are you letting me go?" I asked while the second man unchained me.

"No. We are going to kill you."

What the hell? "I don't understand."

"Draco may be appointed by the gods, but he is also cursed; if he has touched you, no one will allow you to serve in their homes, let alone want to bed you. You are worthless now."

In other words, I was King's tainted sex-goods.

The second man pulled me from the cart by the arm. With my legs half-asleep, I landed with a thump in the dirt.

As he reached down to pick me up, I kicked him in the stomach, and he stumbled back. The first man dragged me by the arms to the fire. I was about half his size, so fighting was about as helpful as singing.

I felt the cold blade of his knife against my throat, and instinctively, I screamed, "Wait! I'll buy my own freedom."

They laughed. "With what?"

"My bracelet. The one I'm wearing right here." I held up my right arm, but was really thinking of a way out. Maybe another curse? Did I have it in me?

"Cheap metal." The leader nodded at the man who held me. "Kill her."

"The punishment for murdering a slave is death," said a deep, dark, and familiar voice I knew like the sound of my own breath.

The leader froze and then dropped to a groveling position in the dirt. "Sir, I meant no disrespect."

"Stand up, Mia." I lifted my head and saw King's magnificent, imposing frame standing in front of me, his hand extended.

As I reached, those black eyes flickered to blue for a split second. I had to wonder if I'd imagined it.

"What are you doing here?" I asked, grateful as hell.

King shook his head. "I don't know. I felt a pull and then…" His eyes darted to the heads of the men who had their faces buried in the dirt. "We shall speak of this later. Right now, I must punish them."

I swallowed, wanting to ask what that meant, but before I uttered a word, King smiled and red light burst from his body. The men keeled over, one by one. I resisted screaming, but the other slaves did not.

As more soldiers showed up to investigate, King merely continued gazing into my eyes, and I felt his torment. And his blinding power. Not one man made it within five feet of us before falling to his instant death.

This is real, isn't it? I'm not dreaming...

Surrounded by a pile of bodies, he drew a deep breath and then gazed up at the starry sky. "No. You are not dreaming. Which is why you should run now, Mia."

He could hear my thoughts again.

"Why should I run?"

"Because after this moment, I will not be letting you go free, and I know not what I will do to you."

That was when I realized it didn't matter what he was or what he said; I was not leaving him. I would rather spend a lifetime trying to fix what I'd done to King than let him suffer like this. It was an odd realization knowing that you can accept someone, the entire someone, and love them unconditionally. Curse and all. I couldn't undo my love. I could only use it to do everything within my power to make things right.

I cleared my throat. "I'll take my chances, because I'd rather die here with you than live without you."

He looked back at me, and his eyes flickered again to a bright blue. "So be it." King went to unchain each and every slave. At first I thought it to be an act of compassion, but he quickly set me straight. Slaves without an owner were granted their freedom by law. I got the impression, however, that being a free slave in these times was like being coated in bacon grease and sent into the lion's den. Without money or an owner to protect them, they would be scavenged upon.

"Where will they go?" I asked.

"This is not my concern."

"Give them money," I said. I needed to know that *he*—the good king—was still in there somewhere.

"Why would I do that?" King asked.

"So they can get the hell away from here."

"I think you mistake me for a man who cares, a man with a soul."

"No. I have no delusions about who and what you are." But I hoped for a sign I could still save him.

He laughed. "Yet you ask this of me?"

I shrugged.

"Very well." King had grabbed one of the soldiers' horses, a big black beast, and waited for me to mount. "I will send my men here tomorrow and take care of any who have not fled."

"That's very kind." And proof that the compassionate man I loved was still inside.

King glared at me.

"What did I say?"

"I am not kind. Do not mistake my interest in you for such foolish emotions." He laced his fingers together and held out his hands. "Get on."

I walked over and looked up at this fiercely muscular, dangerous-as-hell man, wondering what would happen next. "Am I going to wake up from this?"

He frowned. "If you woke, where would you wish to be?"

I had to think about it for a moment. "With you."

He studied me with a peculiar grin and then boosted me onto the horse. He mounted behind me and urged the horse forward.

"You must have a death wish, woman," he said.

Probably, yes. "Mia. For heaven's sake, call me Mia."

CHAPTER SIXTEEN

After we started back toward Athens, I couldn't help but lean back and savor the feel of the man behind me. Yes, King was dangerous and deadly, but in that moment, nestled in his strong, muscular arms, his warm chest against my back and his thighs squeezed around me, there wasn't a safer place on earth. Not in a million years could I have guessed I'd feel this way about *him*. To be clear, *this* wasn't *my* King. He was the worst possible version of the man I'd fallen for: a demon who looked like my King. But once again, I found myself questioning my true feelings. I thought about the time Vaughn had cornered me in a bathroom at a 10 Club party and tried to force himself on me. King's brutality, his willingness to strike quickly and without mercy, had been a godsend. Then there were the multitude of occasions where I'd been losing my mind with grief or fear. It wasn't the kind King who'd held me together, but the one without any real emotions.

So. There it was, the ugly truth: I hated the evil King I'd run from, but I loved King for more than just his "good" side. His dangerous, callous side drew me, too. It was a mess of grays where nothing was perfect, nothing made one-hundred percent sense. But it was what it was, and no amount of thinking or rationalization would change it. I was his. And he was mine. Curse and all.

Who could've imagined that?

Or imagined we'd be riding on a dang horse in ancient Greece, and King wearing a man-frock. A huge departure from tailored suits and Mercedes.

"What is a suit?" he asked, reading my thoughts.

I grinned a little, feeling some strange comfort in the return of our strange mental bond.

"Well?" he prodded.

"Um…" I couldn't possibly tell him what a suit looked like; I'd have to use words like "pants," which would only lead to more explaining. "It's hard to describe—maybe I'll draw one for you later—but you look damn hot in them."

"Why? Are they made of fur?"

I tried not to laugh. I supposed they could be, but that would be kind of weird. "No. I meant, you look extremely attractive wearing one."

"Ah. I see. And this thing you call a Mercedes?"

"It's a car—sort of like a horseless cart. You look hot in that, too."

"Hmmm…I'll try to remember that."

Strange. King seemed so relaxed. So in control. "King?"

"Perhaps it is time you stop calling me that. Though I remain king to some, I am no longer a true king. My people have long since perished."

I was about to say how sorry I was, for them and him. Because he had been a good king and a good man. Instead I said, "Sorry. It's a habit. That's the name you use when we meet."

"I march around calling myself 'King'? That is odd." He paused. "Master, Your Grace, and Draco the Lawgiver, these are all names I understand."

I shrugged. "Yeah. Well, you have—or had—some baggage about Hagne that might've had something to do with it." From what I remember, King's hang-up had been about Hagne refusing to recognize him as the true king, and about how she'd destroyed everything he loved. His name was a testament to his stubborn nature and absolute refusal to allow Hagne's curse to break him. But that had all changed. Hadn't it? Hagne hadn't married King, Callias had not fallen in love—by will or by force—with her, and I ended up being the one to curse Draco because I couldn't bear to let him go.

"Yes, well," he said, "that witch still managed to destroy everything. Did she not?"

I gave it some thought. "Not everything." *Callias lived. I lived. And you're still kicking.*

"Callias is dead," King said bluntly.

"Oh…I guess he is," I said, feeling a sense of loss. Of course, a thousand or so years had passed, but to me, it was just yesterday that I'd seen him.

"Do you know what happened to him?" I asked. "I mean—where he went?" I also wondered if he ever fell in love or had children. That would've been nice.

"I was not fully…" he searched for the word, "*aware* at the time, so I cannot say. I merely know that he is no longer living. I am also aware that you placed a rather harsh punishment on the Spiros family."

Evil bastards were going to slit my throat and kill Callias. "They deserved it."

"Those men, yes, but their entire bloodline?"

"I wanted Callias to be looked after until his time was up." They owed him that much after what they tried to do.

"Ah, but you did not bind them to Callias; you bound them to the king."

"Right. Callias," I said.

"Yes, but I returned. I am, therefore, still the king in their eyes."

Oh my God. The Spiros are bound to King. I rubbed my face. I simply couldn't believe it. Everything I did seemed to recreate the future I so desperately wanted to change.

What if this is the way everything is supposed to happen? My heart began to beat faster, and the ache inside pushed at the walls of my heart. *What if?*

For example, King didn't know about the Artifact yet. If I told him, would it be the beginning of an obsession that would trigger so many horrific events: Justin's involvement with Vaughn, his death, my parents' suffering, my involvement with King?

My heart sank. I didn't know what to do.

You need to think this through, Mia. With a clear head. It was true; I was in no shape to make any rational choices.

"What would you like me to call you now?" I asked, changing subjects to an earlier point in our conversation.

"Master will do."

I laughed.

"You would call me King, but not Master? You are an odd woman." I felt his chest shake a bit.

"You're messing with me, aren't you?" I turned my head and tried to see his face, but it was too dark.

"Perhaps," he replied.

King told a joke. Shocking.

"Yes. It is, isn't it?" he said proudly.

"Why do you seem so different right now?" He wasn't that same evil, scary man who'd dragged me from that dark room in his basement and then fucked me like he'd die if he didn't.

"I would say it is because my tattoo is nearly complete, but I am unsure."

"Tattoo? You mean the collar?"

"Yes. Meketre has been working on it for quite some time. A few minutes each day for several years."

"Who's Meketre?" I asked.

"He is an acquisition from Egypt."

"You *acquired* him?"

"One might say that I am a collector of sorts—of objects and of people with rare gifts that might prove useful."

I knew this story all too well. King's obsession became collecting "power." *So this is how it all started.* I had to wonder if this was the beginning of the 10 Club, too.

He added. "Meketre has helped many to dispel or control their demons."

"So the collar tattoo…" I twisted around a bit. "You're trying to tell me that the collar will help you control the curse?"

"Not the curse, but the violent urges it produces—the curse feeds off of them." He paused. "However, nothing is certain. Meketre has never performed such magic on someone such as myself. I will not know until it is complete, but I do feel at peace. For the moment, anyway."

Holy crap. So when Vaughn took King prisoner and removed his tattoos, he removed King's ability to control his violent side. This was the reason King flipped out and took me to that island. It had to be.

"Can you make me a promise?" I said.

"This depends."

"Do you remember our conversation before you died?"

"How could I forget?"

He said he'd rather die than continue on as a ghost who might one day come back to do something so heinous to me.

"Once the tattoo is done, don't let anyone remove it. Not ever."

"Why would you ask that?" he questioned.

"I think losing it is the reason you attack me."

He was quiet for a very long time, which is when I noticed the eerie silence all around us, the clopping of the horse's feet the only noise to be heard. No cars, no planes, no people. Just us.

"Have you ever considered, Mia, that had I not hurt you, you would have not traveled from the future?"

My mind did a lap, following his logic. He was right. Had he not brought me to that island, I would never have met him as a man. *Hell, I wouldn't even be here right now.*

"No. You would not," he responded to my thoughts. "Which poses an interesting question."

"What?"

"If you could undo the past, would you?" he said without emotion.

I had to think about that. When I'd first arrived to Minoa, I would have given anything to alter the events. But now I knew it would mean never getting the chance to meet King. Now I loved him. So would I do it all over again—go through the pain of Justin's disappearance, which led me to King, and go through that horrible night on the island so that I'd be thrown back in time?

The answer wasn't clear. I could say "yes" to sacrificing myself and reliving my own pain. But if that meant sacrificing the happiness of my family? No. I would only choose to do it all over again if I knew I could bring back Justin, I supposed. In any case, it felt like events were going to play out a certain way, regardless of how I felt.

"Do you think it's possible," I wondered aloud, "that you and I are living a story that's already been written?"

He took a moment to respond. "Yes."

How does it all end?

"I do not know; however, we have little choice but to continue moving forward on the path chosen for us."

Maybe he was right. I didn't know.

"And, as you do not know," he said, "then your only course of action is to make the most of the present."

He certainly was right about that.

"Rest, Mia. We have a long ride back."

"Are you sure it's safe?" *With you*, I added in my mind.

"For the moment."

I felt too frazzled and hungry to question it. Most of all, I needed sleep.

I allowed my body to relax against him. King was like an indestructible war machine from ancient times that no one could touch. Not now. Not in the future. Still, there was that part of him who remained...

Him. The king.

"I still love you," I murmured before drifting off.

King didn't speak but squeezed his thighs tightly around me.

When I woke, we were back in that cold, dark palace. No, I did not recognize the giant bed I was on, or the soft white furs blanketing my body, but the harrowing vibe was unmistakable.

"Mistress Mia, you are awake," said a timid feminine voice.

I glanced over at a young woman dressed in a long flowing black dress, wearing a black headscarf. She stood next to a small table filled with bread and cheese. My mouth instantly watered.

"I am Ypirétria." She dipped her head. "I am here to see that you eat and to help you bathe."

Some things never changed. "That's really kind, but I'm okay. So you are free to go."

Her eyes filled with horror.

"What?" I asked.

"The master will be very displeased if I do not carry out his wishes."

I rolled my eyes. "The 'master' can be displeased with me, then. And—"

"No. You don't understand. Please, do not send me away." She sounded as if she genuinely feared for her life.

Oh Lord. I really needed to talk to King about all this. *After you eat. After.* I couldn't remember the last time I tasted food.

A thousand years ago?

Yes, I really did need something in my stomach. I took a whiff of myself. *And a bath.*

"Okay," I said, "but I am going to speak to him." I would include the topic of, "What the hell are you doing to your people?"

After attacking the food and having a luxurious bath in a stone tub filled with drops of a flowery-smelling oil and warm water that piped in through the wall—dang, the Greeks really had everything—I felt like a new woman. Well, almost. I was dying for a Lady Bic. But Ypirétria did give me a little stick to chew on to clean my teeth, so that was nice.

"Now you are to go to the master's chamber," she said with an accomplished sigh.

"His…chamber?" I questioned.

"It is down the end of this passage, to the right. He said he will be waiting for you."

An uncomfortable glob formed in my throat. There was no point in denying that I wanted him, but the way he'd taken me when I arrived had been pretty rough. What if he wanted it that way again? What if he wanted it rougher?

An image of that whip popped into my head.

I started to sweat, and my pulse accelerated in a bad way. *Okay. Don't think about the island. He's in control of himself, and has been since you got here.* And frankly, I needed to talk to him about the Artifact, but only after I laid out the conundrum we faced regarding his earlier question: if I could choose to let the events repeat, would I?

So what if I told him everything I knew? He could prevent certain events from occurring. Yes, it seemed some tragedies in our story were unavoidable, but I had managed to save Callias. That meant I might be able to save my brother, too.

This was definitely an angle worth discussing.

Wearing a very soft, flowing white dress, belted at the waist, I slipped a pair of skimpy leather sandals on my feet and headed down the hallway.

The palace was extremely drafty and cool with no real windows and large open rooms—a sitting room with musical instruments and a fire pit, a library or study, and another room containing elaborately painted clay pots stacked up along the wall. *The wine cellar?*

Beautiful murals of Greek women coated nearly every wall and reminded me of King's modern-day palace. So did his chamber, actually—soft warm bed with white linens, a giant sunken tub with steaming water, and a balcony overlooking the city. A warm fire glowed in the fire pit and wine had been left out on the table, too. It looked like he planned for us to have a romantic evening.

"King?"

No answer.

I called out once again and waited for a few minutes, but he was nowhere to be found. I decided to go back to my room and ask the servant, but she had left.

I made my way downstairs to the main hall— also empty. "King?" I stood there for a moment listening for anyone, but a sound emanating from a set of stairs caught my attention. They were the same ones King had dragged me up after discovering me in that dark room.

Halfway down the obscure stairwell, I called out for King once again, and in that moment, colors burst from the walls. Reds and yellows—anger and pain. I had to remind myself that the colors couldn't hurt me, but perhaps whatever was down there might, which is why I turned around and decided to wait for King back up in his chamber. Before I made it two steps, a low rumble followed by a faint moan caught my attention.

"King?" I yelled.

Oh hell. Maybe something was wrong. After all, it wasn't like King to leave me waiting. That man was all about punctuality.

I made my way to the landing at the bottom and pushed on the wooden door. It creaked open and inside was a long hallway. At the end, orange light poured through a cracked door. The place was almost exactly like King's modern-day dungeon, and memories of Vaughn bombarded me.

My skin crawled and my hands began to shake as I walked to the second door, where another deep moan blared out. I pushed the door open and held back a horrified scream. An unconscious man with deep gashes on his chest was chained to the wall, his body covered in blood. On the table in the corner, the body of another man lay. It was headless.

Holy fucking shit. That's Blondie. The head of the man who'd sold me as a slave in that market sat topside up in a large clay bowl filled with blood beside the body. The man's eyes looked at me, and his mouth opened as if trying to scream.

My legs nearly went limp beneath my weight, but I willed myself to stay standing. King had done this to these people. King. My King.

I turned and ran up the stairs, unsure of where the hell I would go. I slammed right into King.

"What were you doing down there?" he asked with a smirk.

My mouth opened, but no sound came out.

He crossed his thick, muscled arms. "Answer me."

I stared, unsure of what to say. This was bad. *Really, really bad.*

He read my thoughts.

"So now you know my dirty little secret." He laughed wickedly.

"There's—there's a head. A live one." The moment I said those words, I remembered the two heads in jars—live heads—back in his San Francisco warehouse. The faces had been distorted and the water sort of foggy, but I had no doubt that those warehouse heads belonged to Blondie and the redhead.

More lies. Mack had fed me some bullshit about them being related to one of King's jobs. I'd believed him.

"Why?" I asked.

"They betrayed me. They sold you into slavery when I asked them to take you to safety."

I was about to say that the punishment was just too horrific—two thousand years too horrific—but King didn't give me a chance.

"Do not think to lecture me, woman, about the severity of the punishment. Not after you cursed an entire family for hundreds of generations."

Although it had been by accident, he was right. However, I didn't decapitate them and leave their heads still alive. *Seriously. Who does that?*

"Fine," I said. "I will remove the curse on the Spiros as soon as I figure out how. Please, please undo whatever you did to that man? Just let him die."

"You would beg for this man's suffering to end," he screamed. "You would let him die and release him from the pain, but me...?" he roared louder. "Not I! No! You sentence me to this purgatory, force me to become all that I hated as a man. But this piece of shit," he pointed downstairs, "he deserves your mercy?"

It was King's pain, the curse in control now, triggering this rant. I knew because the calm, rational man inside understood it wasn't the same situation. Hell, he'd been the one to give me the idea to curse him in the first place.

"I will not undo his punishment," King said. "And as soon as I catch the other man, he will share the same fate." King leaned in close, and I could feel the heat of his breath. "They will be part of my collection, their only purpose to serve as a reminder of why I should show you no mercy, why I should loathe you—you selfish bitch." He grabbed the sides of my head and kissed me so hard that my teeth pressed into my lips. I tasted blood in my mouth.

He jerked back and grinned. "Do you love me now, Mia? Do you?"

I wanted to answer, but my mouth didn't want to move. Fear had the upper hand.

He gripped my arms and squeezed so hard that I thought he'd break my bones. "I'll take that as a no."

"Yes!" I barked. "I still love you." Because it was the curse talking, and I knew that somewhere inside was the real man.

"I am real!" he yelled. "And I will teach you to love the true me!" King dragged me down the stairs.

The room. He was taking me to the fucking room!

I fought, twisting my body and kicking my legs, but it was no use against a man like him. Effortlessly, he pinned me with his body and shackled my arms and legs so that my body formed an "X." The man next to me groaned, his body growing pale as he bled out, and the head on the table stared with his wide blue eyes filled with pain and hate. Red and more red. I was certain this was it for me.

"Just kill me. Get it over with," I said, finally understanding why Vaughn had preferred to die rather than be King's torture toy.

"Why would I do that? I'd be missing the fun part. The part where you scream. I'm hard merely thinking about it." He reached for my dress and tore it from my body.

"No!" I screamed, tugging as hard as I could on the restraints, but it was no use.

"Oh yes!" he said, laughing his words.

This can't be happening. This can't be happening.

Of course it can. You ran from him because of this. But I knew it was the curse driving him.

"I know the man I met in Crete is in there somewhere," I said. "And I know he loves me."

"He is not here right now, Mia. I am." He smiled, and his malicious eyes swept over my body as if I were some prized kill. "You should have run when you had the chance."

King walked over to the wall next to the doorway, where knives, large metal hooks, ropes, and chains hung.

Oh God. No. He reached for something, but his large body blocked the view. When he dropped the fabric draped over his shoulder, exposing his bare back, I caught a glimpse of red, crisscross striations on his skin.

Fucking shit.

He began flagellating himself.

My fear for my own safety quickly transitioned to revulsion while I witnessed this man beat himself. How it was possible—he was not truly alive, after all—or why, I could only guess. But I'd seen the marks on his back before. Only, after reading Hagne's journal depicting the original version of this story, I had assumed she'd hurt him with her sharp nails when King had been with her.

Unable to watch, I turned my head.

"Is this what you want?" he yelled at no one, his back still to me. "I can go all night!"

Ohmygod. He's losing it. King was completely consumed by whatever horrible things went on inside him.

"Stop! Just…stop," I said.

"I cannot," he replied and struck himself again. "I cannot let that fucking weak bastard of a king win. He thinks a tattoo will stop me, but it will not."

Holy shit. King wanted to beat the goodness out of himself.

That man is a true king. He is strong and determined. He cared about his people. He would never give in to you or the curse. He would never hurt me. You are a demon. A tyrant. "You are not my king. You are nothing to me."

His head whipped around, and for a fraction of a second, King's eyes turned to a vivid blue.

Yes. He was still in there somewhere—that beautiful man I couldn't help but love.

"I'm sorry for cursing you," I said. "I'm sorry for turning you into this monster."

Anger returned, and so did King's dark eyes. He dropped his whip and reached for a dagger on the table. He studied it briefly and then rushed toward me, plunging for my chest.

I flinched and clamped my eyes shut, but there was no pain. Not even a tickle.

What the hell?

A sharp electrical jolt surged through my body, and I went from being chained to a cold stone wall, to lying naked, face down, on a soft bed, my wrists and ankles bound.

King's heavy form lie on top of me.

My mind took a moment to process. Had I escaped the nightmare I'd been in only to return to another? The one I'd run from to begin with?

I screamed.

"Mia! It's okay!" I heard a familiar voice yell—not King's.

Someone pulled King's body off, and he landed with a thump on the floor.

I twisted my head to see Mack flipping the free half of the sheet over my naked body.

"Mack?"

"You're okay," he said, jumping to unstrap my ankles and then my wrists.

I took a moment to breathe and gather myself. My heart was about to explode.

"It's okay, Mia. You're safe now." I felt Mack's warm hand brush over the back of my head.

But how could I believe that? Nothing made sense, and I didn't know what was real anymore.

"Mia? Speak to me. Tell me you're all right."

Slowly, I turned over, holding the sheet to my bare body. Though there was plenty of light from the torches, it was still pitch black outside. The sound of insects clicking and chirping surrounded us. Yes, I was back on King's private island.

"Are you real?" I asked.

Mack's big blue eyes drilled into me for one intense moment, and then he grinned—that warm, disarming, almost goofy smile. "In the flesh."

Yes, I saw his light. Green—life—and blue—sorrow.

I slowly sat up and studied the limp figure on the floor. King lay there shirtless, wearing a pair of black jeans, his back to me and a dagger sticking from his neck. It was the same jeweled "sleeping" dagger I'd almost used to end my own life.

"What's happening?" I asked.

Mack ran his hands through his messy blond hair. "We're even, that's what happened."

"Even?" I asked.

"You saved my life. Now I've saved yours."

I'd never saved Mack's life. "But—but—I don't follow."

His eyes flashed toward King's body. "Let's just say that my brother isn't going to be happy with me once this all shakes out."

"Your brother..." My words faded away as my mind slid the pieces into place.

"Callias?"

He flashed a sly little grin.

"But how?" I asked.

"I'd love to tell you the full story, but the helicopter is waiting, and I really don't want to spend another second on this island. It's fucking creepy."

He held out his hand, but I couldn't move.

He grumbled something unintelligible under his breath. "Mia, all you need to know is that the Artifact wasn't the first relic King encountered to raise the dead."

I lifted one brow.

"Cleopatra had a necklace."

"You're joking."

He shook his head. "He had to kill her for it. How do you think King got her blood?"

I remember King bartering with members of the 10 Club once, using Cleopatra's blood as his leverage. It was supposedly some sort of crazy youth serum.

I stood from the bed, holding the sheet to my body. "I don't believe it." I slowly reached for his cheek and touched it, expecting him to dissolve.

"Believe it."

"But you don't look like you." Except for his eyes. They were the same vibrant blue.

I covered my mouth in shock and studied him. It all made so much sense now, his lack of judgment and blind loyalty toward King. It was the sort of love only a brother would have for his own.

Mack shrugged. "I was reincarnated—that's what the necklace does—or did. It could only bring back one person. I'm pretty sure Cleopatra had intended to use it for herself."

"So King brought you back and not himself?" Because I had seen Mack's light. He was alive. Very alive.

Mack smiled and bobbed his head. "Yes. About five hundred years ago—a long story. But it was one of his finer moments."

I threw one arm around him and squeezed; the tears trickled from my face. "Thank you, Callias— Mack," I squeezed tighter, "whatever."

"I go by Mack now, short for Macarias, my middle name." He patted me on the back, pulled away slowly, and looked into my eyes, like he wanted to say something.

But there I was, typical Mia, with all the questions running through my head. "How did you find me?"

Mack's eyes flashed to the bracelet on my wrist. "I used it to track you. I knew my brother wasn't right in the head."

"But I thought the bracelet took me back…" I sat down on the edge of the bed and covered my face. "It was all a dream."

Mack sat next to me. "No. You really did save my life that night you cursed the Spiros."

"But how did I get there, then?"

He smiled and rubbed his chin. "You, my dear Mia, are a Seer. A very powerful one."

I stared at him. I really hadn't a clue what he meant.

"You used your gift to travel there."

I blinked. *I was really there. I was really there.* I looked at my feet and then at Mack—shit—I mean, Callias. "Seriously?"

He nodded.

"I can't believe it," I said under my breath.

He added, "But I supposed that's the true definition of a Seer; they have the gift of *seeing*. And you, apparently, wanted to see King for yourself."

Oh my God. He was right; I had wanted to see King as he once was, free from the curse. Alive and happy. And then, when I'd been sitting on that beach, I had wanted to know what had triggered the violent side of King. I'd learned about his tattoo.

"Does this mean I can go back at any time?" I asked. "How do I control it?"

"How the hell should I know?"

"Because you seem to know everything."

"Not everything," he said.

"You knew this," I swept my hand at the room, "was going to happen." Of course, I had told King about it. Sort of.

Mack looked ashamed. "This was never the plan. Ever. King promised he'd never let that part of history repeat, that he'd stay in control and find some other way to get you to go back in time."

"But he didn't stay in control." Obviously, King lost his Egyptian collar tattoo despite my warning, and the events played out anyway. It made my head literally spin. "You could've told me this was coming," I said.

"I tried, Mia. But if I'd told you everything, he would've heard your thoughts and then God only knows what he might've done. My only chance was surprising him—you have no idea how powerful, *truly* powerful my brother is."

I understood his point, but that didn't make reality any less painful. "Thank you, Mack. I really mean that. Thank you for saving me." I'd be dead by now.

He shrugged. "I'm tired of this bullshit. It needs to end."

I couldn't agree more. There had been too much suffering and loss.

I looked at King lying on the floor, still wearing his jeans. "So he didn't…I mean," I couldn't say it. "You stopped your brother before he…"

"Yes. Had I arrived a second later, though…" Mack's face hardened. "Never mind." He stood and offered his hand. "We need to get you both back to the house. It's time to break the curse."

Mack made it sound so good: freedom from all this horror. But then the truth hit me, and I froze. *Oh no.* We were back to square one. And my mind was in absolutely no shape to deal with all this. Justin, my parents' happiness, King's life slash existence ending.

"What's the matter?" Mack asked.

"Justin is still dead, right?"

"Yes. I'm sorry."

I hoped by some miracle, that had changed. It hadn't.

I looked down at the man with the jeweled dagger sticking from his neck. There was no blood, and he certainly didn't look to be in pain. Quite the opposite, actually. It was the most peaceful I'd ever seen King aside from the day we'd made love on the beach.

"I don't know if I can do this." Despite all of the crap I'd been through, I still wasn't ready to let him go. And, yet, I wasn't ready to trade in my family's happiness either.

Mack reached out and squeezed my shoulder. "I'm glad you're back."

I tilted my head.

"The Mia with a conscience," he clarified. "The cutthroat assassin Mia isn't nearly as fun."

It was true; I felt absolutely no anger or resentment any longer.

Well, that's because you gave it all to poor King when you cursed the guy.

I almost had to laugh, really, at the sick irony of it all. It was like one giant, supernatural, vicious circle. Justin getting mixed up with the 10 Club, me getting mixed up with King...Then I'd taken all of those dark emotions and retriggered the events with my curse. I could spend the rest of my life trying to untie the elaborate knots that formed this situation, and I could spend an eternity pointing fingers at everyone—why my life had fallen apart, my brother's death, the pain and suffering I'd gone through—but that wouldn't change the facts: we all made choices along the way. We all played a part.

As for me? I'd made a pretty big mess of things.

I released a heavy sigh. It was time to set things right. But what was "right"?

You should've let King die, Mia. And you goddamned know it.

Mack reached down, effortlessly scooped King up in his arms—I guessed unconscious ghosts didn't weigh much—and looked at me. "Ready?"

"No. I'm not." But it was time to end this anyway.

CHAPTER SEVENTEEN

When the helicopter touched down, I had a whole new perspective on King's palatial Crete estate. It was more than just a house. King had built the home directly over the spot where his real palace once stood. It represented a time when he was good, human, and...well, king.

When I stepped back, I began to see so very clearly the dichotomy that existed within King. There had always been a part of him that was noble, acting on behalf of the deeply loyal, fiercely protective man who existed at the core of his being. Then there was the other man: the part of him that had been corrupted and tainted by the curse. Even from the first moment we'd met, those two sides were always there, always at war with each other. No, my brain hadn't known it, but my Seer side had. King really was evil. But he was also good.

The most disturbing part, however, was that both sides wanted me to love them, to choose one of them. That was why Draco the Lawgiver (evil

King) wanted to kill me; I had rejected him. It was also why on the island he wanted to "break me" and turn me into some sort of cursed companion for his evil self. But I could only pity him, fear him, and feel a morbid fascination for him. The man I really loved was inside.

King.

Me.

I thought hard about the two of us, but there was no separation inside my heart. And that's what my Seer blood had been trying to show me from the first moment we'd met.

So now what?

I don't know.

Leaving the engine on, the pilot emerged from the cockpit and opened the exterior door to the helicopter. He looked directly at me and waited.

Numbed by a full four fingers of scotch and wearing an extra-large white bathrobe with a giant "K" embroidered over the heart (why the heck they had a spa-grade bathrobe aboard was the least of my concerns), I stood. Mack did not.

"Aren't you coming?" I asked.

"Nope. I need to get as far away from here as humanly possible."

"Why?" I asked, as several men boarded and carried off King. They didn't seem at all bothered by his "slumbering" state, or by the giant dagger sticking from his neck. Just another day at the old Spiros office, working for a dead king, I supposed.

"Mia," Mack said. "For a second time in my existence, I've done something to my brother that feels like an unforgiveable betrayal."

"But he was out of control—"

"I know, Mia." Mack held out his palm, urging me to hear him out. "But you don't understand what he went through—what he gave up—to find me and bring me back, let alone free me from Miranda later on."

He was right. I didn't understand, but I could guess. For starters, King had chosen to bring back his brother instead of himself, prolonging his own suffering. It was a sign of King's love for his twin brother.

Then there was the fact that Mack had "belonged" to Miranda—Vaughn's 10 Club wife— *sigh...*—widow after Mack had served in some special ops role. All I knew was that he'd been treated very, very badly, and King freed him. Now, how or why Mack decided to spend his life in the armed forces, becoming a pilot, or how he'd managed to get himself mixed up with Miranda, well, I didn't know. Anyone could see it would be a long, complicated, and very personal story. A story for another day perhaps.

"I'm sorry, Mack. You don't owe me any explanations."

"I did the right thing—no regrets. But I can't stay. Once you break his curse, the Artifact will only allow you to bring back one life."

"But I haven't decided anything yet," I explained.

"Mia, as fucked up as my brother is, as many evil things as he's done, I would still choose him. He's my blood. Which is why I fully expect you'll make the same choice. You love your brother, just like I love mine."

I understood what he said; however, if Mack had to choose between the woman he loved and his brother, his decision might be different.

"You can't leave, Mack. You're the only one who understands the decision I have to make."

He looked down at his feet for a moment, gathering his thoughts. "Mia, after I came back to life, I was not a good person for a long time. I did horrible unforgiveable things. Later, much, much later, my brother rescued me from my own darkness, and it kills me I can't do the same for him now. Because I'm not willing to force you to pick him, and even if I was, it would break him to find out that you didn't choose him freely. That would be the only way he'd be happy with that outcome."

My father had a saying: When something doesn't make sense, it's because you don't have all the facts. And that was why I could never fully understand King's explanation about how the Artifact worked. But now...

"So," I said, "King's line about my having to love him in order to break the curse was complete bullcrap?"

Mack smiled. "I think he just wanted you to..." he paused, searching for the words, "pick him."

All this time, that's what King really wanted. Just for me to love him enough to choose him. "Why didn't he just say so?"

"We're talking about my brother here, Mia. What did you expect him to say? Hi, my name is Draco. You don't remember me, but you and I met over three thousand years ago, and I love you. Oh, and you cursed me, so now I'm evil and partly mad because I've been suffering for just as long. Please ignore my evil tendencies which may be hazardous to your health. Pick me."

I felt like a boulder had landed on my chest, and my eyes began to fill with giant tears. King had just been hoping I'd see through the curse and see him, the real him.

I wiped under my eyes and gave my head a shake, trying to keep it together. "Your brother is a complex man."

"Exactly," he said. "And he would never ask you to choose him over your brother. Nor would he judge you for loving someone so…"

"Fucked up like you once were?"

Mack laughed. "Yeah."

So there it was. I finally had the answers to my biggest questions. Except one…

"What am I going to do?" I said, followed by a long breath.

"Simple. You choose which life comes back."

"How?"

"You're a Seer; you just make it happen with that awesome power of yours." He winked.

That wasn't what I meant—choosing between Justin and King was impossible—but I knew that wasn't a question Mack could answer for me. That said, Mack had brought up a good point.

"You have to tell me how to do this—the mechanics," I said.

"You robbed King of his chosen path in life the moment you made the curse. Breaking the curse gives you the chance to put a life back on course, to undo a wrong."

Okay. Justin was wronged by Vaughn. King was wronged by me. I got those two points, but not how it would bring someone back.

I stared at him, completely confused.

"It's a Seer, order-of-the-universe, balance thing. You displace one thing, something has to take its place. Don't ask me."

"Sir?" The pilot tapped his watch. "We're burning fuel, and we've got quite a distance to cover tonight. Shall I shut off the engine?"

"No need." Mack looked at me. "I really need to go now. I've got something important to do, and it can't wait."

I nodded slowly, avoiding looking at him. The guilt I felt was almost unbearable. He saved me and now…well, I would likely end his brother's existence. "I'm so sorry, Mack."

"I know. But you have to do what's right. And my brother would tell you the same. He really loved you—when he wasn't busy trying to kill you or torture you, of course."

I made a little awkward laugh and moved to the door, then stopped and looked at Mack. "Can I ask you one last thing?"

"Sure."

"Did you at least have a good life before you died—fall in love, have a family?"

Mack's blue eyes looked a bit saddened by the question, but he still smiled. "I traveled for five years and saw the world, went to the most amazing places. But I ended up dying from some fever—probably malaria—in a small village near Palenque."

"Mexico. Seriously?"

"Yeah. How do you think the Artifact got all the way there? It didn't fly."

"Wait. How did you get the Artifact?"

"I grabbed it by accident. Before I left the island that night, I returned to my brother's room to take jewels for money and the dagger he owned. Later, I discovered the stone in the bottom of the basket I'd used to carry everything. I demanded the Spiros take me back to you, but they refused—or couldn't, actually, because of your curse. And since I wouldn't entrust it to anyone, I carried it with me everywhere for safekeeping, hoping someday I'd be able to return it to you. When I died, I asked a good friend, a local man I'd met, to see to it that my things, including the rock, were buried in a marked grave. Hell, I didn't know what else to do, and the Spiros couldn't be trusted to help me once my body was cold."

I could understand why. Once Callias died, that freed them from their obligation to look after him. I bet they'd been on the first frigging canoe, or whatever, home. But that kind of sucked he didn't find happiness. He deserved it. I really felt that.

"Believe it or not, though," he said, "Kan, my friend, ordered the Spiros to have my body brought back to Greece to be buried with my family."

"Kan?"

"The king," he replied.

"King Kan?"

Mack frowned.

"Sorry." I held up my hand, acknowledging that now was not the time to make giant gorilla jokes.

He jerked his head. "No one knows what happened after that; they never made it home— probably died at sea. But my things were buried in Palenque. That's why it took King and me so long to find the Artifact. No one knew the temple existed, or thought to look for it in Mexico. We assumed it was on the bottom of the ocean. By the way, do you have any clue how many dives we've been on over the last five hundred years?"

I shook my head absentmindedly, thinking about how strange it was; the way everything connected. My brother would later be the person to unearth Callias's things. Was it a coincidence?

In any case, I thanked Mack for answering my question and stepped toward the small stairs. "Goodbye, Mack. Thank you for everything."

"Goodbye, Mia. And good luck."

I flashed a meek little smile at him and stepped out. I wondered where he would go next or if I'd ever see him again.

"But, Mia," Mack called out. "I did find a good woman. She just wasn't destined to love me back."

The pilot closed the door, and I stood there for a moment. Had he meant that he'd loved me? But we'd only spent that one evening talking and...

I shook my head. No. *He must've meant someone else.*

He betrayed his brother for you, Mia. Something you said he'd never do.

Callias, I'm so sorry. None of this seemed fair, like we were all destined to suffer. *Fucking Greek tragedy from hell.*

I stared at that helicopter as the blades sped up and whipped the air. Wherever Mack was going, I hoped he'd find happiness.

I turned and headed toward the gleaming white modern Greek palace, with its sharp angles and large tinted windows, perched on a cliff that housed the sleeping cursed king. My King.

෬∘෯

Once inside, I was greeted by Ypirétria number...hell, we had to be up to five thousand or so by now. Stefanos was nowhere to be found, but I assumed he'd show. After all, this was it; the curse would finally be broken and his family would be free.

With a solemn face, she silently showed me to my private room. I wondered if she'd heard the news—what King had done to me.

She turned on the shower and laid out a slip and a simple white dress that reminded me of what I wore in Minoa. I thanked her and shut the door after she left.

I stepped into the shower and let the hot water wash over me. I scrubbed and scrubbed until my skin felt raw, but it was no use. No amount of soap and water would make me feel clean again. Everything felt so…so…poisoned.

I held back the tears, shut off the water, and dried myself. With a towel wrapped around my body, I sat on the edge of the bed and stared at the phone on the nightstand. Slowly, I reached for it and dialed.

Within a few rings my mother's voice came through from the other end. "Hello?"

"Hi, Mom. It's me."

"Dear Lord. Mia, where have you been?"

"I'm sorry. I was…" How long had it been since I'd seen her? In my mind, it felt like ages. But in her reality it had only been about a week. "Taking care of some business."

"You should've called. We were worried sick." I heard my father's deep voice in the background asking if it was me on the phone.

"I know. I just…"

"You don't need to explain, honey. I know this is just as painful for you as it is for us."

She referred to Justin's death. But I'd told them that he wasn't dead. I'd told them that he was fine. All because I'd planned to bring him back.

"But he's not—"

"Mia," she said sternly, "you have to listen to me. He is gone. And he's not coming back. You have to accept it."

I didn't know what to say.

"But I promise," she said, "with time, things will get better. It just won't be today…" Her voice faded into a throaty deep sob.

I could no longer hold back my own tears. "But what if he's not gone? What if you could see him again?"

"Mia, that's not going to happen. So, please, just come home, I'm begging you," she cried. "We need to bury our son."

I underestimated my mother. Instead of completely falling apart, she was trying to help me face my own pain. And in that moment, I felt a great big weight lift from my shoulders. She would be all right. She would make it through this somehow, though it wouldn't be easy.

But that doesn't make your choice any easier. Like Mack, I still loved my brother even though he might have lost his way and done some very, very bad things. But that was where I had to step back. I could not make my decision based on what other people told me, or thought of him. That would be like telling a mother to stop loving her child because he or she committed a crime. Love didn't work like that. As for Justin, I had no clue what he had or hadn't done, so I could only follow what I knew to be true in my heart: Justin was good. And sometimes good people did bad things—no one in this world was completely without fault. No one. But wasn't that the purpose of family? They loved you no matter what. Otherwise, many of us with shaded pasts would be forever lost, with no reason to seek redemption. Love was what brought us back from our darkness, what restored us from the pain of our mistakes.

So maybe that was my true purpose in all of this: To be brave enough to love the unlovable. Only, now I had to choose which man really deserved a second chance.

"Mia? Are you still there?" said my mother.

"Sorry. What were you saying?"

"I'll feel much better once you are home. Where are you?"

"I'm…" *Dammit.* The less she knew the better, but I didn't have the energy to lie anymore. "I'm on the next possible flight home. I'll call you before my flight leaves. Okay?"

"Uh…okay." She knew something was up and that I wasn't going to tell her. "We'll see you soon. We love you."

"I love you guys, too." I hung up and stared at the floor for a few minutes, thinking about Justin. Growing up, he reminded me so much of my mother. Their selfless attitudes. I wondered at what point his life steered off course. If I'd known, maybe I could've stopped it.

That's it. I can save them both. My heart cartwheeled inside my chest. I'd been too tired and too in shock to see the options. If I had the ability to "see" for myself, then I could change the outcome of his fate. At least, I hoped I could.

I threw on the slip and dress, and dashed from the room, not bothering with my wet, sloppy hair. I ran toward King's chamber, hoping he was there.

"Stefanos!" I called out, pushing the door to King's room.

There, laid out cold on the bed, was King, shirtless and wearing his black jeans.

Stefanos stood to his side, still dressed in his police uniform, talking to another man. One of his brothers, I guessed.

"Stefanos, do you have the rock?" Because last I'd heard, King had acquired it, along with Vaughn, who'd had it in his possession.

He looked at me, obviously curious as to why I was so excited.

"Yes. Have you chosen?" he replied.

I nodded. "Give it to me."

He waited, expecting me to speak. I responded by sticking out my hand.

Stefanos narrowed his brown eyes and then pulled the rock from his pocket and handed it over.

I stared at the thing, amazed by how it had colors of its own now as if the thing had a soul. *Red and black.* The colors of death and pain. It made sense given the connection to King and how it bound him to this world even after death.

I sat down on the bed and stared at King's exquisitely handsome face. Even now, it was impossible to believe that he wasn't a real man. But inside him, a war raged between the curse and his soul.

I reached out and touched his face. "I hope you'll forgive me some day for what I put you through."

Likely on his last ounce of patience, Stefanos wrapped his hands around the dagger sticking from King's neck. "Are you ready?"

I looked up at him and nodded. "Ready."

I closed my eyes, focused my energy on the stone in my hand, and squeezed it. *Please work. Please work.* But after a few moments, I realized it wasn't going to crack.

"What are you waiting for?" Stefanos asked.

"I can't break it."

He narrowed his eyes and then glanced at his brother, who hung back near the door. "Get her a hammer."

I smiled sheepishly. "Sorry."

Stefanos continued glaring.

Yeah, I finally understood why they hated me but also felt compelled not to harm me—it was not in King's best interest, and their curse bound them to put his happiness ahead of their own. "I only meant for the Spiros to protect Callias. I swear it."

He bobbed his head. "Did you have to bind our curse to a handful of sand?"

I grimaced. His point was that there was no way to undo their curse other than King's curse ending. "…until he finds peace" were my words.

"I'm sorry. I really mean it." The decision to curse the Spiros had been in the heat of the moment, but that didn't undo the damage. Nevertheless, the only thing to do now was make things right.

His brother returned a few minutes later with a regular old hammer. He handed it to me, and I kneeled on the floor, positioning the rock between my fingers as if holding a nail.

I looked up at Stefanos. "Ready?"

He nodded.

Here goes. I swung hard, and the rock shattered into a million tiny pieces. When I looked up, Stefanos had pulled the knife from King's neck. We exchanged glances—him looking at the clean knife that hadn't left any wounds, me looking at the shattered stone—both wondering why nothing happened.

"Give it a second." I held up my hand to silence him and closed my eyes. *Please come back to me. Please.* I channeled every ounce of love I had for King—my King—thinking of every instance when I'd been offered a glimpse of the sinfully seductive, infinitely powerful man whose fearlessness and loyalty knew no bounds. He was the man who didn't shy away from the hard choices—killing, being killed—or acting ruthless when circumstances required. And despite his situation, he never asked for anyone's pity. Instead, he used his pain and sorrow to his advantage and took control. I not only loved King, but I admired him.

King's aura burst from his chest and swirled around him. Purple at first, then quickly separating to red and blue before evaporating like steam.

"What's happening?" Stefanos asked.

"I think it's working."

King's light transitioned to a vivid apple green. "He's coming back."

But as soon as I said that, the light darkened.

"Oh shit." I didn't know what to say. "I choose you! I choose you to come back." His light faded. "No! No! Goddammit, King. You can't do this to me." Panicked, I jumped up and grabbed the sides of his face. "King. Can you hear me?" I looked at Stefanos. "What's wrong? What am I doing wrong?" We couldn't come this far and fail. We couldn't. "King, you sonofabitch. You arrogant, stubborn bastard." I shook him by the shoulders as his color continued to fade. "I'm choosing you! Take back your life."

He lay there, the color in his bronzed face fading to a pale, pale taupe. "No..." I sobbed. Why didn't it work? "You can't leave. I love you."

I kissed his cool lips and dropped my forehead onto his bare chest. "Please," I sobbed, knowing this was my punishment for what I'd done to him. That's when I realized that no matter what, I would have chosen King. It was the horrible, selfish truth. I could survive anything except losing him again.

"Are you just saying that to be nice? Because I assure you, Miss Turner, your compliments will not buy you forgiveness."

I looked up. "King?"

He cracked open one big blue eye.

"Ohmygod!" I screamed, feeling a happiness I'd never dreamed possible. I leaned forward and squeezed his face. I attacked his plump delicious lips with kisses. "Ohmygod. Ohmygod," was all I could say. I kissed him again and again.

He smiled brightly and slowly pushed me back. "I can't breathe."

I drank him in and sighed with joy. "Your eyes are blue. So damned blue." And his skin had returned to a healthy olive brown. "You're so beautiful."

He flashed that wicked little smile, but didn't speak. Instead, he simply beamed.

"How do you feel?" asked Stefanos.

King glanced up at him. "Alive and…hungry. I'm really, really hungry."

"You're…hungry?" I asked.

He looked at me. "Yes. And not just for food."

My heart accelerated and my core fluttered. Every inch of my body screamed with joy. *Then let's get that man something to eat. He'll need his strength!*

King chuckled quietly, clearly weak.

"You can still read my thoughts?" I asked.

He nodded. "Apparently so."

Then you should know that I'm so, so sorry for everything.

His smile didn't diminish. "We have much to discuss. But later. We will speak later."

Right. He was hungry, and it was time to enjoy this moment.

I stood up. "I'll go tell Ypirétria. What do you want to eat?"

As I waited for King to answer, his light suddenly flickered to blue—sorrow. I froze and his expression turned to horror.

I was about to ask him what was the matter, but then I felt something warm and wet all over my chest. I looked down and noticed I was covered in blood. The blood poured from my neck, and the pain was like nothing I'd ever experienced.

"Mia!" King jumped from the bed and caught me before I hit the floor. Everything was such a blur, but from the corner of my eye, I caught Stefanos. He dropped a small, bloody knife on the floor to my side.

King frantically tried to stop the blood from flowing. "No. No. God dammit, no." I felt the life draining from my body, my fingertips and toes going numb.

"Why the fuck did you do that? I will kill you!" King raged.

"The curse is lifted. You found peace. And I needed to be sure this Seer bitch would never ruin another life."

In the back of my mind, I tried to make sense of what he said. King had found peace. That was my requirement for the Spiros being set free. I never said what sort of peace or that it had to be lasting.

"I will hunt and kill every last one of you!"

"No. You will only kill me and my brother. And we are prepared to die. A small price to pay for justice for my entire family."

I made a tiny gurgle and looked up at King, unable to speak with my mouth. *It's okay, King. It's my karma. Just...promise me you'll look after my parents.*

His hands covered in my blood, he brushed the hair from my face. "You cannot leave me now. You cannot."

I don't have a choice. Can't curse myself.

"I love you, Mia. I will find a way to bring you back. I promise."

No, please. No more. Just...live the life I gave you back.

And just like that, my life faded away to nothing. This time, there was no sense of peace or acceptance, only sorrow. Sorrow and then blackness.

෩෨

My heart cannot begin to comprehend what I see before me. It is a vision of both the utmost horror and of the purest untainted joy a man can experience. Because before me I see Mia. The blood flows from a deep gash in her neck into a crimson pool. Yet, in her eyes I see what a man like me has forever dreamed of: redemption.

There is nothing but love to be seen in those shimmering depths of blue as she looks at me. The sensation is humbling. I do not deserve her love. But I have it. And in me she does not see my past or my crimes. She does not see the actions that will forever haunt me. She simply sees me. A man.

My mind abruptly breaks away from this glimpse into paradise and slams full speed into a place I know all too well. Hate. Rage. Revenge. I may no longer be cursed, but I am still a product of my time, not above violence.

"I will not kill you, Stefanos; I will rip you apart, piece by piece."

He says nothing and lifts his chin. The man knows it is no use to run from someone like me. I am the man who can find anything or anyone.

I look down at Mia and see the light slip from her eyes. I do not want to share this moment, her last breath, with anyone. I want it to belong to me. And only me.

"Leave! I will deal with you later," I yell.

Stefanos and his brother exit the room, the room I built for Mia, my queen. A room that I'd intended to spend long, slow nights making love to her. This was to be her palace, the place where we would rewrite our story.

But there will be none of that.

Her eyes gently close and a subtle smile curls her soft lips. I do not want her to go. I am not ready to let her die. "Mia, I will bring you back."

Gods be cursed. I am King. I possess an ancient arsenal of the most powerful objects known to man. I have lived over three thousand years. I anticipate every outcome and prepare accordingly. Yet this.... I shake my head, cradling Mia's head.

I'd given her a ring to ensure nothing like this ever happened. Why did she remove it?

This is the moment that my mind clicks. My darkness was in control these past days, and I remember very little. However, I know Mia would not remove her ring—a ring I spent three hundred years hunting down for her. A ring made from a stone plucked from the crown of Hammurabi.

I think for a moment, the clock ticking away, her soul slipping from her body.

He took it from her.

I slide my hand into the pocket of my black jeans and feel a small lump. *Fucking hell!* I pull it out and slide it on her finger.

My goddamned hands are shaking. "Please, please come back, Mia. Please return." The ring will only function if worn at the time of death. Not after.

I place my ear over her heart and listen. There is no sound. No heart, no breath.

I shake her by the shoulders, knowing that her soul has not yet traveled far. "Use your power to come back, Mia! You are a seer. *See* the life waiting for you!"

I wait, but she doesn't move.

I grit my teeth and scream toward the sky. All this wealth, all this power…I have everything one man can possibly want, but I failed at obtaining the one thing in this world I need. Her. The hunt for the Artifact was always about that. It was always about us being together.

I lie down next to Mia's now chilling body and know I can do little more than wait for a miracle.

Suddenly, Mia sits up and begins screaming with no end in sight. She yells for me to get away from her, that I am a monster.

I hang my head and think of what he, that fucking monster, has done to her—things no woman should have to endure. Things no woman can forgive.

Fuck. It is exactly as I feared; too much has passed between us, and my curse has poisoned our future.

It's over.

If I care for Mia, even a little, I must let her go.

CHAPTER EIGHTEEN

One Month Later. San Francisco.

I lay on Becca's couch staring at the bright-white ceiling of her apartment living room, sweat covering my body, my lungs barely able to keep up with my racing heart.

"Another nightmare?" Becca groaned from the doorway, just arriving home from work, which meant I'd slept through the day again. "Get off your ass, Mia. You're coming out with me and the girls tonight."

I rolled over and covered my head with the quilt. "I don't feel like it." The fact was, I could barely eat, let alone stand and bathe or get prettied up for a night out with a bunch of Becca's obnoxiously happy friends.

Becca pulled back the blanket and glared down at me with her big brown eyes. "We have VIP passes to a new club."

"I don't want to go out."

"You can't sleep on my couch forever."

"Try me," I groaned and covered my face with my hands.

"Enough, Mia!" Becca barked and flicked my exposed forehead.

I sat up. "What was that for?"

My best friend Becca was one of those women who had a sweet round face and wide innocent eyes that made you want to smile. But when she got angry, her pale face turned tomato red, and that meant you might want to consider fleeing. I knew because we'd been best friends since we were little girls, and I thought of her like a sister. Which was why I'd gone straight to her apartment the moment I'd arrived in San Francisco and hadn't left, with the exception of Justin's funeral. After everything that had happened, my parents needed their grieving space and so did I.

"Mia," she sighed, "I haven't wanted to say anything because I know you need time—time that I'm more than happy to give you. But sooner or later, you're going to have to try to pick yourself up. Justin wouldn't have wanted you to spend the rest of your life on my couch, crying."

I knew she was right, but what she didn't know was the full story. It had been a little over three weeks since we'd put Justin to rest, but I was nowhere near ready to face the toxic emotional cloud churning beneath the surface. This wasn't just about accepting Justin's death, but accepting I'd lost King, too. He'd left me the moment I came back to life. He never loved me. He never cared. He had only wanted his curse lifted.

I lost them both. Both. Something I'd never thought possible. So for the moment, all I could do to hold it together was lie on Becca's couch, sleeping.

I rubbed my stinging forehead. "You're lucky I love you."

She sat next to me and moved the sloppy curls from my face. "Mia, I know you're not telling me everything that happened with King. But when you're ready, I'm here for you." I had told her about King—well, everything leading up to the point before I learned who King really was. A cursed king. A ghost.

She squeezed my hand, and I looked into her big brown eyes. "Thank you," I said, "but I'm not ready to talk about it."

She sighed. "Okay, but…" She stopped, deciding to retreat. "I'm taking a shower. Think about coming out with me."

"But I—"

"I'm not asking you," she said lovingly, "to stop feeling sad. I'm asking you to give yourself the night off. Will you think about it?"

I nodded solemnly, and she disappeared into her room.

Alone again, I slid my laptop from the coffee table and opened it up. I clicked on my email and glanced at the message I'd received from King the day after I'd left Crete. It simply said, "You are safe now."

He didn't have to explain what that meant, because I knew.

When I'd woken up in Crete, his body stretched out by my side, all I saw was blood pouring from my neck. I screamed. I couldn't stop screaming. It was as if my brain had unfinished business, and no matter how hard I tried, it couldn't stop seeing what it wanted: me dying, blood everywhere.

It had taken several hours for King to calm me down with heavy sedatives, and when he did, all I saw were memories of him, the red light circling his body and pouring from his dark eyes as he tried to stab me in Athens. All I could hear was his voice as he tied me up and told me he was going to break me. All I could feel were his hands on me as he ripped away my clothes, intent on violating me.

"I can't make it stop," I'd screamed to him, wanting to claw out my own eyes. "Why is this happening?"

I remembered the sound of his deep voice. Sorrow. As if his entire body was saturated with it. "I do not know. However, I must leave within the hour to attend to urgent business. You will remain here in the compound with Ypirétria."

I said nothing. Not because I didn't care, but because my mind had been filled with so many horrible images and feelings, there was no space left for anything else.

Then after he'd left, I could breathe again. The images stopped. The living nightmares dissolved. I knew, without a doubt, that being near him was the trigger.

And it crushed my heart.

After thousands of years of his suffering, the curse had finally been broken, and I'd miraculously escaped death for a third time. But he was like poison to me.

The worst blows, however, were yet to come.

Later, Ypirétria had cleaned me up and fed me. I arranged for a ticket home, knowing my parents needed me there.

When the car for the airport pulled up, Ypirétria came running after me as I got inside. "Vasílissa!" That meant "queen." We really needed to start using our names.

I looked at the cell phone in her hand and took it. "Hello?"

"You are leaving." King's voice was cold and stark.

"I have to go home. They need me."

"Did the nightmares stop?" he asked.

"Yeah. I'm okay now."

"Good." His question made me start to wonder. "Did you do something?"

"I left," he said.

Shit. So he is the trigger. "What does all this mean, King? What happened to me?"

A long moment passed. "Miss Turner, I have very pressing business to attend to. I cannot waste valuable time discussing topics that have little impact on the present or future."

I was back to being "Miss Turner," which meant he wanted distance between us. I felt my heart crack wide open.

I swallowed back my tears and lifted my chin. "I have to go; the driver is waiting."

"Keep the phone. In case I need to reach you. And you will take my private plane home—it is waiting for you at the airport."

"Thanks, but I already have a ticket." I was about to hang up before I started screaming or crying or something.

"Miss Turner, you will do as you are told."

I felt speechless. I couldn't believe King wanted our relationship to return to this—him acting as if I was his employee.

He added, "The 10 Club is being dealt with, but until then, you must stay out of sight."

"What about the Spiros?" I asked, unsure if I cared any longer about them or anything.

"They will be dealt with as well. All of them."

"They've already suffered enough. Just leave them—"

"Goodbye, Miss Turner." The call ended, and I didn't bother to dial him back. What was the point? King now had what he wanted: his curse lifted and his life back. Nevertheless, he'd gone back to being good old King. Not the man I'd fallen for or the out-of-control monster, but the man I'd first met who was somewhere in between.

Maybe some things couldn't be undone. Maybe his soul had been through too much to go back to being the king of Minoa.

I'd arrived the next morning in San Francisco, feeling like there was absolutely nothing left of me.

The journey had been so incredibly emotional and painful. However, fate wasn't done with me yet.

From the moment I'd left Crete, I began to notice I no longer saw lights or felt things. My Seer gift was gone.

Completely gone.

My only clue to the reason why would later come in my nightmares—new nightmares. I was in that auditorium where Callias beheaded King, standing before those old Seer women. I begged them for my life, knowing that after everything I'd done wrong, I didn't deserve it.

"Nothing is without a price, Mia," said the old woman. "If you wish to return, something must be sacrificed."

"Meaning what?"

"You must leave all of your power here. You must give up your gifts."

That meant I would never have the chance to "see" Justin and save him. But leaving my parents to deal with my death, too? It would break them. In the end, though, it was really a decision between returning without my gifts, or nothing at all. I chose to live.

But you're not really living, are you?

"Are you sure you don't want to go out?" Becca stood in the doorway, wearing strappy heels, tight jeans, and a red silky top. Her brown hair was wound up on top of her head in a giant knot.

"I'm sure."

Becca took a little purple card from her pocket and dropped it on the coffee table. "There's a pass. In case you change your mind."

"Have fun."

Becca disappeared out the door, and I sat there staring at my laptop screen. I closed my eyes and flung my head back on the couch. Honestly, the only thing I wanted was to feel nothing.

Whiskey.

Yes, great choice.

I got up from the couch and dug through Becca's cupboards, finding only a bottle of white wine. "Shit, Becca. Really?"

I looked down at my ratty tee shirt and sweats and thought it over. *You can do this, Mia. You can pretend for one night that you're not dead inside.* Not to mention, they'd have real alcohol at the club.

An hour later, I found myself walking past a long line of stylishly dressed people toward the entrance of the dance club. The bouncer, a large man with a shaved head, wearing a red tee and jeans, looked me over. I wore a short, backless black dress I'd borrowed from Becca's closet and red Manolo heels. I had my blonde hair pulled back into a sleek bun at the nape of my neck and added gold hoop earrings. I'd also managed to throw on a little mascara and shimmery pink gloss. I didn't feel human, but I looked like one again.

The bouncer took my pass and let me inside, where the loud music blissfully drowned out the sound of my own thoughts. I stood at the entrance for a few minutes, allowing my eyes to adjust to the darkness and flashing lights. The club was packed with wall-to-wall sweating bodies gyrating to the hypnotic, invigorating bass beat.

I felt my blood pressure shoot up. *I can't do this.* I turned toward the door and felt a soft hand grip my wrist. "Mia! Ohmygod! I can't believe it!" Becca squealed and hugged me tightly.

"I—uh…don't think I'm staying," I screamed over the music.

She frowned. "Like hell you're leaving! Come on." She dragged me through the crowd to a small table toward the back where her friends—I couldn't remember their names—a blonde and two brunettes—sat with five guys. They were doing tequila shots and laughing.

"Everyone! Look who's here!" Becca pushed me down into a seat. I smiled politely and made a little wave. The guy next to me, with a brown buzz cut and big blue eyes, immediately scooted closer. Becca shoved a full shot glass into my hand and said, "Mia, this is Grant. Grant, Mia!"

"Nice to meet you." He grinned. "Come here often?"

I resisted rolling my eyes and instead threw back the shot.

"Let me get you another!" he said, speaking loudly. He handed me another drink from the full tray at the center of the table.

Becca leaned down and spoke into Grant's ear, no doubt giving him some sort of instructions, such as, "Whatever you do, make sure she has fun and doesn't leave."

After five shots, I felt the weight of my anxiety lifting and the ache in my heart numb just a bit.

Bliss. I reached for another shot.

"Hey," said Grant, "not that I'm opposed to your getting hammered or anything, but you might want to slow down."

I was about to snap at him, but when I looked into his big blue eyes, they reminded me of King. "Do you want to dance?"

"Sure."

I took his hand and negotiated our way to the middle of the floor. Grant wasted no time at all placing his hands on my hips and pressing his body to mine.

I lifted my arms and closed my eyes, focusing on the sensation of our bodies moving together in a primal, erotic rhythm. I couldn't help but fantasize they were King's large hands on my body, his muscular arms gripping me to him, grinding our hips intimately together.

When I opened my eyes, however, it wasn't King. It was Grant, his handsome face not possessing even a tenth of the beauty.

"Miss Turner." I heard that deep, dark voice from behind me. I whipped my head around and felt my body lock up.

Standing in front of me, angular, unshaven jaw ticking with anger, was a towering mass of lean hard muscles draped in a sleek black suit.

"King?" I gasped.

His brilliant blue eyes bored into me with utter fury.

"What are you doing here?" I asked.

"What. The. Fuck. Are *you* doing here?" His eyes flashed for a moment over to Grant.

"Uhh…" I blinked.

King leaned forward and spoke into my ear. "As usual, Miss Turner, I am wondering how I've managed to get myself an assistant who lacks the ability to speak."

"Hey, is this guy bothering you?" asked Grant.

I looked at Grant and saw the irritation in his eyes. He didn't know who the hell he was messing with. King could cut him down in a heartbeat.

"Um, no. This is my…" *Fuck. What do I say?* "This is my boss. I'll see you over at the table in a minute."

Grant nodded slowly and disappeared in the crowd.

King grabbed my wrist, and the moment he touched me, jarring images bombarded my mind. Memories of him and I on the beach, of the two of us in that hotel room in Edinburgh where he'd crawled inside my body, of us…lying together in his bed, surrounded by a pool of my own blood…

I tried to pull away, but King had his iron grip placed strategically over my "K" tattoo. He leaned in close and whispered something strange into my ear, but it felt like his words simply passed right through me. Then my wrist began to burn like hell. I tried to jerk it away, but King stared into my eyes and held on tight.

"You will stop fighting," he commanded.

I couldn't believe it. Even now, even with him back in a human body, he still had the power to control me.

Well, why the hell not? After all, it had never been his curse or his incorporeal state that had given him power. He had his abilities in spite of them, to overcome them. *He's probably more powerful now that he doesn't have a handicap.*

"There. It is done," King snarled.

"What's done? What're you doing here?"

He grabbed my arm and dragged me to the back of the club, through a back door, into a dark stairwell.

I looked up at his beautiful face with thick black stubble and sensual lips.

"What are you doing here with that man?" he growled.

"You don't own me, King. I can be here if I want."

"I don't own you?" He laughed that deep, sadistic chuckle into the air.

I jerked my arm away. "No. You don't."

His smile melted away, and a predatory gaze took over.

It was a look that made my heart race with fear. I stepped back, and fury filled his eyes.

"You are afraid of me?" he asked.

Holy shit. "Yes."

He ran his hand through his hair.

"I thought you were cured," I said.

"Cured? Of what? Of my torment? Of my memories, Miss Turner?"

"Mia. For fuck's sake, my name is Mia!" I punched his chest.

He looked down at the spot and grinned wolfishly.

"Yes," he said slowly, "and we had a deal; you are mine."

"You left me! And our deal is over. Way, way over!"

"I did not leave you. I had to take care of a few things."

"You mean kill some people?" I yelled.

"What the fuck do you think, Miss Turner? You are mine. No one touches what's mine." He reached for me and pulled me into him. His lips crashed into mine, and his hot tongue delved into my mouth. His taste, his heat, his smell overwhelmed me.

I wanted to fight him, but my body didn't have the strength to resist what it so badly needed. He spun our bodies around and pinned me against the wall with his hard frame. His hands reached between us, freeing his hard cock, and then grabbed for my thighs. He lifted me up and positioned me just right. "Slide your panties aside," he growled.

Longing for his thick, long shaft to extinguish that hollow, erotic ache, my fumbling hand removed the barrier, and King thrust the silky head of his cock inside me.

Heaven and sin, lust and love. Feeling King plunging himself into my needy body felt like all of those.

He groaned with a deep masculine breath and pounded into me with fierce hard strokes that stole my breath. This wasn't like the time he'd taken me in Athens, nor was this like the time he'd first made love to me on that beach after having thought he'd lost me. This time, he claimed me, each penetration of my soft needy flesh a reminder that only his cock could deliver what I needed, and no one could make me feel like he could.

My muscles contracted with that rapturous, almost unbearable tension, and my nipples hardened to sharp tingly points. Meanwhile, King's hard frame flexed and pushed as his hips hammered into me. "Come for me, Mia. Come hard."

I couldn't hold back any longer. Every muscle in my body flexed, preventing me from moving as the release tore through. King's head bowed back, and he leaned his hips forward, thrusting the tip of his cock as deeply as it could go. His throaty groan was so male and primal, so sexy, that the mere sound triggered another euphoric contraction.

For several moments, we clung to each other, and I savored the sensation of his erection pulsing inside me, releasing those final drops of cum.

He moved his lips to mine, and our panting breaths mixed the air and heat from our lungs.

"God, I missed you, Mia," he whispered.

Mia. I was Mia again.

My head slowly drifted down from the sinful place he'd taken me as King applied lazy, sensual kisses to the corner of my mouth.

I didn't want to come back to earth, but it couldn't be helped.

"King, please, put me down."

He stilled for a moment, resting his forehead to mine, but then pulled out and slowly lowered me.

I yanked down my dress while he put himself back into his pants and straightened his blue silk tie. The knot was crooked, but I didn't say anything. The little imperfection in his appearance felt comforting somehow, a reminder that he was no longer the cursed man who demanded perfection.

But he's still King. I couldn't help but be in awe.

He flashed one of those wolfish, sly grins. "Like what you see, Miss Turner?"

I ignored his arrogant little comment. "Why are you here?"

His black silky brows knitted together. "I am many things, woman, but a welsher I am not." His blue eyes flashed to my wrist.

I held up my arm and noticed the missing "K." Hagne's spit tattoo remained, however.

"I don't understand," I said.

"We made a deal. You would give me one night of what I wanted, and I would give you your freedom." It was a deal we'd made a while back, long before my trip to Minoa.

"But my nightmares of the blood and the things you did to—"

"Those were not *your* nightmares, Mia; they were my memories. With the curse lifted, I must now deal with three thousand years of them."

My eyes drifted back to my wrist. "I was seeing *your* thoughts?"

He nodded. "I did not realize it at first, but the facts spoke for themselves. You are too strong a woman to allow the past to consume you as it does me."

I cupped my hands to my mouth. "I'm so sorry, King." He'd suffered enough as it was, and now hearing that his past, his guilt, would continue to haunt him...well, it was profoundly unfair.

He stared at me with those fierce blue eyes. "Yes, well." He cleared his throat. "I hope that with time, my old memories will be replaced by new ones. Speaking of, Miss Turner. It is now time for you to choose."

"Choose what?"

"You and I made a deal, and it still stands. I said I would free you to make your own choice in exchange for," his eyes swept over my body, "getting what I wanted. And that was one hell of a fuck."

This was his way of asking if I still wanted him. It was such a King move.

I stepped in closer and gazed up at that perfectly masculine face. "I'm not sure."

His blue eyes widened a bit. "Not...sure?" he growled.

I reached for his tie, pinning him with my eyes. "I might need another...fuck."

The side of his mouth turned up. "Perhaps we can renegotiate our deal, then." His voice was deep and seductive.

"Yes. But," I wiggled the knot of his tie and planted a sensual kiss on his full lips, "you should know I'm already spoken for by a dangerous, sexy man."

King grinned. "I can take him. Rumor has it, the man is a bit…old."

I laughed. "Crazy-old. My great-grandfather's socks are spring chickens compared to him."

A subtle twinkle of joy sparkled in his eyes, and he slowly lowered his slightly swollen lips to mine. "I love you, Mia."

I felt the tears welling in my eyes. "I love you, too."

He pulled back. "Then it is settled."

My eyes shifted a bit. "What?"

"You have chosen, so do not think of welshing. You know what will become of you if you do." He tugged me back inside the club, and we bumped into Becca as he dragged me toward the front door.

"Mia?" she said.

I waved at her as her jaw dropped. "Is that King?" she mouthed.

I nodded and made a phone sign with my hand to tell her I'd call later.

Once outside, King walked over to a very expensive-looking, black Mercedes sedan with tinted windows. He opened the passenger door and turned around.

"Get in," he said.

"Where are we going?"

"To put the past where it belongs and make new memories. We start tonight with a clean slate."

I took a moment to digest the sight of this tall, deadly, elegant man who'd lived over three thousand years, ruled an ancient civilization, died, and had come back to life, now standing next to the car, waiting for me like an eager puppy. Not in a million years could I have imagined that we'd make it. But here we were. I wanted to cry and laugh and kiss him and scream and…

"For fuck's sake, Mia. Are you going to stand there all night?" The stern look in his eyes and those muscles flexing beneath his black-stubbled jaw indicated he was about to carry me off if he had to.

I laughed. "You are going to have to work on your impatient streak, King. And that mouth. Jeez. Don't let my mother hear you talking like that."

He grinned and dipped his head in a way that indicated he might make me pay for that little comment. I was really looking forward to it.

EPILOGUE

Six months later.

My beautiful king and I were married on an unusually warm winter day, standing over the same spot where we'd first made love roughly three thousand years earlier, near his home in Crete. At first, I wondered why he'd insisted on this location—after all, we were busy making new memories now. But he'd simply said it was the one memory he would never replace: the moment he fell in love.

No woman in her right mind could argue with that.

It was a simple, quiet ceremony with a minister, my mother and father as witnesses, and Becca acting as both maid of honor and best man as Mack was…well, I didn't know where, and King wouldn't talk about it. Yes, more secrets. But I'd learned I would have to accept that about King. He wasn't evil anymore, but he was still King. The man would always have his secrets.

Anyway, despite the obvious absence of both our brothers, the event marked a new chapter in our lives, one filled with a quiet joy that we'd made it.

As for the Spiros family, King had not wiped them off the face of the earth as I'd thought, but I didn't doubt King had shown no mercy to Stefanos or his brother. I didn't know what to think about it, but King assured me that the family was no longer a threat. I'd simply have to trust him on that.

As for the 10 Club, King had decided to come clean the night after he'd found me in the club. He was, in fact, the man behind the giant smoke screen, the wizard secretly pulling all of the strings. I suspected that the psycho Vaughn had figured it out and that was what he'd meant to say before I killed him.

"But why in the world did you start something like that?" I'd asked King.

"It began after I tried to kill you in Athens," he'd explained. "You disappeared, and I needed to find a way back to you. I needed a cure for this curse."

I cried after hearing that news, but it was what it was. The silver lining was that King was in a position to slowly dismantle the Club and "deal" with the members. I suspected, however, that his monster-slash-curse had created a monster of its own that would never go away entirely. Corrupt people like that, with more money and power than they knew what to do with, would exist whether he charged a membership fee or not.

But, again, it was what it was.

As for facing all of the lies and deceptions cursed-King had orchestrated around me during his quest for the Artifact, there were simply too many to count, and it was now a moot point. King, my King, simply explained it as such, "I loved you, and when *he* was in control, I never wanted him to know how much you meant. But every step of the way, I did what I could to show you, to tell you I was there. I hoped you'd see past his evil and see me. Waiting for you. Waiting for the chance to end him."

King also explained that had I surrendered to my own darkness and demons, I might have ended up loving the cursed King more than him. If that had happened, the monster would have come to life in his place. Thankfully, I'd fallen in love with the right King, for the right reasons.

After that revelation, we made a promise to put the past in the past. I knew, however, that King still carried a tremendous amount of guilt for everything he'd done, despite knowing he'd not been in control. Anyway, that became my unspoken quest: to help him forget and fill that arrogant, sexy, cocky head of his with new, beautiful memories.

So, that left us where we are today: our extended honeymoon. Six months traveling around the world on a five-hundred-and-thirty-foot yacht. Turns out that King did own one, something he'd denied once. And it was a floating slice of heaven, staffed with a gourmet chef, three butlers, an eight-person crew, one Ypirétria, and a helicopter pilot. Yeah, it was really, really over-the-top extravagant, but I wasn't going to complain. I needed some serious pampering.

"Mia? Are you coming or not, woman?" King screamed from the aft deck, his voice pouring into our suite above through the open balcony doors.

I smiled and finished tying up my too-tiny white bikini and then strolled outside onto the private terrace. There, standing shirtless in black board shorts—too cute—was the most beautiful man in the world. He was also loyal, determined, loving, and dangerous as hell. Yeah, like I suspected, removing the curse only made the damned man that much more powerful. I wasn't going to complain. His powerful side—now not so evil—gave me a sort of comfort that allowed me to feel safe, allowed me to lick my own wounds and heal.

I sighed and beamed down at him.

He lifted a pair of diving flippers and jiggled them at me as if to say, "I'm waiting."

We were anchored in the Bahamas this week, and he'd promised to teach me to dive today.

"Almost ready!" I held up my index finger, watching as his smile melted into a look of pure irritation.

I turned away from him, stopped at the foot of the bed, and untied my top, grinning like a fiend as I lay down in the bed. *One, two, three, four, five, six—*

The bedroom door burst open, and there was King, his broad, bare chest heaving, his eyes completely furious.

I smiled up at him. "You are so predictable." He hated to be kept waiting.

The moment he registered my topless body, breasts waiting with perky hard nipples, his look once again shifted. This time into lust. Pure and simple lust. Topped with a heaping helping of love.

His beautiful blue eyes narrowed, and he cracked a wicked little smile. "That was a dirty trick."

I shrugged and grinned.

"I might have to punish you for that."

"I kinda hoped you would," I said.

King was on me like a hungry wolf, tearing his cock free from his trunks. He positioned himself between my thighs and tugged on the side string of my bikini bottom, effectively removing the barrier between us. Gazing into my eyes, he gripped his long, hard, thick shaft in his hand and watched with erotic fascination as he slowly guided himself into my ready entrance.

I flung my head back on the pillow and savored the sensation of his stiff hot flesh entering my body. Inch by inch he fed himself into me until he could go no further.

Still arching over me, he pillared his arms to either side of my head and gazed into my eyes. "I will never get enough of you."

"You have no idea how sexy you are, do you, King?" His large lean frame was every woman's sexual fantasy. He fucking rocked my world in bed. And as long as I wore the ring and he wore his, the one he'd had made—yes, in hopes that this day would come—we'd never grow old. We'd never die.

"I think I like punishing you." He pushed his hips forward sharply to apply exquisite pressure on all the right spots. I orgasmed instantaneously, gripping fistfuls of sheets.

He watched with pleasure as he repeated the movement and made me come again.

How he did it, I didn't know. But I didn't care. The man could practically make me come for him on command. *Okay, yes, his sensual mouth or huge penis is normally involved, but there was that time with his hand when he—*

"Silence, woman," King barked and thrust again. "Or I will not make you come again."

Oh, yeah. And then there was that. I'd made King put back his mark. I'd told him that whatever pain he had, I wasn't going to let him live it alone. I was his, and he was mine. Anyway, he was back to listening in. Not always a good thing when he was working…down there.

I snapped my mouth shut. "Silencing. Not another peep."

He smiled with that sensual, wicked grin and lowered his hot mouth to mine, pumping and licking with a leisurely pace.

I felt the tension coil deep within once again and then…*Heaven*.

Sensing the contractions, King pushed the tip of his hard shaft forward and stoked the flames, making the experience a seemingly never-ending, mind-blowing event. As usual.

The moment my inner walls clenched around him, he began to pump fiercely—one, two, three thrusts—and came hard deep inside me. He released a throaty groan and collapsed.

"Careful," I said, "don't smoosh my stomach."

He chuckled and rolled to my side. "You are far too paranoid."

I rubbed my tummy and grinned. "Well, he is a miracle." And I knew that King would make sure there'd be a ring waiting for him, too, when the time was right.

"That he is." King kissed my bulging stomach and then reached for the phone next to the bed.

He paused for a moment, waiting for the galley staff to answer. "Hello, Paolo," King said in the deep, velvety voice that made my toes curl. Pause. "Yes, Mrs. Minos and I are fine, thank you."

Oh, yes. I forgot to mention that. His last name, as it turned out, was Minos. (Mee-nus.) As in King Minos. Homer would later embellish on local folklore and turn my King into a fictional character—a god—who also sparked the legend of the Minotaur. Yes, I found excessive amounts of humor in that he would most be remembered for working for Zeus, but it was weighed down by the historical references tied to Draco, the Lawgiver. Both were extreme fictionalizations of the real man, but I guessed it couldn't be helped. After all, King was larger than life.

"Yes," he said to Paolo, "it is a beautiful day, indeed. Could you ask Ypirétria to leave a bottle of sparkling water outside the door for my wife and some champagne for me?" Pause. "Thank you, Paolo. We'll be down shortly for our excursion."

One might wonder why King had insisted on bringing Ypirétria—a seventy-year-old Greek woman who'd served in his house since the age of eighteen. That too was a pleasant surprise. After my trip to ancient Athens, when I'd been taken as a slave, King kept his word and sent his men to give money to those freed slaves. With nowhere to go, many followed his men home and insisted on staying. King said they worked harder and were more loyal than any "help" he'd ever had. From that day forward, he began paying all of his people. "It made good business sense," he said. But I think a part of him did it because it felt good. Anyway, Ypirétria, as it turned out, earned about one hundred grand a year, plus benefits. She'd paid for college for her six children, and now that they were all grown, she'd decided to stay with King. She liked "the adventure and danger," she'd told me, compliments of Hagne's spit tat that ironically translated every language. Yes, I decided to keep the damned thing. It was a handy little piece of magic and reminded me of my time in Minoa, something I never wanted to forget.

I looked at my king and grinned. "You ordered champagne. You haven't had that in a while."

"Well, I used to drink it just to piss *him* off, but I find myself missing the taste."

I laughed. "You're telling me that all of those bottles you had were there to torment evil King?" That was what I called him now.

He shrugged those bronzed wide shoulders taut with muscle. "Yes. He didn't much like it. Seemed like a better choice versus whipping him back."

I tilted my head and stared at this beautiful man, understanding another tiny piece of the puzzle. Evil King had tried to beat the goodness out of him. How insanely righteous that the good King tried to fight back with champagne.

"Drink all the champagne you want. After our son is born, I'll drink a glass with you, too. But no cigars, they smell disgusting."

His blue eyes glimmered with joy. "I love you, Mia."

I cupped his cheek. "I love you, too." *More than anything you could possibly imagine.*

"More than anything?" he asked and placed his warm hand on my belly.

"Okay. You're tied."

He laughed. "Well then, are you ready?"

"For what?" I hoped he meant more sex.

"To go diving." He sounded like a little boy eager to find a hidden treasure.

"I can't go deep, but yeah. Sure. What are we diving for?"

"It is the Incan Chalice of Life," he replied.

"Uh-uh. No. You promised your 'relic hunting' days were over."

"But this object is for us. Something we need."

"And why would we *need* that?"

King was quiet for a moment. "It has the ability to bring a person back to life. Specifically, those who have unfinished business and are tormented souls that remain in limbo."

"But you're alive alrea…" My voice trailed off. *You mean…for Justin, don't you?*

King nodded. "Mack and I had been searching for the chalice for a very long time—as a backup, of course. And as luck would have it, I received an email last week, containing the location of the Spanish vessel rumored to have been carrying it."

"Mack sent you an email?"

King nodded.

"What did it say?"

He scratched his chin. "It simply said, 'Tell Mia thank you.'"

Wow. I could only assume he'd meant "thank you" for saving his brother. He now meant to give me back mine. There were no possible words to describe how grateful I felt.

"And," King added, "I suppose it seems only fair that your brother be given a second chance. After all, where would we be if someone hadn't fought for our souls?"

It was true. King had brought back Mack. I brought back King. King had brought me back. And I wasn't simply referring to our lives.

"Thank you, King." I hugged him tightly. "Thank you for giving my family a chance to be whole again." We'd have to get very creative with the story we told my poor parents, but we'd figure that out.

"You may thank me properly," he said, with a deep, sinful voice, "after we've retrieved the chalice."

"But it's going to work, right?"

"Of course," he said, sounding almost offended that I would doubt him.

"God, I love you." I couldn't believe it. After all the pain I'd gone through trying to let go, I would get Justin back. No, he wouldn't be without his baggage and issues, but it was all anyone could ask for: a second chance. And with King by my side, I had no doubt in my mind that we would set Justin straight. We would fix him.

"However, first we will need to break him," King said, reading my thoughts.

I blinked. "Did you say 'break' him?"

King grinned and then shrugged. "Sorry. Old habits die hard."

"Let's just leave the breaking and torture in the past."

"If we must." He reached and nuzzled my neck. "But then you'll have to give me some other way to occupy my time."

With pleasure, my King. "Right after we go diving."

THE END

AUTHOR'S NOTE

Hi All!

Welcome to the end of the book! I hope you enjoyed the King Trilogy. And before anyone asks, I am thinking about writing a story for Mack. No firm decision on that yet, though, as I already have so many exciting books planned for 2015 (revealed in the back of this book!).

Anyway, with each and every book I write for you, my goal is always to surprise. (It's not easy! You folks read a lot of dang books!) To do this, sometimes I create characters who may leave you feeling conflicted. Sometimes, I create characters you downright want to strangle. ("No, stupid! Don't go down into the basement! What are you thinking?!!) But one of my biggest thrills as a writer is getting the reader to change their minds about a character they hate as the real pieces fall into place. (Remember Chaam from *Accidentally...Evil*?) But even better is when a reader takes a leap of faith and continues reading when all seems hopeless. Hopefully, in the end, the story leaves you smoking a mental cigarette and wondering what the hell just happened. But in a good way.

I want to thank each and every reader who trusted me and came along for this journey. I hope you enjoyed the ride.

HAPPY READING!

Mimi

P.S. Want to listen to the music I had piping into my ears while writing this book? Here you go! Get out those hankies!

PLAY LIST

"Goodbye My Lover" by James Blunt
"Changing" by Airborne Toxic Event
"Black Sheep" by Gin Wigmore
"Wise Up" by Aimee Mann
"If Only" by Gin Wigmore
"Hold the Line" by Pilot Speed
"Bluff" by Pilot Speed
"Do You Feel Me" by Anthony Hamilton
"Feelings" by Maroon 5
"Unkiss Me" by Maroon 5
"Save me" by Aimee Mann
"My Heart is Open" by Maroon 5
"Be Still" by the Killers
"Won't Go Home Without You" by Maroon 5
"Take Me to Church" by Hozier.
"Happy Ever After" by Gin Wigmore.

ACKNOWLEDGMENTS

A HUGE thank you to the folks who helped get this book out the dang door! (It was a tough one.) Vicki Randall (Oh look! I made you read another one! LOL), Dalitza Morales (I so love your OCD tendencies), and authors Kylie Gilmore and Elizabeth James (Thanks for taking time out of your busy writer schedules!).

Also, I really need to recognize the folks who put so much effort into the production part of this series: Su at Earthly Charms (awesome cover!), Stef at Writeintoprint.com (please don't EVER retire, you're the best), and the ladies who provided multiple layers of awesome editing—Latoya Smith (I miss you!), Tessa Shapcott (I hope that wasn't too painful?) and Pauline Nolet (Did I seriously misspell that word? Oh Lord.).

AND…my guys. As always, you rock.

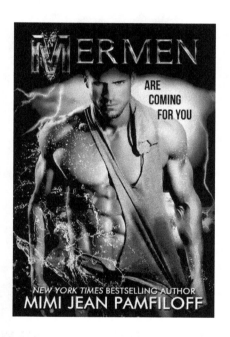

CHECK OUT OTHER MIMI JEAN TITLES

FATE BOOK TWO
COMING DECEMBER 2014

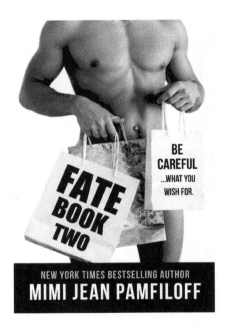

BE CAREFUL WHAT YOU WISH FOR...

Despite every bad guy in the world wanting her dead, nineteen-year-old Dakota Dane believes she's finally found her "happy ever after." Until Prince Charming (aka her hot Italian bodyguard) bolts from the church two minutes before the wedding.

Was it something she said?

Dakota doesn't know, but she's not about to let him off the hook. Because he loves her and she loves him.

Right?

But when Dakota finally catches up to Mr. Cold Feet, she'll find herself wishing she'd let him go when she had the chance.

IMMORTAL MATCHMAKERS, INC.

COMING SPRING 2015!

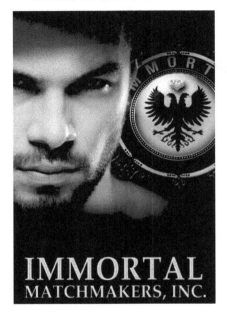

BECAUSE...dysfunctional immortals need love, too.

ANDRUS

Once the most powerful immortal assassin ever to exist, this demigod now spends his days pining for the girl who got away: Helena. Doesn't help that he's also Helena's full-time nanny slash bodyguard. But now that the apocalypse is over and her husband, the vampire general, has returned home for good, it's time to move on.

But can Andrus let go of the woman he secretly loves?

Cimil, Goddess of the Underworld and owner of Immortal Matchmakers, Inc., knows the solution is finding another gal. The right gal. But getting a woman to date this callous, unrefined, cold-hearted warrior will prove to be the biggest challenge of her existence. Good thing they're in L.A.

When aspiring actress Sadie Townsend finds herself one week away from being thrown out on the street, the call from her agent is like a gift from heaven. But when she learns the job is teaching the world's biggest barbarian how to act like a gentleman, she wonders if she shouldn't have asked for more money. He's vulgar, uncaring, and rougher around the edges than a serrated bread knife. He's also sexy, fierce, and undeniably tormented.

Will Sadie help him overcome his past, or will she find her heart hopelessly trapped by a man determined to self-destruct?

ABOUT THE AUTHOR

Mimi Jean Pamfiloff is a *New York Times* & *USA Today* bestselling author of Paranormal and Contemporary Romance.

Her books have hit the Amazon and B&N top-100 lists multiple times and have been #1 genre sellers around the world. Both traditionally and independently published, Mimi has sold over 500,000 books since publishing her first title in 2012, and she plans to spontaneously combust once she hits the one-million mark. Although she obtained her international MBA and worked for over fifteen years in the corporate world, she believes that it's never too late to come out of the romance-writer closet and follow your dreams.

When not screaming at her computer or hosting her very inappropriate radio show, (Man Candy on Radioslot.com!), Mimi spends time with her two pirates in training, her loco-for-the-chili-pepper Mexican hubby, and her rat terrier, DJ Princess Snowflake, in the San Francisco Bay Area.

She continues to hope that her books will inspire a leather pants comeback (for men) and that she might make you laugh when you need it most.